Surprise Party . . .

Hunter pressed himself against the wall, watching the sector between the west and north of the building. The rest of the team, keeping low, walking quietly and swiftly, proceeded to their assigned positions. Travis went to the second door on the left. Jen and Jack ran to the door straight ahead—the general sleeping quarters. Sam and Sarah took the first doorway to the offices on the left, and Stan went right.

Travis waited until he knew each team member was in position, then whispered, "Kaboom," voice-detonating the fuse on the Semtex outside. He looked down the corridor, heard the explosion, and saw the flash of light.

Travis gave the order, "GO!"

All hell broke loose.

DIRE STRAITS

Cliff Garnett

A SIGNET BOOK

SIGNET
Published by New American Library, a division of
Penguin Putnam Inc., 375 Hudson Street,
New York, New York 10014, U.S.A.
Penguin Books Ltd, 27 Wrights Lane,
London W8 5TZ, England
Penguin Books Australia Ltd, Ringwood,
Victoria, Australia
Penguin Books Canada Ltd, 10 Alcorn Avenue,
Toronto, Ontario, Canada M4V 3B2
Penguin Books (N.Z.) Ltd, 182–190 Wairau Road,
Auckland 10, New Zealand

Penguin Books Ltd, Registered Offices:
Harmondsworth, Middlesex, England

First published by Signet, an imprint of New American Library,
a division of Penguin Putnam Inc.

First Printing, February 2001
10 9 8 7 6 5 4 3 2 1

People sleep peacefully in their beds at night only because rough men stand ready to do violence on their behalf.

—George Orwell

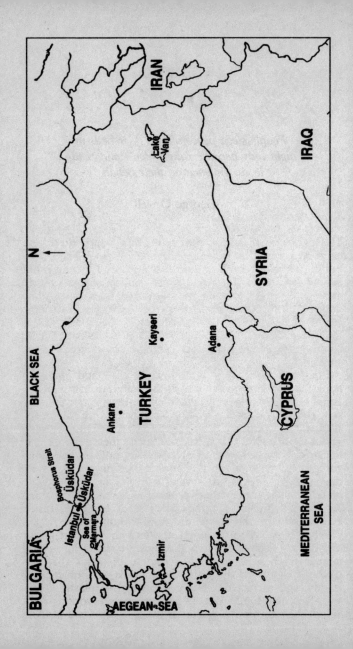

Prologue

The man was dressed entirely in black battle dress, the exposed areas of his bearded face smeared with black shoe polish. It was a very dark, overcast night and drizzling, but he needed to avoid reflecting the artificial lights on and around the Bosphorus Bridge, one of the two bridges connecting the city of Istanbul, in European Turkey, with Asia and the great bulk of the Turkish nation. The traffic at this time of night was not as heavy as during the day, but he could still hear the rumble of cars and trucks crossing the span.

Equipped with lightweight climbing rope and grappling hook, he had laboriously scaled the southern tower of the Istanbul side to a location at which the tower met the support girder. The grappling hook was coated with rubber for silence. He had tied a loop around himself with a bowline under the armpits. The drizzle had made the steelwork particularly slippery, so the climb had been difficult and slow-going: hand over hand, arm muscles burning with strain, thighs aching, progressing several feet, sliding back a couple of feet. He was perspiring profusely, the sweat streaking his blackened face, soaking his clothing from the inside even more than the drizzle did from the outside.

When he reached the point at which the support girder met the tower directly below the deck, he rested for several moments. Then he reached around to the pack that was strapped tightly to the back of his waist, to prevent any jarring, and extracted a melon-sized ball of plastic explosive. He could barely discern his companion working right across the way on the northern tower. While still holding on with legs and right hand, his left hand molded the C-4 plastique until it formed a salami shape. He affixed the explosive to the deck with duct tape.

He then attached to it the coupling assembly and M-1 firing device, a four-inch-long metal cylinder. Directly behind the coupler was the primer, which, upon explosion, would detonate the plastique. He pushed the timing device, already set for 10:40 that morning, into the plastique, secured it with duct tape, and connected the wire to the M-1.

He knew that five of his comrades were working on other strategic sections of the bridge, according to instructions supplied by the engineer known to him only as Enver "Mühendis," not his family name, just the Turkish word for "engineer." He also knew that another team of six were conducting the same operation on the Fahti Sultan Mehmet Bridge, the other span connecting Istanbul with the rest of Turkey.

10:30 A.M.
Üsküdar, Turkey,
across the Bosphorus Strait from Istanbul

The café was on a breezy promontory in the city of Üsküdar. It had tables and wooden folding chairs on the terrace. The *Kahve Güzel Manzara* lived up to its name: Beautiful View Café in English. It afforded an excellent vista of the Bosphorus and the city of Istanbul on the opposite shore. The muscular forty-five-year-old man with the hawk nose leaned back in his chair, nursing a lemonade. He wore an orange sports shirt, jeans, and sneakers; he wanted to be taken for a tourist, a man on holiday. It was a pleasant spring day.

The man gazed at the sparkling blue of the water that separated Asia from Europe, and the heavy shipping passing below, en route from Black Sea ports in Georgia, Russia, Ukraine, Rumania, and Bulgaria to the Mediterranean, by way of the Bosphorus right below him, and from there to the Sea of Marmara, the Dardanelles, and the Aegean. He observed the traffic on the bridges connecting the two continents. The Bosphorus Bridge, he knew, was the longest suspension bridge in Europe, with a total span of 5,118 feet. His gaze shifted to the great city across the water. Through the light haze he discerned the domes and minarets of Istanbul among the urban sprawl. He could hear the motors and horns of heavy traffic, muted by distance, rolling across the water.

He stroked his neatly clipped black beard as he gazed at Istanbul. *Beautiful, beautiful, those rounded domes, those magnificent mosques surrounded by their minarets. Minarets soaring heavenward like the prayers of the faithful . . . And like nuclear missiles reaching out to destroy the unbelievers.* Rauf Karahisarli, known to his followers as Rauf Pasha, had resigned from his position as colonel in the Turkish Army several years before.

The army discouraged what they called "religious fanaticism." True, it allowed the men to worship as they pleased and to study Quran—after all, almost all Turks were Moslems—but it did not tolerate Islamists, those who insisted on having the strictest rules of Islam incorporated into the laws of the Turkish state. The military and the largely secular government stubbornly refused to force women to stay at home or to cover their bodies and faces if they had to appear on the street. It permitted them to go to school, to hold jobs, and to drive automobiles as if they were men. It even allowed them to mingle shamelessly with men in the marketplace, at the cinema . . . Everywhere! This was evil and could only lead to the destruction of Turkey.

Worse yet, the military refused to heed the warnings of the faithful to break its compact with the unbelievers, to drop out of NATO, that unholy alliance. All the other nations belonging to NATO were lands of the infidel, especially their hated neighbor, Greece, an enemy of longstanding. This made no sense. It turned Turkey into a whore, in bed with those who despised her.

The Turkish Navy was presently holding joint sea maneuvers with the worst of the Westerners, the United States, the Great Satan. And with Israel, the Little Satan, which was like a cancer planted by the West in the heart of Islam. The Turkish government allowed the United States to have bases on Turkish soil, as at Incirlik, bases from which they had attacked Iraq, an enemy of holy Iran, true, but a Moslem nation, nonetheless. The Turkish Air Force was conducting maneuvers in Turkish airspace with the demonic

Israeli Air Force. This was too much to bear. All this would have to end. It *would* end.

Rauf Pasha looked around him. His dark eyes narrowed. They radiated hatred. It was hard to conceal his outrage at what he saw: fellow Turks—Moslems—with their families, drinking coffee with cognac! In spite of the Prophet's interdiction of alcoholic beverages. Did they think they were Greeks? Or Americans? Or Jews? They were Turks! They were speaking Turkish. They called themselves Moslems. And yet there they were, chattering away, joking in public with their wives or girlfriends, or harlots . . . Shameless women with faces uncovered in public, smiling lasciviously, unconcernedly gesticulating with their bare arms, glittering bracelets adorning and calling attention to those arms, their hair uncovered, shining in the sunlight . . .

The women were demons who would tempt men to sin, lure them into the lair of Satan. They should stay at home, in the kitchen, taking care of their children, having many children, serving their husbands, not conducting themselves as equals to men. They behave like harlots; they should be treated as harlots.

And the men: disgusting. They lower themselves to the same level as the women, rather than maintaining their rightful position as superior to females. They probably even allowed the women to be on top when they fornicated. They were no better than pimps, displaying their women in public to the lascivious stares of other men. Or, God only knows, maybe they were homosexuals or even eunuchs, who felt no passion for their women, had no jealousy concerning them. He would have liked to strangle those sons of pigs with his bare hands . . . after castrating them with a blunt knife. He made a supreme effort to calm himself. Well, no matter; they would all burn in Hell for eternity.

Rauf Pasha had recently returned from abroad—eighteen months in Iran where he received religious indoctrination in the holy city of Isfahan and political instruction in Tehran. Six months in southern Lebanon with the Iranian-backed Hizbollah, where he instructed the mujahideen, holy warriors, in military tactics and where he, for his part, gained practical experience in guerrilla warfare against the Zionists. Having returned to Turkey, he and his men had engaged in small hit-and-run raids on isolated villages whose inhabitants were overly fond of Western ways. The army never knew where they would strike and always arrived too late, much too late.

Just three months before, Rauf Pasha's men had taken control of a little village for one hour. In that hour they taught a lesson to all of Turkey. Girls are to stay home and learn to be housewives, not sent to school like boys. A smirk spread across his lips as he recollected the raid. They had shoved and dragged by the hair the ungodly teachers and their female students, aged fourteen to sixteen, into the courtyard. They forced the defenseless villagers—including parents and other family members—to watch as they raped the girls. Then they slit their throats as though they were slaughtering sheep. Naturally, those who tried to interfere were killed.

The rape was necessary, of course, to dishonor their families, those families who suffered from pride, who shamelessly sent their daughters—faces and arms uncovered—to study like men. The dishonor would burn the sin of pride from their souls, and teach them humility. In the end, it was for their own good. This he learned from his beloved mentor and spiritual leader, Najatollah Yazdi, the sixty-nine-year-old Iranian mullah sent by Tehran to guide Rauf Pasha and his men in their holy mission.

Rauf pasha was proud of his men, as was the mullah. It takes courage, great courage, to spill the blood of young girls, pretty girls, girls they had just raped and who were weeping and pleading piteously for their lives. But his men were steadfast, brave, committed. They were true mujahideen, holy warriors. If they felt pity, they hid it well. They were avenging angels and showed no mercy. They did their duty. With dedicated heroes like these, they would win their struggle. Turkey would return to the fold of the true believers and would even make war against the infidel West. And with the most fearful weapons available.

Rauf Pasha was buying military supplies of all kinds, including portable missiles, missile launchers, and nuclear warheads, from the greedy Russian entrepreneurs and from Kazakhstan. The funds were generously donated by the Iranian government and by the elusive Saudi millionaire, Osama bin Laden.

Rauf Pasha, after destroying the bridges connecting Europe with Asia and eliminating the Turkish military personnel and equipment rolling across those bridges, would be taken seriously by the government in Ankara. Then he would demand that the military step down within five days and install an Islamist government, which would enshrine the strictest Islamic rules as part of the law of the land. If they refused, he would destroy Athens, capital of Greece, as well as Tel Aviv, the heaviest population center of Israel, with nuclear weapons. It would be *jihad*, holy war.

A horrific event of this kind, of course, would completely discredit the ruling Turkish government. NATO would expel Turkey from its midst, and his country would be shunned by the West. Perhaps NATO would retaliate by destroying Istanbul with nuclear weapons. All the better! It would be the wrath of God against all those Westernized, dissolute, so-called Turks living in the Westernized cesspool of corruption, the den of sin that Istanbul had become, with its discos and bars and movie houses. Not to mention the infidel foreigners. And if true believers among them were among the dead, then as martyrs they would immediately ascend to Paradise. If the mosques must be sacrificed, that would be truly a pity, but, after all, they are only buildings, constructed by human hands. We do not worship architecture. Not carrying out the mission because of those buildings would be a sin; it would be a form of idolatry.

If the Turkish government, or NATO, or Israel, or anyone at all, attempted to interfere and came close to doing so, he would unleash his weapons before the five-day period of grace. Of course, this was only the beginning. Once he controlled the Turkish government, he would have infinitely more power, infinitely more financial resources at his disposal. He would be the head of government of a sovereign nation, with armies, navies, and air forces. He would buy more and better nuclear weapons and scientists. Ultimately, he would be able to threaten all of Europe with nuclear annihilation, and finally cities like Boston, New York, and Washington, D.C., the head of the American serpent.

Rauf Pasha returned to the present and focused on the bridges several miles away. Civilian traffic had been halted on the Bosphorus Bridge and the Fahti Sultan Mehmet

Bridge to allow the passage of armored personnel carriers and tanks on their way to joint NATO maneuvers in the south, near the Syrian border. *Maneuvers! They're looking for me, no doubt. But they won't find me and my men until I want them to. And on my terms.*

He took another sip of lemonade, replaced the glass on the metal table, and checked his watch. Two minutes to go. He restrained himself from concentrating on his watch. He looked around him at the cognac drinkers and their sluttish bitches. They would soon see a sight that would shock them. It took a great deal of discipline, of willpower, to force his taut muscles to relax, to appear completely at ease. Discipline, in order to relax! The irony almost made him laugh. He forced himself to sip his lemonade and appear to enjoy the view. It was difficult, maintaining the appearance of calm and relaxation, when every nerve in his body vibrated with anticipation.

10:35 A.M.
The Aegean Sea

The large American container ship was en route to the Turkish port of Izmir. Forty-three-year-old Captain William Lopez sat on his swivel chair on the bridge, his eyes half closed, calmly sipping a cup of coffee, smoothing his dark mustache with the fingers of his left hand. The vessel was sailing due north through the island-studded Aegean. Lopez enjoyed reciting the names of the Greek islands hugging the Turkish coast as the vessel slid past them: Astipalaia, Kalimnos, Leros. The ship had just navigated between the islands of Patmos and Samos. *Yeah, that good dry wine from Samos,* Lopez reflected. Ahead, but not yet in sight, lay the narrow passage between the Turkish headland to starboard and the Greek island of Khíos to port. Once through the passage he would order the helmsman to come sharply about to 90 degrees, and soon after to 135 degrees in order to enter the Bay of Izmir.

The water was calm. Even without the aid of binoculars, Lopez could easily see fishing vessels in all directions. With binoculars he saw that some flew the Greek flag, others the star and crescent of Turkey. *Good thing they aren't fitted with guns; they'd probably blast each other out of the water.* He chuckled thinking about Greece and Turkey both belonging to NATO, yet each country constantly looking over its shoulder at the other, because of centuries-old hatreds.

Why couldn't they be more like Mexico and the United States? These two countries on both sides of the Río Grande got over that nineteenth-century war between them. Well, more or less, he figured. Maybe even more than the South ever got over the Civil War, according to his wife, one set of whose grandparents were from Tennessee. Bill's parents were Tex-Mex and his wife's maiden name was Henderson. And he and Kathy had three beautiful little children. He couldn't wait to get back to his wife and kids in Houston. People said the eldest boy took after him, with his dark good looks and prominent jaw. Looked like him except for the mustache, he would joke. The younger boy looked more like Kathy: he had a tiny nose, and was blond and very light skinned, a *huerito*, as Bill's father affectionally called him. The girl, eight years old, was going to be a heartbreaker, he figured. She had his dark eyes and complexion, and his wife's delicate features. In fact, she was getting a little too flirty, he thought. He had recently seen her in front of a mirror, practicing to walk with a sway. He'd have to keep an eye on that one.

He reflected on the night before he left, when Kathy had been particularly passionate in their lovemaking. Well, she usually was, the night before a voyage, but this time her passion had seemed even more urgent than usual, almost desperate. So much so that he noticed it. And wondered about it. And she had finally fallen asleep with her arms locked tightly around his neck. He finally had to gently extricate himself from her embrace in order to get even a few hours sleep.

He kept picturing Kathy when he last said good-bye to her and the kids. Her long blonde hair shone in the sun as she waved good-bye on the pier in Galveston. The kids looked more interested in the ship than in him. Well, what the heck . . . They were kids. And they were great kids. He'd bring them back some presents from Izmir.

Before he went aboard his vessel, Kathy had kissed him and said, "Be careful, Bill." Not the way she usually said it, but with a worried look on her face. He told her he was always careful and asked her if she was worried about anything in particular. She just shook her head and smiled. But the smile seemed forced. Sometimes he jokingly called her his *bruja*—witch—because she sometimes had premonitions and sometimes they came true, but mostly, he told himself, they were just superstitions.

At the outer rim of his consciousness, Lopez noticed that one of the fishing boats had been gradually moving closer to his own ship, even discounting the northward progress of his vessel, while the other fishing craft seemed not to move at all. When first sighted, the Turkish fishing boat had been about thirteen nautical miles almost dead ahead. It was now about five miles distant at a relative bearing of forty-five degrees. Lopez raised the binoculars to his eyes and read the vessel's name: *Kara Kale. Hmm . . . Turkish for "Black Castle." Is there a town in Turkey by that name? Sounds sinister. Probably too many vessels and not enough fish where it had been. Still . . .*

On the horizon, Lopez could make out the distant shores of the Greek island of Khíos and the Turkish coast. Dead ahead the sea met the sky where his vessel would pass between the island to port and the mainland to starboard.

This evening he would enjoy a good restaurant in Izmir. One with music and dancing girls. Kathy would fold her arms across her chest and screw up her face when he mentioned that. But, what the heck, she didn't really object. He'd go to the Kirmizi Çiçek, the Crimson Flower. First, *yelanji dolma*, stuffed grape leaves, with the rice wine called *arak*, then a main course of grilled lamb with rice, sweet peppers, onions, and tomatoes, enhanced by Samos wine, and finally the honey-soaked, almond-filled pastry called baklava accompanied by thick, sweet Turkish coffee. Maybe he would even let someone tell his fortune by turning the cup upside down and then reading the patterns formed by the syrupy coffee. He didn't really believe in that hocus-pocus, but it would be entertaining to think you could actually foretell the future. It sure would be useful to know the future.

Out of the corner of his eye he noticed movement. *Kara Kale* had seemed to pass Lopez's container ship; it was heading south while his own vessel sailed north. *Kara Kale* was well abaft the starboard beam at a distance of only three miles now. The movement Lopez noticed was the fishing vessel's sudden change of course; it veered toward the American ship and suddenly gunned its engine from what he estimated to be ten knots to thirty knots. *A fishing boat moving at thirty knots?!* Simultaneously, Lopez heard the lookout's alarmed report on the intercom, "Captain, fishing vessel closing fast, starboard!"

Lopez jumped to his feet. "What the hell?!" Then he heard what sounded like two champagne bottles being uncorked one second apart. He saw the two splashes and the two whitish trails being blazed through the blue water toward his vessel. He heard the lookout's incredulous cry, "Torpedoes, Skipper, torpedoes!" as *Kara Kale* veered sharply in a 180 degree turn and sped away.

Lopez knew intellectually that it was no use, but he instinctively gave the helmsman the command to come about from zero degrees to 130 degrees at full speed. His reflex response was to attempt to have his ship present as small a target as possible by bringing its bow about to face the torpedoes. He knew, of course, that objects moving through water, especially very large objects, like a huge container ship, respond sluggishly to course changes. It's not like tire against asphalt; very little friction is present. It's almost like objects floating in a space module.

The captain gave orders for the crew to lay down to their abandon-ship posts and to ready the lifeboats. He heard the explosions and was dashed against a bulkhead by their force. Blood trickling from a gash in his forehead into his eyes made him wonder if he really saw *Karakale,* about five miles away, veer again, bringing her prow about to face the doomed ship once more.

10:40 A.M.
Üsküdar, Turkey,
across the Bosphorus Strait from Istanbul

For a few moments the patrons of the outdoor café kept up their friendly chatter. The sounds at first didn't register. Distance made the explosions sound like a series of remote thunderclaps. But in two seconds their instincts told them this was something different, especially since the day was clear and sunny. When they turned toward the sounds, they incredulously witnessed, as though in slow motion, the Bosphorus Bridge seeming to lift upward at three points, flinging troops and vehicles into the air as though they were toy soldiers in toy vehicles. Puffs of gray smoke appeared, then spread and thinned. Then, still in slow motion, they saw the toy soldiers, armored troop carriers, and tanks falling back to splatter and bounce on the bridge. It seemed to them that those blown to the side floated down toward the water below.

A few seconds later the almost identical scene was played out on the Fahti Sultan Mehmet Bridge. The shocked spectators' minds adjusted to the events and the action sped up to normal, as they instinctively jumped to their feet and focused their attention on the catastrophe.

10:40 A.M.
The entrance to the Bosphorus Bridge, Istanbul side

Major Serdar Aksu, Turkish Army Intelligence, had been sent as an observer with the troops on their way to maneuver with NATO Forces in eastern Anatolia. The armored car in which he sat had been rolling along, just entering the unsuspended side span of the Bosphorus Bridge. He saw brief, blinding flashes of light, then heard a deafening roar that seemed to continue forever. After the initial shock, he realized they were a series of explosions, separated by seconds. He felt the roadway vibrate under his Humvee, making his teeth chatter. He was transfixed as he looked down the length of the bridge in front of him. The section of bridge less than 1,000 feet ahead of him seemed to thrust itself up into the air, accompanied by a puff of smoke, throwing Humvees, men, and tanks even higher. Huge hunks of concrete and steel sprang into the air. These men, along with the armored vehicles, appeared to be suspended in space for what seemed like an eternity, then fell heavily back like a motion picture in reverse, bouncing against what remained of the roadway, then plunged through the gap resulting from the blast, to rain down on the water and the oceangoing vessels below. Huge water spouts were sent up from the narrow channel, while seamen and parts of superstructures of the oceangoing vessels below were knocked into the water, churning up yet more white foam.

Before the men, equipment, and sections of bridge began to drop back, Aksu's eye suddenly focused further forward on the middle of the bridge, which went through the same process, followed closely by the end closest to the Asian shore. Seeing all this, Major Aksu had the fleeting impression of a snakelike monster engaged in some kind of violent, lurching dance. A tank rolled over the side of the bridge and landed on an oil tanker, causing another explosion, a bright blast followed by thick black smoke and orange flames.

Aksu's eye was caught by movement to the side. He turned his head and, although he could not hear the sound of the explosions, observed the Fahti Sultan Mehmet Bridge through a light haze a few miles distant, dance to the same macabre beat, sending objects that must have been men and equipment up into the air, and then down to the channel below.

Through his shock, Aksu was aware of the eerie silence that now pervaded the atmosphere. Except for the faint hum of distant traffic, anyone and anything near enough to have witnessed the catastrophic events or heard the blasts were shocked into silence. No one spoke. All motors were cut off. After a silence that seemed to last forever, Aksu became aware of the moaning of wounded soldiers lying on the approaches to the main span directly in front of him, some of them crushed under overturned armored vehicles. Then the frenzied shouting of the troopers around him, and finally, the barked commands of officers attempting to restore order and help the wounded.

Major Serdar Aksu suddenly remembered that his eighteen-year-old brother, having joined the army eight months before, was among the troops in front of him. One of those thousands of human beings, and body parts, had to be his brother Selim, the brother he had encouraged to join the armed forces. *Oh, God, God! Selim, Selimcik, my baby brother. Why? Why?* Aksu stood and repeatedly slapped his own face with both hands to stop the burning tears of rage and sorrow from streaming down his cheeks.

10:40 A.M.
Üsküdar, Turkey

At the *Kahve Güzel Manzara*, Rauf Pasha sprawled back in his seat, his head thrown back. He had been awaiting the event with mounting anticipation. Now, as he watched the bridges rise, then collapse, the soldiers and armor tossed into the air like toys, then plummet to the Bosphorus below, he breathed faster, more heavily. His eyes then half closed, a look of unutterable ecstasy etched on his hawk-like features.

Chapter 1

People streamed out of their homes and into the streets and squares of Istanbul. They gathered on the grounds of mosques and public buildings—Taksim Square, the Grand Bazaar, the Spice Bazaar, the campus of Istanbul University, even the grounds of Dolmabahce Palace and Topkapi Palace. They spilled over onto Sultanahmet Square, which contains the immense architectural jewel of the Aya Sofya Museum, and the Sultan Ahmet Cami, with its many domes, its six graceful minarets reaching heavenward, its walls covered with blue Iznik tiles. Also called the Blue Mosque, its vast courtyard was surrounded by a horseshoe-arched collonade, and was now filled with an agitated crowd of people.

A multitude had gathered in the Misir Carsisi, the Egyptian Bazaar, in the Eminonü District. Crowds filled the spaces between the stalls filled with spices, dried fruits, cheeses, olives, towels, slippers, baskets, and jewelry.

There was something about the press of tightly packed humanity that made a man feel larger, stronger, than when he was alone. And there was something about the smells filling the air: the strong coffee, the roast lamb in the *sis kebap*, the charcoal smoke, the garlic, onions, anise, basil, bay leaf, cardamom, fenugreek, cinnamon, cloves, black pepper, red pepper, coriander, ginger, powdered mustard, and a host of other aromatic herbs and spices.

Adding to the turmoil was martial music issuing from a radio turned way up. A low-pitched wind instrument wailed a single note, a drone against which higher-pitched wind instruments, interspersed with the plucking of a lutelike string instrument called the *oud*, wove a wild melody to the frantic accompaniment of drums.

The merchants had been jittery enough because of the blowing of the bridges, but now they were doubly nervous because of the look of the crowds. These people were not buying or inspecting the merchandise. They looked as though they were on the point of exploding. All it would take, thought Zia the gold merchant, would be one spark.

That spark was not long in being ignited. Ahmet was nicknamed "Kasap" not because he was actually a butcher, but because he was a clumsy barber. His heavy hand with the straight razor left him with few customers, only those whose courage matched their financial straits.

Ahmet "Kasap" saw the distraught crowd milling aimlessly about, wanting to do something but not knowing what. This, he felt, was his opportunity to become an important person in the community. He mounted a wooden case of dried apricots and yelled, "Attention, Turks! Attention, Turks!" He waved his hands above his head, and the radio volume was turned down to become background music.

The murmuring receded as all gave him their attention.

He looked at the hundreds, perhaps thousands, of faces turned toward him. It made him feel important. He said, "Why are we just standing around like headless chickens?" He looked around and saw blank faces. "You're thinking, 'What *should* we do?' Well, I'll tell you."

The throng surged forward to hear better.

He shouted, "A terrible crime has been committed against the entire Turkish nation. You all know who did this to us: the Kurds! Isn't it bad enough that they rebel against our government in the eastern provinces, where they fight hit-and-run battles with our troops? Isn't it bad enough they commit acts of terrorism against civilians out there in the east?"

A murmur of assent swept through the crowd.

Encouraged, he continued more vehemently. "Now they strike at us right here in this great city. And you know why. It is because we have captured their leader, Abdullah Ocalan, who is rotting in jail. It is time we taught the Kurdish dogs a lesson. We must avenge the deaths of all those soldiers, the cutting off of Istanbul, this, our greatest city, from the bulk of the country. Tourism, which is like bread and butter to us, will cease. Investment by the Europeans will come to a halt. We will be laughed at and despised by the world."

Voices in the crowd shouted their outrage. One man called out, "But our troops are fighting the Kurdish rebel forces in the east. What can we do here?"

Ahmet slowly repeated the question with heavy sarcasm. " 'What can we do here?' " He laughed disparagingly. "They have blown the bridges. While our troops were crossing! If they would do such a terrible thing as that, they will stop at nothing to destroy us. There are Kurds right here in Istanbul. The enemy is living in our midst, right under our noses. Next they will blow up our public buildings, our marketplaces, the place we are standing in right now when it is filled with people! They will bomb our schools, our homes. They will kill our children. They will rape our women. And they are right here in Istanbul!"

A woman in the crowd timidly said, "But the Kurds who live here are law-abiding citizens. They have businesses, professions . . ."

"You just *think* they are. They *act* that way so that we will allow them to carry out their bloody acts of treason. No! No, I tell you. They will murder you in your beds if you let them. They are laughing at us because we stand around doing nothing. Let us avenge the deaths of our soldiers!"

"Yes!" cried the throng.

"Let us avenge the terrible damage to the Turkish nation!"

"Yes, yes!" Fists were raised. Teeth were bared.

Breathing the spice-filled air, the mob's passion grew as they continued to hear the inflamed message of hatred against the background of martial music.

"Let us teach them a lesson before they hurt us any more. Enough is enough!"

"What should we do?" several voices called out.

Ahmet said. "There is a Kurdish neighborhood just blocks from here in the Süleymaniye District, right behind the Süleymaniye Cami, the local mosque."

Voices in the mob called out, "Let's get them!"

The merchants became even more nervous. One of the gold merchants called out, "The Kurds who live here are peaceful people. I know many of them."

All heads turned toward the merchant. Ahmet said,

"You deal with traitors, enemies of the nation, murderers? Maybe you yourself are a Kurd?"

The merchant's protests were drowned out by angry voices. Someone threw a stone through the merchant's window, which shattered, cutting some of the bystanders. There were many people in the crowd who felt as the merchant did, but seeing the mood of the others, they held their peace.

Ahmet pulled out his straight razor, opened it, and brandished it over his head. He yelled, "Come, loyal Turks, let us deal with the Kurdish enemy. Follow me!"

Filled with pride at having inspired the crowd, feeling as though he were the *atabeg*, the supreme military commander of the fifteenth-century Ottomans or the earlier Seljuks swooping down from the plains of Central Asia, he jumped down from the apricot crate and led the mob out of the marketplace and into the streets toward Süleymaniye.

People ripped legs off the stalls to use as clubs, sending piles of red, yellow, and black spices flowing to the ground. Others broke into the sword shop, knocked the protesting owner to the floor, and made off with costly swords and curved scimitars of finely tempered Damascus steel, with hafts of cloisonné enamel and silver gilt. Some preferred to show their patriotism by breaking into the shop of the gold merchant who had protested, knocking him senseless, and stripping the place clean of gold bracelets, rings, earrings, and chains. These opportunists thought it better to go home with their patriotically inspired gains, rather than join the frenzied mob in pointless mayhem.

Those who thought this behavior was wrong were intimidated by the more violent among the crowd. Once outside the bazaar, they furtively slunk away to their homes. But the most impressionable, the misfits, those dissatisfied with their lives, needed to take out their anger and frustration on someone. The Kurds were a good choice.

11:25 A.M.
Süleymaniye District, Istanbul, Turkey

The street had shops with Kurdish names on the windows and apartments above the shops where the owners lived.

An old man in baggy pants hummed a merry tune as he swept the street in front of the dry-goods store. Mehmet Ali Yazoglu was seventy-two years old and hard of hearing. He was a Turk who did light part-time work for the Kurdish textile merchant. He liked the merchant, who often sat down to have coffee with him and talk of their families, or the weather.

Mehmet Ali did not hear the angry roar of the crowd that surged through the streets toward him until they were twenty feet away. He turned, puzzled, and through his cataracts dimly saw a mass of people rushing toward him, waving objects above their heads. He thought it was some kind of celebration, perhaps a wedding. So he stopped sweeping to smile at them. Then he felt as though a hammer had struck his forehead, and everything went black.

Someone had thrown a stone at the old man's head. When he fell, dazed, they trampled him. The mob ran through the street, smashing the windows, stripping the stores bare, and setting fires with improvised molotov cocktails. The most violent dragged the merchants out of the shops and pummeled them mercilessly. Others went up to the apartments, where they beat the occupants, raped the women, and looted the personal jewelry and electronic appliances. They pulled drapes down, ripped up mattresses and pillows, and threw furniture out of the windows into the street below. In some cases, skulls were crushed, people tossed out of windows to the cheering mob below. Ahmet the "butcher" gave new meaning to his nickname; he slit throats on purpose this time and performed a couple of castrations, one on a corpse, the other on an unconscious man.

Police tried to intervene, but they were beaten by the mob, and their weapons taken from them. This resulted in the shootings of other Kurdish citizens. Other policemen, hating the Kurds as much as this mob, simply stood by. Finally, a detachment of Turkish Infantry arrived and fired into the air. Many of the rioters then took their booty and fled. The sergeant then gave orders to fire directly at the remaining rioters. His men hesitated, feeling that the Kurds deserved this treatment.

The sergeant extracted his sidearm from its holster and placed it against the temple of the man nearest to him. He then said, "We are here to do our duty and restore order. I'm going to give the command again. If any son of a bitch refuses to fire, I will put a bullet through him." He glared at them, and added, "And shoot straight, damn you, because if you don't, I will."

The troops respected this hardened warrior. Looking at the fierce expression on his face, they knew he meant what he said.

Then the sergeant hurriedly shouted, "Ready. Aim. Fire!"

The troops fired and the remaining looters began to fall. Those who did not fall, fled. But the damage had been done. The wounded and dazed survivors tearfully surveyed the corpses of loved ones and the destruction of their shops and homes. Several of the bodies, it was later discovered, belonged to the attackers as well.

11:30 A.M.
The Roofed Bazaar, Istanbul, Turkey

A huge crowd had gathered in the Kapali Carsisi, the immense roofed bazaar in the Beyazit District, just blocks south of the Spice Bazaar. It was a labyrinth of over 4,000 little shops located on narrow pedestrian walkways. They streamed in from the Cagaloglu gate and the Beyazit gate. Some had brought their great-grandfathers' swords and were waving them over their heads. "Death to the Kurds!" they chanted over and over.

On the street of the carpet merchants, music issued from one of the shops. The *dombeg*, the deep-toned hand drum, provided the slow, insistent rhythm against which the female voice wove a sultry, hypnotically monotonous melody, filled with intricate trills and passionate whimpers that suggested sexual desire. The Turkish words spoke of love, desire, and the longing for the beloved. The deep twanging of the stringed *oud* and the mellow tones of the wooden flute filled the gaps left by the human voice. People were quiet, some with their eyes closed, swaying gently to the music. The song came to an end.

"Hey, look there!" shouted a short, thin man, pointing

to the carpet shops. Edip was an unemployed baggage handler who had been fired from his job at the Atatürk International Airport for repeated lateness and discourtesy to passengers. The crowd on this street looked and saw the exquisite handwoven carpets with their intricate geometric patterns and swirls, their colors like those of fruit cakes. The carpets were Turkish, Azerbaijani, Persian, Afghan . . . Unfortunately, some were labeled "Kurdish."

The little man twirled the end of his handlebar mustache and in a shrill voice shouted, "Those are Kurdish carpets! Destroy them, rip them to shreds!"

The mob surged toward the shops, smashing the windows, but they did *not* rip the carpets to shreds. The first to reach the carpets shoved the shopkeepers back against the far wall and seized the carpets. More practical minded then Edip, they did not limit themselves to the Kurdish carpets; they took *any* carpet they could get their hands on.

"To the Kurdish quarter!" Edip cried out, waving his sword above his head. But fighting had erupted among the looters for possession of the luxurious carpets. Soon a roar went up, and the mob began running through the maze of roofed streets, smashing windows, stripping shops bare of jewelry, handwoven textiles, brass artifacts, carved meerschaum pipes . . . The fighting among the looters for the disputed booty became more widespread. Most of the people fought their way out and headed for home, horrified by what they had witnessed, considering themselves lucky to escape in one piece.

The unemployed baggage handler was followed by only a small portion of the huge crowd that had congregated in the roofed bazaar. He was followed by a group of ferocious misfits looking for blood to calm their feelings of inferiority. He and his band of fifty-odd thugs headed for the streets. They turned north at the Beyazit Mosque, continued past Istanbul University until they reached Süleymaniye, where they saw a crowd fleeing toward them.

Thinking they were Kurds trying to escape some other mob behind them, the little man with the big mustache shouted, "Death to the Kurds!"

Edip and his band were unaware that the crowd running toward them was the remainder of Ahmet Kasap's mob, fleeing from the scene of their crime, escaping from the

bullets of the Turkish troops. The mustached man led his
followers onward, waving his sword, but as he came within
twenty feet of the opposing mob, he turned white with fear.
He turned around and tried to flee, as did the men immediately behind him, when they saw that the other side had
swords, knives, clubs, and a couple of pistols. But it was
too late. The momentum of those in the rear pushed those
in front into the oncoming rabble. Without understanding
what they were doing, people clubbed, beat, stabbed, and
shot each other in the panic. Another detachment of soldiers charged to within fifty feet. Then they were given the
order to fire.

1:00 P.M.
The Presidential Palace, Ankara, Capital of Turkey

The ornate reception hall, with its magnificent chandelier,
oak paneling, and oil paintings of former Turkish leaders,
was filled with reporters and television cameras. President
Erdogan Oguzcanoglu stood at the podium. He wore a
double-breasted gray suit that matched the circles under his
eyes. He looked haggard, worried. This was a live broadcast
and would be heard on television and radio throughout
Turkey.

"Attention! Attention, please!" He paused to clear his
throat. "My fellow Turks, listen very carefully to my words.
The bridges over the Bosphorus have been destroyed and
thousands of our gallant troops, with their armor and weaponry, have been lost. They were on their way to join our
allies in NATO maneuvers.

"Once more, I beg you to listen very carefully to my
words. This horrible crime was *not* committed by Kurdish
agents. I repeat, it was *not* committed by Kurdish agents."
He paused for the message to sink in.

"We have had a message from the perpetrators of this
heinous crime. They have revealed their identity. It is a
militant Islamist organization called as-Saif al-Islam. They
have also sunk a container ship belonging to our great ally,
the United States, that was about to reach our port of

Izmir. Then these cowardly terrorists machine-gunned the crew in the water.

"These people threaten even more violence if we do not give in to their demands." He took a handkerchief from his breast pocket and mopped his forehead. "Their demands are nothing less than that we hand the government of our beloved country to them, so that they may institute *shari'a* as government policy. If they do this, if they make strict Islamic law the law of the land, as they intend, we will be like Iran or Saudi Arabia. The progress instituted by our beloved reformer, Mustafa Kemal Pasha, whom we lovingly call Atatürk, will be reversed. We will be expelled from NATO, from dealings with the European Common Market, with all dealings with the West. We will march, not forward to the twenty-first century, but backward to the fifteenth century. But I say to you, we will not permit this to happen.

"Unfortunately, there have been riots and massacres all over Turkey directed at our Kurdish minority. These acts are being committed by the dregs of our society. This must stop immediately! There is a Kurdish political group that has been at war with the government. But that is just one political group! They do not represent the Kurdish people. Even if this crime were committed by agents of that group, it would still be completely unjust to blame the entire Kurdish people. But it was *not* committed by Kurds at all, but by the same fanatical Islamic extremists who have been terrorizing our countryside.

"The rioting must cease immediately! The looting and anarchy of all kinds must come to an end at once, so we do not appear to be barbarians to the rest of the world. Our troops are seeing to it that order is restored.

"Loyal Turks, go to your homes and carry on with your normal lives. Our allies in America, in Europe, in Israel, as well as our friends in Japan, have all offered to send men and supplies to aid us in our time of need, just as they helped us after the terrible earthquakes. We all remember their dedication, their hard work, and their warm friendship. Let us not ruin those friendships by acts of barbarism. In the meantime, we are dealing with the Islamist threat."

President Oguzcanoglu bowed his head and was silent for a moment. Then he raised it and looked directly at the cameras. "In the name of the Turkish nation, I extend my sincerest sympathies to our loyal citizens of Kurdish origin and offer my humble apologies to them. Please forgive us."

The president then said, "Thank you," and turned to walk away. Reporters began to shout questions, but he told them they would be informed of developments as he himself became aware of them.

He lied. He did not tell his audience the terrible secret. He could not tell them, because to do so would have caused pandemonium. He had to bear the burden of the fearful threat almost alone, sharing it only with his most trusted top officials . . . and the president of the United States. He did not even tell his wife. Nuclear war loomed on the horizon.

1700 hours
Turkish Army Intelligence Center, outskirts of Ankara

The soundproof, bullet-proof walls of the conference room were one foot thick, constructed of steel wrapped in concrete. The additional two-inch layer of soundproofing material was concealed by oak panelling. Running down the center of the room, a lustrous ten by forty foot mahogany conference table contained now empty water pitchers at convenient intervals. The two men sitting beside each other looked incongruous in this room meant for large groups.

General Süleyman Denktash, Chairman of the Turkish Joint Chiefs of Staff, was sixty-two years old, but was as vital as the most vigorous forty-year-old. His bemedaled khaki tunic did not entirely conceal his broad shoulders and massive upper-body strength. He turned to the man seated beside him and finished giving him his instructions.

Major Serdar Aksu of Turkish Army Intelligence was young for his position; he was thirty-nine years old. Only five foot, five inches tall, he was slim and wiry. His mental acuity, however, was matched by his physical agility and endurance. His dark complexion and black brush mustache made him resemble, at a quick glance, Saddam Hussein, a man he despised. His full head of thick dark hair, his courtliness, and his wild sense of humor were known to have charmed many beautiful women. At this moment, listening intently to General Denktash, no humor was visible on his face.

Denktash spoke in hushed, confidential tones, "Major Aksu, I have called you here for a reason. This is something we must discuss in person."

The major nodded and kept his eyes fixed on his superior.

"The general continued, "You have heard President Oguzcanoglu's press release."

"Yes, General."

The general placed his hand on the younger man's shoulder and lowered his head. "Do you know why I've asked for you today?"

Major Aksu shook his head. He looked up and said, "No, General."

"You attended college in the United States, Northwestern University near Chicago, before attending our military college. Your English is excellent, I am told. In addition, you have a good working knowledge of the Kurdish language, and of Persian."

"Yes, and most of the few inhabitants of the sparsely populated southeast region are either Kurds or Azeri."

"Right. And, of course, Azeri is basically a dialect of Turkish, and not too difficult for us to understand." The general paused. "Your military experience, your patriotism, and your loyalty are well documented and beyond question."

"Thank you, General."

"The thing is, you have valuable contacts in southeastern Turkey who have supplied you with information on the Kurdish rebels as well as on Iranian and Iraqi troop movements along the borders."

"They are simple shepherds who easily travel across borders with their flocks. Most of them are Kurds, but don't care about politics."

"I understand they engage in contraband as well."

"Yes, they do a bit of harmless smuggling as well."

The general nodded understandingly. "Anyway, the reports we have received from villagers all indicate that as-Saif al-Islam's headquarters are somewhere in southeastern

Turkey, but no one seems to know exactly where. I want you to do surveillance and to put yourself in contact with your sheep herders to see if you can pinpoint the location of the terrorists' headquarters."

"Shall I leave tomorrow morning for the border region?"

"No, immediately. Right after we finish this little talk. There is no time to spare."

"Yes, General, I can imagine."

"I'm afraid you really cannot imagine the truth."

Major Aksu looked puzzled.

General Denktash looked up at the ceiling, as though talking to himself, and murmured, "You have not heard the worst, Major."

Aksu's head snapped up to look into his general's eyes. He waited.

Denktash gazed at the portrait of Mustafa Kemal Pasha, the man who brought Turkey into the twentieth century at the end of World War I. "He must be turning in his grave. We do not give him the title of Atatürk, 'Father of the Turks,' for nothing. By sheer force of will, he dragged us from the swamp of feudalism, ignorance, poverty, and corruption, and brought us into the modern world."

"He was a patriotic Turk," Major Aksu affirmed.

"Yes, and a true Muslim as well, by Allah. And now these Islamists want to plunge us back into the Middle Ages, keep women in the harem, the part of the house reserved for women, if you can believe it."

"Yes," said Aksu. "So many of those restrictions are not really part of Islam; they are merely ancient traditions, which are outdated. And not our own Turkish traditions either, traditions borrowed from the seventh-century bedouin of the Arabian Desert."

"Of course, Major. And are we not good Muslims? Do we not pray to God five times a day? Do we not observe the fast of Ramadan and keep every Friday as a holy day? And if there are Turks who are lax in these matters, or who take a little beer or *arak* on occasion, who are we to force them to abstain? That is between the individual and God. This is a democracy."

Major Aksu steered the conversation back to more practical matters. "General Denktash, you were going to give me bad news. I believe you said I had not heard the worst . . . ?"

The general turned to Major Aksu and sighed. "Brace yourself, Serdar Aksu . . ." He paused. "The as-Saif al-Islam have purchased nuclear weapons, missiles, and launchers."

Major Aksu's eyes widened. "Yes . . . ?"

"They threaten to use them on Athens and Tel Aviv if we do not hand the government over to them."

Major Aksu could not speak for several seconds. Then he said, "If that happens . . ."

"Yes," the general said, "the full consequences are unforeseeable, but necessarily catastrophic. They are insane." He paused. "Of course, we could hand the government over to them, as they want . . ."

"But who knows what they would do once in power?"

"Exactly."

"Besides, the Greeks and Israelis . . ."

"Yes, we belong to NATO along with Greece, and just recently have started to have a genuine rapprochement with the Greeks. It's shaky, but we've taken the first steps.

"And Israel is our military ally. Not to mention a true friend. They were the first to send their army disaster units and medical personnel to help us after that terrible earthquake."

"And, of course, it is almost certain that Israel has nuclear weapons. If they are attacked with weapons of mass destruction . . . It would be only natural . . ." The general sighed. "The situation as it is right now is intolerable."

"What is the deadline, General?"

"April six, at sunset. You leave immediately. A jet is waiting to take you to Diyarbakir. From there a helicopter to Hakari. From Hakari you'll be taken by Land Rover, accompanied by the driver and two privates, over the Büyük Zab Irmak to just beyond Geliashin Dag."

"Yes, the Great Zab River, and Mt. Geliashin. That mountain rises to almost fourteen thousand feet high. I know the region well."

"Will you be able to do the job?"

"Yes, General."

"Good. Remember, all we want is to pinpoint the location of their headquarters." He paused. "Now, Major Aksu,

I know you. I have already told you why you are the best man for the job. But you have one flaw: you are too heroic."

"Too heroic . . . ?! I am a soldier, General."

"Yes, I know. But keep in mind what the objective is, and go no further. Don't let that flaw be a fatal flaw. You are too valuable a man to lose. Just find out where the bastards are, relay the information to me, and get the hell out of there."

"Very well, General."

The general studied the major's face and then said, "All right. Time is running out. Allah be with you."

Chapter Two

Major Serdar Aksu had bought traditional Kurdish attire of the region from the shepherds. The brown trousers were tight at the calves, but baggy from calves to waist. He wore sheepskin boots, with what looked like a long white shirt hanging over the trousers to midthigh. Over the loose shirt he wore a lambskin vest, and on his head a brimless karakul cap, his dark hair protruding from under the curly gray fur. At his hip under the loose shirt was a sidearm.

He reached into the pocket of his vest, took out a cell phone, and pressed several buttons. After several buzzes, he heard General Denktash's voice, "Yes."

Aksu said, "General, I hope I haven't awakened you."

"You have, but I welcome your call. Report."

"I've been a guest of a band of shepherds. Some of them and I knew each other from a couple of years ago."

"Were they helpful?"

"Yes, sir. After I apologized and commiserated with them for the massacre of Kurds in western Turkey and distributed some legal tender, their old goodwill returned."

"Good. Continue, Major."

"A building has been erected in the last eighteen months in what had previously been uninhabited mountains. They have tried to approach it, to trade with the occupants, but they have been warned off by machine-gun fire. One man got too close and was blown up by a land mine. They avoid the place now."

"Where is the place?"

"They say it is four or five kilometers over the border into Iran."

"It's inside Iran!?"

"I'm afraid so, sir. I've changed into local civilian clothes, and I'm going to get a look at the place and report the exact location."

"If you cross into Iran, Major, and you're taken prisoner, we know nothing about you. You understand?"

"Of course."

"Well, then, good luck." He added, "Be careful, my boy."

"You can count on it, General."

0910 hours
Near the village of Selime, fifty miles southwest
of the city of Kayseri, Cappadocia region, Central Turkey

"I feel like we're on a different planet," Mary Cavanaugh said, as she surveyed the landscape. Mary was forty-four years old, with dark brown hair, sparkling blue eyes, and a trim figure.

Her husband, Bob, slowly nodded his head as he looked around him. "Amazing," he said. He was forty-eight and looked as though he were accustomed to daily workouts.

On this bright, clear day, the tourists could see the snowy peak of Mount Erciyas shimmering in the distance, almost 13,000 feet high. They stood in a weird landscape consisting of strange, gray conical formations rising from a beige plain of volcanic soil, flanked by steep cliffs on both sides of the valley. On closer inspection, the tourists could discern holes, openings in these rough-textured volcanic cones. There was no sound of traffic, no sound of insects. Other than the brushing of feet against the sandy soil and the comments of the tourists, there was no sound at all. The air was dry and irritated the nostrils.

"Very impressive," Ronald Billings quietly said to his wife, Clara. The distinguished-looking man in his early fifties was tall, slim, and had a full head of white hair.

Clara smiled, "It certainly is. But you should have had some security people with you, Ron."

"Please. I'm tired of all that nonsense. Besides, no one here knows who I am. I've been U.S. ambassador to Turkey for the last four years and never had any problems. And you and I have never seen anything of the country in those four years except for dreary Ankara and occasional trips to Istanbul. Now, Istanbul's an exciting place. But there's so much to see of the country. Like here, for example. I'd hate to think that thousands of tourists come here every year to see these wonders, and that I . . ." he whispered the next four words, ". . . the ambassador to Turkey," then continued in a normal voice, "never saw the place."

Ten-year-old Billy Lopert gazed at the conical formations. "They look like giant sand castles," he said, his voice disappearing into the vast silence. His parents, thirty-five-year-old Kathy and forty-one-year-old Dave Lopert, agreed.

"It's too hot," complained Billy's fifteen-year-old sister Kerrie. She squinted at the formations and shaded her eyes with her hand.

"Those cones look like the headgear of Armenian priests," Harry Sebouhian said. "Or hooded monks. And those openings look like their eyes, noses, and mouths."

Henry Snyder, a thirty-five-year-old computer expert, was on vacation with his wife, Carol. He turned to Sebouhian. "Did Armenians live here?"

Perry Stein, Ph.D., eminent Ottoman historian, quietly commented, "Of course there were Armenians here. Up until the Massacres." Stein, in his mid-forties, had a full black beard, graying in part. He was five-foot-seven, but what he lacked in height he made up for in girth.

They had arrived by bus from the city of Kayseri, fifty miles to the northeast. When they had alighted from the dust-covered vehicle, they noticed two empty Land Rovers parked nearby, but no other tourists. Okan Altiparmac, the rotund local guide in his mid-fifties, had squinted at the Land Rovers, wrinkled his brow, and looked around. Seeing nothing untoward, he shrugged.

Clara Billings asked Altiparmac, "Who do you think the Land Rovers belong to?" She sounded nervous.

"Who knows?" He shrugged. "Maybe some private tour."

"But where are the people who came in them?"

"I don't know. Probably inside one of the caves."

Ronald Billings put his arm around his wife's shoulders

and squeezed. "Come on, now, honey, don't be paranoid."
Yet he furtively scanned the area with his steel-gray eyes.

The sun was already gathering strength, and the fifteen
tourists were feeling it. Ruth Johnson, a forty-year-old so-
cial studies teacher from San Francisco, wished she was
someplace air-conditioned.

Okan Altiparmac mopped the perspiration from his
round face with a handkerchief and announced, "Ladies
and gentlemen, look around you. Here we are in the Peris-
trema Valley. See the steep cliffs on either side of the Mel-
endiz River, how they are riddled with cave dwellings. The
terrain in this valley consists almost exclusively of a fine-
grained, compressed volcanic ash. This comes from repeated volcanic eruptions from fifty to one hundred fifty
million years ago." He paused for dramatic effect, to let
the numbers sink in.

"And this valley sits among the foothills of the Hasan
Dag, the southernmost of the now-dormant, thank God,
volcanic mountains that created this distorted landscape.
And then millions of years of erosion carried away the
softer ash, creating these conical formations."

"Back in the Göreme Valley yesterday we saw those so-
called 'fairy chimneys,' " said Otto Dierkes, a stockbroker
from New Jersey. "What about them?" Dierkes tried to
keep a straight face. "Do you have many fairies here in
Turkey?" He lit a pipe filled with Yenidji tobacco, releasing
pleasant aromatic fumes into the dry air.

"Ah, yes," said the guide. "In that region of eastern Cappadocia, a layer of nonvolcanic rock often remains, eroded
into columns, each one supporting a volcanic cone. Those
are the 'fairy chimneys.' " He paused, put his finger to his
nose, and added, "By the way, Göreme, the name of that
valley, is Turkish for 'unseen,' or I guess 'invisible' could
be the word. But there are so many tourists there now that
it is probably the most *seen* of all Byzantine sites outside
of Istanbul." He chuckled.

Clara Billings had an unpleasant thought. She said, "Mr.
Altiparmac, are there Kurdish guerillas in this area?"

"No, no, of course not. They are much further east. We
would not be conducting tours in this area if it were a
war zone."

"What about the Islamist terrorists?" Harry Sebouhian asked.

"Of course not. What would they be doing here?" Altiparmac said.

"Well," Mary Cavanaugh said, "they don't exactly love Americans. And here we are, a whole bunch of us."

"No, no, they would not dare to bother foreign tourists."

"Uh, you were talking about the formations right here . . . ?" Otto Dierkes prompted. He then resumed puffing on his newly purchased meerschaum pipe with the amber stem. A lifelong nonsmoker, Dierkes had bought it in Istanbul several days before as a souvenir. Later he decided he ought to smoke it a bit, so he took an occasional puff just to keep the tobacco burning, but without inhaling.

"Yes, of course," Okan resumed. "There are entire cities built in the tenth and eleventh centuries . . . No, I should not say *built*, to be accurate, but rather *carved* out, of these volcanic formations: living quarters, granaries, churches, stables . . ."

Harry Sebouhian interrupted, "Armenian churches?"

The guide frowned. "No. There were no Armenians here."

"Hell, they weren't Lutherans, were they?" Sebouhian had an edge to his voice.

David Juhl, a middle-aged Lutheran minister from Brainerd, Minnesota, raised an eyebrow, looked at Sebouhian with distaste, then removed his steel-rimmed glasses to wipe them with a handkerchief.

The guide forced a laugh. "No, they were certainly not Lutheran. They were Byzantine. This was part of the Byzantine Empire." He paused. "Now, in the fourth century, this region produced three of the church fathers: Basil the Great, Gregory of Nazianzus, and Gregory of Nyssa. Yes, the two Gregorys. But the buildings, whole cities, carved out of the soft *tufa*, were done between the tenth and eleventh centuries."

"Soft what?" asked Mark McCain, a college senior.

"*Tufa*, it is called. And 'Negative architecture' is the technical term for this scooped-out kind of structure."

Harry Sebouhian said, "Yeah, but what kind of people built these cities?"

"For a long time, the general opinion was that they were

built, if I may use the word 'built' with reference to this
negative architecture, by ascetic Byzantine monks who
wanted to get away from the world. But very recently this
theory is being attacked. The latest theory is that these
troglodytes . . ."

"These *what*?!" Harry asked.

"Troglodytes, cave dwellers. That they were actually sol-
diers, aristocrats and farmers placed here to protect the
Byzantine Empire against invading Arabs coming up from
Syria."

Okan Altiparmac paused. "But come, we now enter this
tunnel at the base of the cliff, to make our way up 300 feet
to the Selime Kale."

"Three hundred feet? It'll kill me!" An overweight
woman in her fifties moaned as she shaded her eyes and
looked up at the steep cliff looming above her. The huge
mass with its series of openings, plus the heat, combined
with the idea of climbing three hundred feet, made her
think, for a moment, that it resembled a grinning death's
head. A feeling of approaching doom seized her. She shuddered but said to herself, "Get a grip, Betty Martin."

"Don't worry, it is a gradual ascent, and we will go
slowly. I am not exactly an athlete, myself." Okan patted
his ample paunch and laughed.

"What is the Selime Kale?" asked Tracy Licata, an an-
thropology major in her junior year at Miami University of
Ohio. The young woman tossed her dark hair as she waited
for the answer.

"The Selime Kale is the largest, most intricately planned
complex here at Selime. On ground level here there are
stables and granaries. We shall pass through them and proceed through the entrance tunnel cut through this rock until
we enter courtyard number one, to the west of the courtyard, that is, to our left, will be the kitchen. Not like a
kitchen in a tiny modern apartment. No, a large kitchen."

Okan Altiparmac moved forward and announced, "We
now make our ascent through this tunnel." As they leisurely walked, he continued his patter, one he intended to
repeat once they were in the chambers he was now describ-
ing in advance in order to entertain the tourists as they
climbed through the rock tunnel.

"To the east, our right, we shall enter one of the two

very large halls. A tunnel at the end of the first hall leads into yet another hall, and at its northern end is a room, which may or may not be a sleeping chamber. There is a cross carved into the ceiling, practically the length and breadth of the entire ceiling. Perhaps the cross on the ceiling, rather than on a wall, might have been carved there so that people lying in bed could look up at it."

Ten minutes later they emerged from the tunnel and found themselves in a spacious area carved out of the rock. Okan provided a running commentary, "All this has been carved out of the soft volcanic *tufa*, this malleable volcanic material. This is one of the two spacious courtyards in this complex. We shall turn to the right and enter the first great hall of the Selime Kale."

The tourists gazed in wonder all around them at the large, rectangular room with a flat ceiling, six barrel-vaulted niches, three carved into each of its long sides.

Okan pointed ahead and announced, "Ladies and gentlemen, at the end of this hall, you will see another barrel-vaulted niche flanked by two tunnels. Now, these two tunnels climb to the upper galleries. If you look up you will see that these galleries consist of arcades with arched openings that are around us on three sides. From up there, as you will soon observe, one can watch whatever is happening throughout this spacious hall."

Okan continued, "We will soon pass on to the Selime Kale Kilise, and . . ."

"The what?" asked Harry Sebouhian.

"Ah, yes, that is what we call it. It means the church of Selime Castle. It is very interesting, as you will see. It has alternating round columns and square piers, and it has three barrel-vaulted aisles. The walls are covered with frescoes, most of them quite deteriorated, depicting scenes from the life of the Virgin Mary, and . . ."

At that moment, they heard hurried footsteps. They turned and saw three men in fatigues, carrying Kalashnikov semiautomatic assault rifles, rushing into the chamber from behind them. They leveled their weapons at the tourists. The Americans turned back toward the tunnels and saw that the two tunnels were guarded by an armed man at the entrance to each.

"Stand right there and wait!" a loud voice shouted from

above, echoing against the stone walls. They looked up to the arcaded galleries of the second tier to see three armed men dressed like the others. The scar-faced one who spoke English was Rauf Pasha's Libyan lieutenant, Mahmoud ibn Hassan el-Badawi.

The three men turned and disappeared. Soon the tourists heard footfalls echoing in the tunnels leading from the upper galleries and then saw the three men stride toward them.

"Really, gentlemen, I must protest . . ." Okan Altiparmac didn't get to finish his sentence.

El-Badawi offhandedly fired a burst from his AK-74 assault rifle at the guide, who fell backward, his chest ripped open, blood spurting from the wounds. The noise from the burst reverberated throughout the stone chamber. El-Badawi then calmly looked at the horror-stricken tourists. Bob Cavanaugh held Mary close as she sobbed. Tracy Licata instinctively shrank back behind the others, away from the men in fatigues. Fifteen-year-old Kerrie Lopert stood stiffly, staring straight ahead at nothing in particular while she whimpered. Her brother Billy stared at the corpse, then at the armed men. He kept mumbling, "Oh shit oh shit oh shit oh shit." Betty Martin screamed, and then continued screaming. She seemed unable to stop.

"Silence, American sow!" barked el-Badawi.

The Reverend David Juhl took Betty's hand in his two hands and whispered, "There, there, Betty. Calm down, now. Calm down."

El-Badawi said something to one of his men, who walked over to Reverend Juhl and shoved him back away from Betty Martin. Juhl's steel-rimmed glasses fell to the stone floor. When he bent down to retrieve them, the man put his hand against Juhl's face and pushed him further back. Then he smiled and deliberately smashed the glasses with his booted foot.

Betty Martin screamed even more loudly. El-Badawi walked up to her and smacked her hard once. Twice. A third time. She started to fall backward, but Harry Sebouhian and Otto Dierkes caught her, Dierkes's pipe falling to the ground. Betty finally stopped screaming, but was hyperventilating.

Ambassador Billings was about to interfere, but Clara
sank her fingernails into his arm, and he held his peace.

Bob Cavanaugh noticed with revulsion that el-Badawi
had been smiling as he slapped Betty. He seemed to enjoy
the activity. El-Badawi noticed the disgusted look on Cavanaugh's face. His smile became a scowl as he fixed his
penetrating eyes on Cavanaugh for several seconds. Cavanaugh realized he was in no position to antagonize their
captor; he looked down.

El-Badawi gave a command and his men shoved their
prisoners toward the exit tunnel, nudging them into a run
with the barrel of their weapons. When they emerged from
the Selime Kale, they heard the repeated *thwock thwock
thwock* of helicopter blades. They looked up and saw the
huge chopper descend at a spot a few hundred meters from
where they were standing. The men in fatigues urged the
prisoners into the whirlwind of volcanic dust churned up
by the helicopter blades. They cast openly appreciative
glances at Tracy Licata and Kerrie Lopert and winked at
each other, exchanging comments in Turkish. One of them
seemed more interested in Billy.

The tourists were shoved and prodded toward the helicopter. When they reached the door, they were pushed
from behind and pulled by other men into the chopper. The
captors lingered a little longer than necessary, it seemed to
Mark McCain, when their hands were on the girls' buttocks, helping Tracy and Kerrie to climb in.

They had difficulty getting Betty Martin into the chopper.
She was too stunned to cooperate, and her excessive weight
made it difficult for the terrorists to lift her easily. El-
Badawi grunted, "Baah!" and strode over to her, taking
his Colt .45 automatic sidearm from the holster. He placed
the gun to her temple and fired. She lurched to the side
and fell to the ground. Her blood spattered against the
fuselage of the helicopter and el-Badawi's hand and
forearm.

Ron Billings couldn't restrain himself. "My God, man!
You'll pay for that!"

Clara sank her nails into Billings's arm and said, "Shut
up, shut up, shut up!"

El-Badawi stared at him through half-closed eyes for several seconds. Then he spoke in English, "I know who you

are, Mr. Ambassador. And the only reason I haven't killed you on the spot is because you have a certain value. However, if you push me too hard, I might kill your dear wife."

Then el-Badawi addressed the entire crowd. "Chopper would never be able to take off with her in it, anyway," el-Badawi said in English, chuckling and smiling at the other tourists as though he had just cracked a good joke. Seeing the horror on the faces of some, the anger in the eyes of others, his smile disappeared. "*Yallah, yallah!* Go, go, go!" he barked.

0940 hours
In the mountains of northwestern Iran,
26 kilometers west of Dazgir, Iran

Major Aksu lay prone on a windy height overlooking the mountain valley below. He was led to this spot by the herdsmen and left there as they traveled on. He extracted his binoculars from under his shirt and studied the compound below. Then he called General Denktash on the cell phone.

"Yes?"

"Aksu here. I am inside Iran and looking down on what must be the terrorists' headquarters."

"I'm listening."

"There is a gray building, probably concrete, within a compound that is surrounded by an outer and an inner perimeter of what appears to be razor wire. The shepherds call the place Kara Kale. The building is one story high, but could have subterranean levels. In one part of the compound I see two helicopters. I can't tell from here what kind."

"What are the exact coordinates of the compound?"

Aksu provided the general with those coordinates.

The general said, "Very well, Major, you have done excellent work. Now return to Turkish soil immediately."

"But, General, if I can get closer and give more details, it will be better for an attacking force."

"No, Major. Besides the fact that you are too valuable a

man to risk, we don't want to create an international incident. Return immediately."

Aksu rubbed the cell phone against his lambskin vest to create sounds similar to static. Then he said, "I'm sorry, General, I'm having difficulty receiving you."

"Major Aksu . . . Major Aksu . . ."

Aksu pretended he didn't hear the general. "General . . . Hello? Hello? Are you there?"

Then he cut off the communication and began the descent into the high valley.

1005 hours
Two kilometers from Kara Kale

Major Aksu had come as close as two kilometers from the outer perimeter of Kara Kale when he heard the crackling of broken twigs above and behind him. Gravel scraped and trickled down toward him. He looked up and saw three men in camouflage uniforms just thirty yards above him.

"Hey you!" One of them shouted in Turkish.

His first inclination as a soldier was to take cover and use his weapon. But he could not let the terrorists know that they were in danger. He couldn't let it be known that a member of the Turkish Army had crossed into Iran. Battle, then, was a total impossibility. Instead, he quickly tossed his pistol with its holster, the cell phone, and the binoculars into the brush.

Pretending he was a local shepherd, he yelled to them in Kurdish, "Can you give me a hand?"

"Wait there," they commanded in Turkish.

When they reached him, one of them said, "What the hell are you doing here?"

Purposely speaking in broken Turkish, to sound like a Kurdish shepherd, he explained that he had been chasing some lost goats for the last three hours and had become separated from his fellows.

They looked at him suspiciously. "How do we know you were not spying on us?"

"Why would I do that? I am just a humble shepherd."

"You shepherds are smugglers as well. Everyone knows

that. You would buy and sell anything, if it paid, even your mother. Maybe the Turkish Army is paying you for information."

"Turkish Army . . . ? I am a Kurd. And a smuggler. The last thing in the world I want to see is a Turkish soldier."

"He has a point," one of them said to the others.

"Who gives a damn! We can't take chances. Anyway, they've been warned."

"Yeah," the third man said. "Shoot the stupid bastard. One less Kurd. One less pain in the ass."

Aksu knew he was finished. He was not going to die without fighting. He thought of diving for his weapon, but he could not use the pistol he had thrown into the brush, because that would warn the terrorists that they were actually in danger. One of the terrorists yawned and lazily started to unsling his AK-74. Aksu swiftly reached for his hunting knife. He knew the knife was the kind used by the shepherds, and it would be perfectly natural for one of the smugglers threatened with death to use it.

In one motion he whipped it out and thrust it into the throat of the man who was unslinging the Kalashnikov. The man's eyes bulged, as he staggered backward, gasping for air, the blood gurgling into his lungs, and crashed to the ground, rolling down the hillside.

Before the man even hit the ground, Aksu had drawn the knife from his throat and shoved it under a second man's sternum, serrated blade upward. Before he could extract the knife from the fatal wound, the third man managed to unsling his assault rifle and fire several bursts at point-blank range into Aksu's chest as the major turned to face him. Aksu was thrown backward and fell heavily to the ground. Then he rolled downhill through the scrub and dust.

Chapter 3

Sam Wong sat among the banks of computer screens, key-boards, switches, and trac-ball devices in the darkened communications center. Sometimes, during the brief periods in which there was no particular emergency, he felt weightless, disembodied, as though he were floating in limitless space, in everlasting darkness with no anchor. The walls of the communications center seemed to melt away at those moments. There were no limits. But not now. Now, he was acutely conscious of the walls. He was firmly anchored. He had just received an urgent TAD, as he called it: a TALON Action Directive.

Sam broke into a sweat. He always did when he received a TAD. He was well aware that, as always, the directive had originated with the Chairman of the Joint Chiefs of Staff (CJCS), General George H. Gates, had been passed on to the Commander in Chief of Special Operations (CINCSOCOM), General Samuel "Buck" Freedman, and after consultation with the CIA, the NSA, and the Department of State, was delivered to Brigadier General Jack Krauss, Commander of the Joint Task Force known as TALON Force, of which Sam was a member.

Sam knew that these consultations, and the passing on of the TADs, took place with the utmost speed, because any directive for TALON Force was a response to an urgent need for military action with life-and-death consequences for the United States.

Sam Wong, computer expert, communications wizard, techno-geek par excellence, was responsible for bringing together the seven members of TALON Force Eagle Team as quickly as possible. He was also responsible for maintaining contact among members of the task force and between them and General Krauss. He was aware that this was a lot of responsibility for a twenty-three-year-old. So Sam sweated when he received the latest TAD on the computer zip line. Especially after he digested the content.

This small-boned young Chinese-American was five-foot-six, and looked more like a chess player than a warrior, yet, through sheer determination, he had made it through the most rigorous weeding-out process and training and had become one of the select few to be chosen for TALON Force. Since then, he had proven himself a valuable member of Eagle Team in many dangerous operations.

So he sweated. But wasted no time. As soon as he received the directive, he pushed his glasses back up to the bridge of his nose and got to work. He keyed the buttons, and a map of the United States appeared on the screen. He eyed the little symbols, red bird claws—TALONs—, at six different locations across the country, indicating where the other members of TALON Force Eagle Team were at that precise moment. There would be only a few seconds between each member's receiving the notification. Still, the boss came first: Major Travis Beauregard Barrett, U. S. Army/Special Forces. Then Lieutenant Commander Powczuk, U.S. Navy SEALS, second in command to Eagle Team. After he alerted them, he would contact the four other members of the team.

0615 hours PST
The Horny Bull Bar,
50 miles south of Edwards Air Force Base,
Area 51 (Groom Lake), Tonopah, Nevada

Captain Hunter Evans Blake III, U.S. Air Force, was one cool customer. He was an Airborne Rescue Pilot and was Ranger qualified. He had flown Piper Cubs when he was ten, and by the time he was seventeen, could fly anything that had wings, including a 1911 Bleriot with wingwarping, built before flaps were invented. He acquired these skills during a summer job working on vintage aircraft engines at the Rhinebeck Aerodrome on the Hudson River in New York State.

During the Gulf War he had flown an F-117 Nighthawk Stealth fighter/bomber. Even though the plane was practically undetectable, a concentration of Iraqi antiaircraft fire had unwittingly hit his craft while firing wildly into the night sky. His instruments indicated that he was rapidly losing fuel. In this situation the safest thing was to turn back immediately and make for the base. But not Hunter Blake. No, not Mr. Cool. He had some installations to destroy, and he was confident he could somehow make it back to safety.

He fired his air-to-ground rockets toward the targeted SCUD missile launchers, destroying them. Only after determining that the targets had actually been neutralized did he turn back. The last five minutes of flight were on empty. Most pilots would have ejected, but Hunter was confident that his experience with every type of aircraft in existence, including helicopters and gliders, would bring him in for a safe landing and save this very expensive piece of equipment for Uncle Sam at the same time. He was right. Barely. He managed to bring the plane to a halt just about a hundred feet short of the control tower.

When he alighted from the plane, he looked around at the fire engines and ambulance and calmly said, "Hey, guys, have a little confidence." Then he turned to a member of the ground crew and offhandedly murmured, "I believe the tank's been hit."

His present job was test flying an experimental F-120 Stealth bomber/fighter for the Air Force. He had been flying during early evening of the previous day and had slept soundly from around midnight until a half hour ago. He had awakened, feeling restless, as though something important were in the offing.

Off duty until evening, he had been letting off steam driving his Dodge Viper at a hundred miles an hour along a secondary road to nowhere in particular. He enjoyed observing the change from hurtling through an indistinct gray world to a more solid reddish one, finally seeing the parched and dusty brown landscape appear. When he spotted the neon sign proclaiming THE HORNY BULL BAR and in smaller letters, misspelled OPEN TWENTY FOR OURS, he decided to stop for a cup of coffee and some local color.

Hunter pushed open the door and looked around. He saw a wide, squarish room with the bar on the left and pine tables and chairs to his right. The head of a longhorn bull gazed down from the wall behind the bar. The smell of stale beer was cut by the aroma of fried grease and tomato paste issuing from the kitchen in back. *Way too early,* he thought, but he sat at the bar and ordered a cup of coffee.

With Hunter's chiseled features, slicked-back sandy hair, and silver tongue, the women always took notice.

"That your Dodge Viper out front, Mister?"

Hunter turned, stood, and slowly took in the flaming-red hair, the boobs bursting out of the halter, the tight cut-off jeans, the shapely legs . . .

"That's right, darling. How did you know?"

She took a step closer and was only six inches from his face. When she opened her mouth to speak, her breath reminded him of the aroma that would hit him when he opened a bottle of gin. "I know most everybody around here. Nobody I know drives a Viper."

He pushed his ever-present sunglasses down from the bridge of his nose and peered over them at her face. She had big blue eyes, a tiny freckled nose, and she ran her pink tongue along her succulent bottom lip as she waited for his response.

"Well, tell me, darling, am I squeezing you?"

She cocked her head and smiled quizzically.

He corrected himself, "I mean, is my car parked too close to yours?"

"Oh, no. It's just that I never saw that kind of car before, in person."

He laughed. "In person, huh?"

By now, her left hip was pressed up against his right thigh, and her face was less than three inches from his.

"My name is Kate. What's yours, Mister?"

"Nice to met you. I'm Hunter."

"Hunter, heh? What do you hunt, Hunter?"

"Well, that depends where I am, sweety. Once, in Tibet, I went hunting the wild ass."

She put her hand on his and squeezed. In a slow, sly tone, looking him up and down, she said, "Oh, I'll just bet you *have* done that kind of hunting more than just once. Lots more. And not just in Tibet."

"Hey, Kate, what the hell are you doin'?" The booming voice issued from the mouth of a man who Hunter thought looked a lot like the Hulk, only not green. Wearing cowboy boots, Levis, and a buckskin jacket, fringes and all, he was six-foot-one, and had shoulder-length black hair. He was so broad he had to come through the door sideways. He looked around, then strode up to where Hunter and Kate were standing. He did not look happy.

Kate seemed scared. "I'm not doing anything, Willie, honey," she whined. "We're just talking is all."

"Yeah, I'll bet that's all you were doin'. Hey you, pretty boy, move off, you're annoying my girl."

"Oh, now, I don't think I'm annoying the lady."

The Hulk wasn't accustomed to this kind of response. He was used to a man taking one look at him, shrugging his shoulders, and quietly moving away.

The Hulk took time to digest this turn of events. He scratched his three-day growth of beard, then said, "Well, you are. And now you're annoying me, dickhead. And I don't like to be annoyed before havin' my eggs. It upsets me."

"Sorry to hear that." He turned to his coffee and took a sip, ignoring the Hulk.

Kate looked worried. She backed away from the two men. The Hulk moved closer to Hunter and continued, "Yeah, and you know what annoys me most about you, pretty boy?"

Hunter was getting a little irritated, but prided himself on his self-restraint. He turned toward the Hulk and very calmly and deliberately, as though he were explaining a complicated concept to a student, said, "No, actually, I don't know. But would it surprise you very much if I told you I don't give a rat's ass about what annoys you? Or about what you're having for breakfast, or what your favorite wine is . . ."

"Oh, you're real funny, dickhead. I'm gonna tell you anyhow."

Hunter sighed. "Yeah, I kind of thought you would."

"I don't like to see some asshole who's prettier than she is talking to my girl."

"Well, then, you're the perfect match for her."

The Hulk looked puzzled.

Hunter was starting to get irritated. "Let me explain that to you. It means you're an asshole who's definitely not prettier than she is, you ugly son of a bitch, so you ought to be very happy."

The Hulk paused to process this information. Then his face lit up with comprehension, and he took a wide swing at Hunter, who ducked and grabbed the other man's wrist.

Hunter spoke calmly and deliberately, "Look, shit-for-brains, I feel it's my duty to warn you that I'm a real good fighter. Really. I am. I'm not bragging, just stating a fact. And if you force me to, I'll have to hurt you pretty badly, because I have a duty to protect myself." He paused, still holding the Hulk's wrist, to see if he was getting through. "Now, I'm being sincere with you. So, why don't you let me buy you a drink and then I'll be heading out of here, and we'll both be happy. Okay?"

By now, a crowd had gathered to watch the action. Hunter judged that most of them hadn't yet gone to bed, and only a few had recently left their beds. He figured there wasn't much excitement in this part of the country. The Hulk seized a bottle from the bar, and in one fast movement smashed it against the bar and lunged for Hunter's face with it. Hunter ducked and brought his fist up hard into the Hulk's groin. The Hulk groaned and doubled over. Hunter clapped his hands against the other man's ears, brought his knee up against the Hulk's chin, then chopped the back of his neck with his right hand. The Hulk collapsed, smashing his face against the floor.

Hunter looked at Kate and very sincerely said, "I didn't want to have do that. Really." He paused to look at the prone Hulk. Hunter shook his head and murmured, "What a waste."

Then Hunter readjusted the shades on his face, smoothed his hair, and sauntered toward the door.

"Well," Kate said brightly, "y'all come back, now. Okay?"

Hunter raised an eyebrow, shook his head, and kept walking. Then he stopped in mid-stride when he felt the vibrations emanating from the beeper at his waist. He concentrated on the decrypted morse signals.

b-i-r-d-m-a-n//f-l-y//q-u-i-c-k//c-h-o-p-s-t-i-c-k-s///

Hunter quickened his step, opened the door, rushed to the Viper, put pedal to the metal, and left in a cloud of dust.

One of the bar patrons, observing that the Hulk was starting to regain consciousness, commented loudly, "Yeah, the coward *better* run before Big Willie gets ahold of him."

0915 hours EST
U.S. Army Center for Health Promotion
and Preventive Medicine (USACHPPM),
Aberdeen Proving Ground, Maryland

Captain Sarah Greene, U.S. Army, stood at the front of the classroom. At age thirty-four she had an impressive medical background: doctor of medicine, board-certified surgeon, microbiologist. Beyond these accomplishments, she was resourceful; she could whip up medicines as well as poisons, plus their antidotes, from whatever plants and animals might be at hand. Not to mention a mean chicken soup. She had special proficiency with infectious diseases and epidemiology. She also had expertise on the medical aspects of chemical, biological, and nuclear warfare.

The one hundred-odd young soldiers listened to her lecture on chemical and biological warfare in rapt attention.

"Why me?" she had asked her commanding officer. It was an elementary course that could have been taught by so many less-qualified instructors. You didn't have to be a brain surgeon to teach this course.

"Because some of these young kids let their attention wander, damn it," he had told her, "and I want to make damn sure they pay close attention."

She had an idea about what he meant, but she asked him anyway, just to be sure. "Damn it, Captain Greene," he had muttered, banging his fist on the desk, "you know damn well what I mean!" He paused, looked her up and down, and resumed, "Look at you. Green eyes, freckles, your short black hair, that pixie look. You look ten years younger than your age. And," he let his gaze wander up and down her shapely legs, "well, hell, you're a damn fine-looking woman, Captain Greene. If I may say so."

She drew herself up to her full five-foot-four stature. "Major," she had said stiffly, "if I may speak frankly, that kind of talk is sexist and uncalled for." She saw his jaw drop in surprise and embarrassment, his ruddy face turn a shade redder under his bushy white hair, and she relented. He didn't have a clue, she thought, and he means well. "But, I'll just take it as a compliment, while registering my protest at the assignment. It's a waste of my talents, sir."

"I know, I know, Captain. But it'll take only two weeks of your time. Humor me."

So, here she was, teaching the ABCs of nuclear warfare to a bunch of kids. At least it would be for only two weeks, and this was her third day.

"All right," she announced, "we've been talking about the immediate effects of nuclear bombs on people and buildings. We've taken the specific cases of Hiroshima and Nagasaki, and we've gone into how much more powerful the present generation of nuclear weapons are than those relatively primitive ones."

She swept her gaze over the class and saw that everyone was hanging on her every word.

She continued, "I'd like to talk now about some of the nuclear accidents that have taken place, and could still take place, and long- as well as short-term effects of those accidents."

Sarah wasn't accustomed to standing still. Her legs were not only shapely, they were strong from years of snow-boarding in her native Vermont. Her arms were strong as well, from years of chopping firewood. She had done some skydiving and was a highly proficient martial artist too. She was accustomed to physical activity. So she paced back and forth in front of the class as she spoke. She noticed with some annoyance as well as some secret satisfaction that their eyes followed her intently as she moved about. *Horny bastards,* she thought. But she had to smile.

"You've all heard of the accident at Chernobyl. Well, as recently as October 1, 1999, a nuclear affairs official near the accident site reported that it was raining and that radio-active particles were coming down in the rain."

A murmur went through the class. "Yes, the effects of

nuclear leaks are long lasting. You can imagine, then, the effects of the explosion of one of the most powerful modern nuclear bombs. Now, so far, there have been no nuclear bombs used in warfare since the end of World War II. I'm not talking about atomic bombs, like in World War II, but hydrogen bombs, or thermonuclear devices."

A young man who looked like a high school quarterback said, "Yeah, but the Russians are sloppy about security, and they're selling material and know-how to countries like Iran and Iraq."

"Oh, yes. The danger for nuclear war is real, very real. But that's a political matter. The fact is that nuclear accidents have happened, many more than the average person knows about, and the potential for many more is there."

One of the few female members of the class had been sitting there silently for the entire period, a sullen expression on her pretty face. "What about the effects of these accidents?" she asked.

Sarah cleared her throat. "When the Chernobyl accident took place, two workers were taken to the hospital showing all the signs of radiation poisoning. They suffered from nausea, vomiting, diarrhea. The level of these symptoms and the rapidity of its development depends on the size of the exposure."

She put her hands behind her back and strode back and forth while concentrating on the floorboards, as she continued to speak. "After that, maybe ten days, two weeks, people recover, or *seem* to recover, and there are no outward signs . . . But then the blood cell counts will be down, and people will be very susceptible to infections during that period. Then from two to three or four weeks later, they'll contract other infections and . . . well, die. Do you know why?"

The annoyed young woman student said, in a bored tone of voice, "Because their immune systems are shot to hell. In fact, they won't have an immune system."

"Yes, exactly."

"What about long-term effects?" The freckle-faced boy who asked the question let his gaze run from her dark hair and green eyes to her hips and legs.

"Good question. It could take five, ten, fifteen years to

notice an increased risk of thyroid cancer and leukemia in the affected population."

"Captain Greene," a student said, "you had mentioned after the atomic explosions in Japan, even children who weren't born yet had brain damage. Is that likely in the event of an accident like Chernobyl?"

"It's certainly possible. It depends on . . ."

Sarah stopped speaking to give her full attention to the message vibrating under her blouse at the waistline:

s-o-r-c-e-r-e-s-s-//h-o-u-s-e-c-a-l-l//c-h-o-p-s-t-i-c-k-s///

Her class was instantly dismissed. Ten minutes later, she was in her yellow Volkswagen New Beetle, having passed through the holding barrier, tearing up the road northward.

1715 hours
Mountains of northwestern Iran, 26 kilometers
west of Dazgir, Iran, 7.8 kilometers from the Turkish border

Six hours earlier, the tourists had been herded past the outer gate through the circular razor wire, then through the inner gate past more razor wire, and into the inner compound. They had been sitting on the ground huddled together for warmth on this cloudy afternoon. They were surrounded by guards in camouflage fatigues. The temperature was now sixty-six degrees and dropping as the sun dipped behind the mountains of Turkey to the west. Shadows grew ominously longer. The prisoners were hungry. Since being captured, they had been given only the chance to drink brackish water from a trough, on their hands and knees, as the guards stood by and laughed.

They had been told nothing up until this moment. Now Mahmoud ibn Hassan el-Badawi strode out to them and barked, "Welcome to our humble abode, American pigs." He swept his gaze over them and smiled. "Now, all men will line up single file over there." He pointed to an area a few meters to his right.

The Cavanaughs started to walk in the direction indicated. El-Badawi gestured to the guards. One of them seized Mary by the hair and pulled her away from Bob. Bob attempted to help her, but was struck in the ribs by a rifle butt and punched in the face by another guard. He slumped to the ground, blood trickling from his nostrils. Mary's blue eyes widened in desperation, but she restrained herself from a strong impulse to call to him. She did not want him to struggle and be beaten more, or killed.

El-Badawi said, "Am I not speaking English, fool? I said *men* will line up over there. I did not say *women*." He thought for a moment, smiled, and added, "But, if you think you are a woman, maybe we will treat you as such." He smirked and looked around at his men. He repeated what he had said, but in Turkish. At this his men laughed raucously.

Kathy and Dave Lopert were still standing together, holding hands, looking at each other's faces. Several terrorists pulled them apart, shoving Dave toward the spot indicated. Kathy took a step toward him, and one of the terrorists, standing behind her, put his arms around her to hold her in place by grasping her breasts. She struggled desperately, but her captor held fast and laughed. Dave turned to go to her. A terrorist kicked his legs out from under him, and he landed on his face in the dirt. Another man then kicked him in the stomach and said something unintelligible to him, while pointing in the direction that el-Badawi had indicated. When he struggled to his knees, one of the guards kicked him at the base of his spine, so that he toppled over.

"Please, gentlemen . . . ," the Reverend Mr. Juhl meekly said to no one in particular. Without his glasses, it was difficult for him to identify the man in charge. They shoved him in the proper direction.

Mark McCain, a college senior, shuffled toward the lineup area. Then he heard Tracy Licata plead, "No, don't. Don't!" He turned to see one of the guards with his hands between her thighs. He couldn't help himself. He was seized by a sudden impulse. He whirled in her direction, and, fists clenched, started to run toward her. A guard struck him in the temple with the rifle butt, forcing him to slump to his knees. As he knelt in this dazed condition, another guard viciously struck him across the face with the back of his hand. He fell backward and was dragged to the appointed spot by two guards grasping his arms.

Harry Sebouhian was walking to the area indicated, cursing under his breath. Perry Stein sighed and followed him. Stein saw that Henry Snyder seemed frozen in place. His wife, Carol, was wringing her hands. "C'mon, Hank," Stein quietly said as he passed close to him, "don't play games with these characters."

"No talking!" yelled el-Badawi.

Henry seemed to snap out of his daze. He turned and followed Stein.

Ten-year-old Billy Lopert held his mother's hand. A husky man in camouflage gear, with a close-cropped beard and shaved head, approached Mahmoud el-Badawi, pointed to Billy, and asked a question.

El-Badawi smiled indulgently, but shook his head. "Not yet, Azzam," he said. "Send him with the men."

Azzam Hamal walked over to Billy and Kathy Lopert, lifted a terrified Billy by the collar and the seat of his pants, disregarding Kathy's protests, and carried him over to the men, where he roughly deposited him like a piece of cheap luggage.

The men stood in line, except for Mark McCain, who was unable to stand. Bob Cavanaugh was dazed and barely managed to stay on his feet.

El-Badawi arrogantly strode over to them. He stood silent for some moments, looking the rest of them over. The expression on his face was that of a man inspecting a pile of manure that had been standing in the sun too long.

Finally, he announced, "Welcome, gentlemen. Never mind to where, but welcome." In a tone that suggested humor, he stopped in front of each man and said, "Passport, please." He studied each passport, which he then confiscated, and examined each man's face.

When he studied Sebouhian's passport, he then looked at the man's face and said, "Haig Sebouhian, eh? Armenian?"

"American."

"Yes, I can see you are a U.S. citizen, but you are Armenian." He paused to look him up and down. Then he continued down the line.

When he came to Perry Stein, he examined his face and said, "Stein, eh? Could be a German name. Could also be Jewish, no? Yes, I believe you are a fat Zionist pig." He grasped Stein's beard and pulled him closer. "Am I right, Dr. Stein?"

Stein answered sharply, "Hey, I'm not fat. Portly, perhaps, but not fat."

El-Badawi scowled, "A portly Jew! Indeed. You have a sense of humor. Good, you will need it."

When el-Badawi completed his inspection of the men, he stepped back and announced, "You men need to be disinfected. Remove your clothing!"

The men looked at each other, alarmed.

Reverend Juhl looked at el-Badawi and said, "But . . ."

El-Badawi stopped him by holding up a hand. Then he walked over to the reverend and struck him across the face with his swagger stick, leaving a burning red welt. "No one told you to speak, *Reverend*." He pronounced the last word sarcastically. The reverend's eyes teared with the pain, but he stood erect and stared straight ahead.

"Remove your clothing, American pigs!" el-Badawi repeated, more loudly.

A knot of terrorists had gathered around them, leveling their weapons at them. The men sized up the situation and resignedly began removing their clothing, despite the fast-dropping temperature and the embarrassment. They helped the dazed Mark McCain do the same. Two of the guards picked up the clothing and carted it away. The men stood in line, shivering, looking up at the cloudy sky. Billy looked at the ground and wept.

"Very well, now we disinfect." El-Badawi motioned to one of his men, who trained a fire hose on them. When he had finished hosing them down, to the laughter of the others, the American men stood there shivering violently.

"Now, gentlemen," announced el-Badawi, "you will soon have dinner, such as it is in our humble abode. But first begins your training. The most important thing for you to learn is obedience. Americans are not accustomed to this concept. But you will learn. This I promise you." He smiled as he watched them shiver.

He continued, "First, you must understand—thoroughly understand—that you must obey orders. Without question, and immediately. I believe I once heard an American noncom, who was training us in Afghanistan, say, and I quote, 'If you hear me say *shit!*, I want to see you squat and strain.'" El-Badawi paused to allow his sense of humor and his command of the American English idiom to be appreciated.

Then he continued, "To bring this concept home to you, a concept so difficult for you arrogant Americans, we must give you an idea, merely an idea, of the consequences of not obeying. So, although you have not done anything seriously wrong, what is about to happen is merely in the way of demonstration. Just a free sample, so to speak." He smiled broadly and glanced at the women. "The women will benefit from witnessing this demonstration as well."

El-Badawi called to Ronald Billings, "Mr. Ambassador, come over here. I have to show some delicacy in handling you. You can watch."

"I prefer to stay with my fellow Americans."

El-Badawi said something in Turkish to one of the men. This man walked over to the women and smacked Clara Billings's face. Billings started to run toward his wife, but was stopped by two guards and pushed toward el-Badawi.

El-Badawi looked into Billings's eyes and said, "I warned you. That slap was nothing, you arrogant American dog. Now obey, if you value your wife's person."

Then el-Badawi told Billy, "Come here, Billy, beside me, and watch." Then he nodded to three of his men. Two of them held whips. The third held a truncheon. They casually strolled over to the American men and began laying into them.

The women began to scream and weep. Kathy Lopert fainted. Billy tried to look away, but el-Badawi held his head between his two hands, forcing him to face his father and the other men. At the end of five minutes the moaning men were lying in a heap, battered and bleeding.

"Very well," el-Badawi announced to his men, "initiation is over. Now, quickly, get them to their quarters, dry them off, and dress them again. I need them alive. Or at least most of them." He sent Billy and Ambassador Billings with them.

El-Badawi then strutted toward the women. When he reached them, he barked, "Line up, American sluts!" When they had lined up, he said, "Don't worry, you will not be subjected to the same kind of brutality you have just witnessed your effeminate menfolk submit to. Who else but helpless women would submit to that kind of treatment without resisting. They are spineless cowards, your so-called men! But *we* are real men," he said, sweeping his arm in a gesture that included himself and his men. "As you will have the honor to find out." As he said this, he grasped his crotch. He paused to enjoy the effect of his words. "So don't be afraid. Cooperate and you will be all right."

El-Badawi loudly said something to his men in Turkish, nodding toward the women. The men responded with chortles and leers.

Fifteen-year-old Kerrie Lopert and her mother, Kathy, were weeping, their arms around each other. El-Badawi looked at Kerrie, pointed at her, placed his index finger over his lips, and said to his men, "*Söyleme bise. Çocuk var burada.*"

They laughed even louder at the idea that he was telling them to watch their language because children were present.

Chapter Four

1930 hours
Mountains of northwestern Iran, 7.8 kilometers
from the Turkish border

The gray stone fortress blended in with its rocky surroundings. Only a handful of the members of as-Saif al-Islam knew its location.

The mountains themselves formed a natural barrier against the outside world. To anyone penetrating the mountain barrier, and then looking down at the fortress, it gave the appearance of a grim and fortified Shangri-La.

Rauf Karahisarli thought of himself as a traditionalist; others considered him a romantic. His spacious reception hall in the center of the otherwise bleak fortress was furnished and decorated in the style of an affluent eighteenth-century Turkish living room. This room, the *selamlik*, was where Rauf Pasha received his associates and conducted his business while at the fortress. In a traditional home, a door would lead from this center of male activities to the harem, where the wife, or wives, and daughters would receive friends. Female, of course. Men, no matter how close friends they might be, would never enter the sacred precinct of the harem, the women's quarters. But this, of course, was not really a home; it was a fortress. As such, there was no wife, no daughter, and, therefore, no harem.

Rauf Pasha's *selamlik* was carpeted with beautifully patterned woolen rugs from Turkey, Iran, Azerbaijan, and Uzbekistan. As in the days before Western influence entered the Middle East, there was no furniture in the center of the room. Instead, a long line of couches covered with colorful soft cushions extended around all four walls. Small tables were placed in front of the couches at intervals of three feet. Several nargilehs, the water-cooled pipes that could be used for smoking tobacco or hashish, were strategically placed around the room. Several tubes extended from the water-containing base so that more than one man could smoke from it at the same time.

Since this reception room was placed in the center of the first floor below ground level, there were no windows. Instead, false windows had been painted on two opposing walls. The visitor could gaze at these "windows" and see painted mountain scenery. Mahmoud ibn Hassan el-Badawi was amused and at the same time somewhat irritated by this indulgence in nostalgia for an era his leader had never experienced. The Libyan had to force himself to use the pompous title "*pasha*" or the rather formal term "*efendi*," equivalent to English "sir" or "mister," when addressing his chief. But, he consoled himself with the knowledge that Rauf Karahisarli was totally devoted to the Cause, was a brave warrior and a superb military strategist. These virtues allowed el-Badawi to overlook his eccentricities.

Rauf Pasha, in camouflage uniform, sat cross-legged on the sofa, sipping from a tiny cup of syrupy black coffee. While in this room, and only in this room, he incongruously wore an old-fashioned red fez with a golden tassle. Mahmoud el-Badawi, also in camouflage, sat on the couch perpendicular to his chief's, his cup of coffee on the table before him. He leaned back against the cushions, his legs stretched before him, and lit a Turkish cigarette. A very old man with a long white beard, wearing a black turban and a flowing black caftan, sat erect on the rug-covered floor. This was the mullah Najatollah Yazdi, the Iranian cleric who served as the spiritual guide of the as-Saif al-Islam organization.

The mullah, who had been sipping from a glass of orange juice, glared at el-Badawi, pointed at the cigarette, and shook his head. The Libyan remembered the prohibition, so poetically put, on allowing hashish, and by later extension, tobacco, to "touch the lips," so he grudgingly extinguished the cigarette in the palm of his hand. The nargilehs, called *hookahs* by the Arabs, were invented to circumvent the prohibition against smoking, since the substance being smoked would not actually touch the lips. However, el-

Badawi was not in the mood to fiddle with a nargileh. He was more interested in getting down to cases.

He said to his chief, "Your Turkish government has not yet responded to our demands, *efendi*. And April six at sundown is the absolute deadline. What do you plan to do, Rauf Pasha?"

Rauf Pasha stared at Mahmoud el-Badawi through half-closed eyes for several moments, as though he were observing some animal he could not identify. Then he spoke very slowly, very quietly.

"How can you ask me that question, Mahmoud? Have I not announced to the government what I would do?"

El-Badawi's mouth fell open. "You mean, you would actually use the nuclear weapons on Athens and the Zionist entity?"

Rauf Pasha's voice was low and menacing, "I cannot believe my ears, Mahmoud." He glared at his lieutenant. "You thought I was bluffing? Have you ever known me to bluff? Tell me, Mahmoud, have you?"

El-Badawi stared at the swirling patterns of yellow, blue, black, and burgundy of the rug beneath his boots.

Rauf Pasha prodded him, "Mahmoud . . . ?"

El-Badawi looked up at Rauf Pasha as though he had awakened from a dream. "No, *efendi*, I have never known you to bluff. That is true."

"Do you object to killing the infidels?"

"No, by Allah, I do not! I take great pleasure doing just that, as you know."

"Then what?"

"It is the world's reaction I'm thinking of."

"Bah! Allah will protect the faithful. The unworthy—and there are many of them in Turkey, too many—will burn. We and ours will be spared. It will be a land of true believers, and *shari'a*, the sacred law, will be the law of the land." Turning to the Iranian cleric, he asked, "Is that not so, my master?"

Najatollah Yazdi stared straight ahead, as though his gaze penetrated the painted window on the wall and saw the future. "Yes, my son," he intoned in Persian-accented Turkish. "The wicked will burn twice: first in the earthly nuclear conflagration, and then eternally in the fires of Hell. The majority of the faithful will survive and prosper. But even those of the righteous who die in battle will live forever in Paradise, among the sweet flowing waters, the fruitful date palms, and the long-haired, dark eyed, forevervirgin *houris* who will satisfy their every whim.''

El-Badawi raised an eyebrow and stared at the wizened old man in black, at his long white beard. He was struck by the way the old man sat erect on the rug and stared unblinkingly ahead. There was no denying it, he admitted to himself, this frail old man radiated some kind of power, some kind of charisma. It burned in his unblinking eyes; it resonated in his surprisingly powerful voice. His entire being seemed to glow with an aura of otherworldly luminosity. When he spoke, others were transfixed.

"Besides," Rauf Pasha explained, "the West will know we mean business. They will fear us. We will be like a scimitar prodding into the heart of Europe. We will take back the Balkans, the Caucasus. Our armies will take Vienna, and then all of Europe. And the infidels will know we will hesitate at nothing, and will be afraid to oppose us."

Najatollah Yazdi intoned, "The world is divided into two parts: *Dar al-Islam*, the Abode of Submission to the will of God, and *Dar al-Harb*, the Abode of War. There is no middle ground. When we win, we will establish the *khilafah*, the Muslim state, in Turkey. But we will not stop until we conquer the whole world. It is the will of God. There can be no compromise."

1535 hours
Kara Kale, northwestern Iran

Outside the razor-wire perimeter of the Kara Kale compound was a level field. This afternoon men had set up poles to indicate the limits of the playing field. The men had measured off 140 yards to fix the length of the field. The game, in celebration of the taking of hostages, was about to begin, and the men gathered around the edges of the playing field. At each end of the field there were seven men mounted on fine Arabian horses and holding five-footlong wooden javelins in their hands. The horsemen were attired in shirtsleeves, baggy trousers that were tight at the calves, and goatskin boots. The seven men of one team wore green cloth wrapped around their heads, while their opponents wore red ones.

Looking down from one of the guard towers were Rauf Pasha and Mahmoud ibn Hassan el-Badawi. The Turk was explaining the game to the Libyan.

"See, Mahmoud," Rauf Pasha said, "how each man holds a javelin? The game is called *cirit* because that is the Turkish word for 'javelin.' This sport has always been very popular in Eastern Turkey, especially in the villages. Our Turkic ancestors in Central Asia practically lived on horseback. Adults ate, drank, conducted business, held meetings, and even slept on horseback."

El-Badawi felt like saying, *I'm surprised they didn't fuck on horseback,* but held his tongue. His mind lingered on the thought; the ramifications were fascinating.

Rauf Pasha continued, "They would put little children on the backs of sheep before they could walk, to get the feel of riding. They were the first people to use bow and arrow while in the saddle. At top speed, mind you. And they were very accurate. They were the terror of the world, sweeping across the steppes of Central Asia and what is today Russia, and through Iran, the entire Middle East, and the Balkans. Right up to the gates of Vienna by the sixteenth century. And the Chinese had to build a wall to protect themselves from us. The Chinese called us the 'horse barbarians.'"

"Are they going to rush at each other, trying to run the opponent through?" El-Badawi smiled with pleasure at the thought.

"No, no, Mahmoud. There is more skill and agility involved. Each man will make a series of passes, trying to hurl his spear so that it will hit his opponent. That is the main object. When he hits his opponent, he gains six points for his team. But it is not easy, my friend. These horses are lightning fast, can accelerate to great speed in just a few strides, and can stop short in a second. And they are trained to perform some very intricate maneuvers."

"I imagine it is something like polo, which comes from India or Pakistan."

"A little, but in polo you just hit a ball. You don't throw

spears at your opponents." He laughed. "It is not warlike enough to suit us. Not manly enough."

El-Badawi nodded in agreement, then looked closely at the horses. "Magnificent animals."

"Yes, of course. In my home village near the city of Bayburt, I used to play from the time I was twelve years old. I am still quite expert, and I expect to be so twenty years from now. Men of all ages engage in this sport in the villages of Eastern Turkey."

"Why aren't you playing today, *efendi*?"

"I wanted to explain the game to you as it unfolds. Now watch."

Rauf Pasha held a blue cloth aloft and waved it back and forth to get the teams' attention. He saw that all eyes were trained on the cloth. Then he flung it down, and the men and horses went into motion. Clouds of dust rose into the air above the players. Rauf Pasha smiled ferociously and cried out, in imitation of the ancient Ottoman cavalry commanders, "Come on, my wolves, come on!

"Notice," Rauf Pasha said, "at first, the two teams move straight toward each other at a walk, then a canter, and finally a gallop. But see? As they approach each other to within javelin-tossing distance, the horses and riders execute intricate maneuvers, weaving in and out, changing speed, backing up, moving forward again. See?"

"Yes, *efendi*, it is really an impressive show of skill."

"You see the two nearest to us? See how they twist and turn, back up, go from canter to gallop in one second, trying to disorient the other man's horse. Ah, see! The green throws his spear. But the red pulls his mount to his left and the spear sails harmlessly by. He spins the horse in a 360 degree movement in just—what?—two? three? seconds, spurs the horse forward at a gallop, and flings his javelin at his retreating opponent with all his might, as he stands in the stirrups and leans over the horse's head. The javelin flies toward his opponent, and . . . yes! He hits him! The green man was not paying enough attention. That is six points for the red team."

They heard cheering from the spectators.

"Look there, Rauf Pasha," el-Badawi cried, pointing to the opposite side of the field. Through a cloud of dust, they saw a man of the red team hurl his spear. His opponent made his horse rear up, and the spear passed harmlessly in front of them, but when the horse's front hooves crashed back into the dust, the rider lurched and fell to the ground. Choking in the dust, he rolled out of the way of his mount's hooves but into the path of a teammate's horse. The teammate pulled his horse sharply to the left to avoid trampling him, and crashed into the horse of a red horseman at the moment this man hurled his spear at a green rider, making the spear go off course and shoot past the intended target's shoulder.

Rauf Pasha said, "The one who fell off . . . he cost the green team three points. But worse than that, it costs him the respect of the people watching. Turkish warriors do not fall off their horses. They are supposed to be as one with their mount."

El-Badawi heard the crowd jeer the fallen rider. Some of them called out the most insulting things they could think of under the circumstances:

"You are not really a Turk, Mustafa! You are a Greek!"

"You ride like a Persian!"

"No, he must be a Syrian!"

"No, an Egyptian . . . belly dancer!"

"Look there," Rauf Pasha said, pointing. A man was struck with a javelin full in the forehead, just an inch above the left eye. His head snapped back, and blood began to flow from the wound into the eye, but he kept his seat, turned to face the man who had thrown the lance, and chased after him, his spear held in position for throwing.

The crowd cried out, "*Hay, hay, hay! Iyi! Çok iyi!*"

"Yes, very good," Rauf Pasha said with satisfaction, "that is a real Turk."

1800 hours
Rauf Pasha's office, Kara Kale

The office was ten by thirty feet. A reproduction of an oil painting representing a proud yet benign Süleyman the Magnificent, sultan of the powerful sixteenth-century Ottoman Empire, in rich robes, lavishly large turban, and costly jewels, hung on one wall. A black-and-white photograph of the somber Ayatollah Khomeini, white-bearded, in black robe and turban, malignantly glared down from another wall. Rauf Pasha sat behind his ornately carved mahogany desk.

Mahmoud ibn Hassan el-Badawi entered the room. He felt a chill when he noticed the old man in the black robe and black turban standing motionless in the corner behind and to the right of his boss. He looked like the reincarnation of the Ayatollah Khomeini.

"You sent for me, Rauf Pasha?" el-Badawi asked.

"Yes, Mahmoud. Take a seat, please."

"*Shukran, efendi.*" The Libyan thanked his chief and sat on a wooden chair in front of the "pasha." Mahmoud said, "The time is getting close, *efendi.* Has there been any response to our demands yet?"

"There has not, Mahmoud." Rauf Pasha's voice betrayed irritation. "Whatever is fated to happen will happen. It is kismet."

"No, not kismet. The will of Allah," intoned the surprisingly powerful voice of the frail Iranian mullah.

Rauf Pasha nodded in recognition of the correction, then spoke to el-Badawi. "Still, I have taken an added precaution. I have raised the stakes a little. Only a little, mind you."

El-Badawi looked quizzically from Rauf Pasha to Najatollah Yazdi. Seeing no expression in the cleric's face, his questioning gaze returned to Rauf Pasha.

"Maybe the Americans don't care about the Greeks or the Jews to put enough pressure on the Turkish government. Probably our Turkish government doesn't give a damn about our vaporizing the accursed Greeks, our traditional enemies for centuries. They might care about the Zionist entity, since they have developed such a strong political and military alliance with them, but . . ."

"But, *efendi,*" el-Badawi interrupted, "they do care about nuclear retaliation against Turkey, and their involvement with NATO and the European Union . . ."

"Yes, yes, of course. But then why have they not turned the government over to us? Perhaps they would rather burn than see our holy organization take its rightful place."

"One way or the other, they *will* burn," assured the Iranian cleric in Persian-accented Turkish.

Rauf Pasha continued, "You successfully led a mission to kidnap the American ambassador, Ronald Billings and his wife, who, according to our spies, were foolish enough to sign up for a tour of a very picturesque part of our country. We have them and the other American tourists who were with them."

"Yes, *efendi*, except for an unfortunate accident resulting in the death of one of them."

"Accident, yes . . . Well, I've been thinking. The more pressure, the better. The ironic part is, the governments of France, Russia, China, and much of the Third World are putting enormous pressure on the Turkish government to accede to our demands. So, perhaps at the last minute . . ."

"But, so far, nothing."

"Correct. As you know, I'd rather take over the government without using the nuclear devices. For now, that is. But, if we have to, we shall. Meanwhile, the ambassador and the other tourists in our power will help. Billings is an old friend of the American president, and his wife has family connections with some very important people in the United States."

"They have only three days to comply." El-Badawi shook his head.

"Yes, and I have decided to raise the stakes even higher. And in the bargain to possibly acquire some important information."

"Well, Rauf Pasha, in what way have you raised the stakes?"

"We are going to have another guest to join the others."

"But, how is one more hostage going to matter?"

"This person should be very important to the Americans. As important as the ambassador. Possibly more important. He is none other than Lieutenant Commander Bernard Schraer, U.S. naval attaché to the embassy of the United States in Ankara. Furthermore, he is related to the president of the United States by marriage."

"That won't make any difference to the Americans."

"You think not?" Rauf Pasha was irritated. "Lieutenant Commander Schraer has many military secrets in that head of his. I expect to get those secrets out of him. Especially anything that has to do with American plans for dealing with us. If we know what they intend to do, we can better prepare for it."

"But, *efendi*, it must be next to impossible to capture him. All their security . . ."

"Leave that to me. You see, Schraer has a weakness. He has a Turkish mistress, some filthy whore that he seems to actually be in love with. He evades most of his security people and even disguises himself in civilian clothes, a fake mustache and beard, to visit her. But he does take four trusted bodyguards with him. The same four each time. So these are people he really trusts, apparently."

"Are his visits consistent in days of the week and time of day?"

"I'm afraid not. But our people have been keeping surveillance on him. It's at least worth a try, Mahmoud, don't you agree?"

Chapter 5

The seven members of Eagle Team were gathered in a close knot near the empty fieldstone fireplace in the former hunting lodge. They were suited up in their TALON Force Battle Ensemble, which, constructed of lightweight but tough synthetic fibers, afforded full body armor protection, monitored life functions, and provided immediate and automatic medical trauma aid, body temperature control, voice, digital and holographic communications, and high-power optical sensing.

It also had "brilliant camouflage," the capability to make the wearer practically invisible by day, and just about fully invisible by night. It worked something like a chameleon; when the Low Observable Suite was charged up, microsensors woven into the bullet-proof fabric of the ensemble would automatically analyze the visual background and copy the exact shade of color and luminosity of that background. As a result, all that anyone might see of the trooper camouflaged in this way might be a slight shimmer. When charged, the wearer literally would blend in with the background for a limited period of time.

"Okay," Travis ordered, "helmets on, and use the net-com system."

They put the camouflage helmets on and extended a wing arm that had been recessed in the side of the helmet shells. The little arm rested at a point just above the left eyeline.

Sam manipulated the buttons and switches of the panel in the case he held. He slid a diskette into an encrypt/decrypt radio computer he had in a small, black waist pack. He pulled the tiny, almost invisible, antenna up out of the computer body, buckled the durable pack around his waist, the pouch in front, and pressed some small buttons inside it.

The team members looked up toward the little monoclelike device extended above their eyeline. This immediately placed them in a virtual-reality visual theater produced by the action of a holographic image projected directly onto the retina of their eyes. They saw small, red, digital lettering above and below the images projected. To clear this image, they had only to lower their gaze to a normal angle. In two seconds, the images of three-dimensional photographs appeared before them. They were high resolution, so that what they saw was absolutely clear, vivid, and detailed.

Travis explained what they were seeing. "This is a map of the area we're in. Down in the southeast quadrant is this hunting lodge. Everybody see it?" He looked around to see them nod their heads.

"Okay, look seventy kilometers to the northwest. What you're looking at is a compound surrounded by razor wire. There is one entrance; it's on the west. The compound is heavily guarded, but I haven't been told in what way. Since we know so little about our actual target in Turkey, we might as well know nothing in training either. As you can see, though, the area is being guarded by forty-two Army Rangers.

0944 hours
Sangre de Cristo Mountains, New Mexico

High altitude, low-opening parachute jumps were tricky and certainly hazardous. Bailing out at an altitude high enough to not be detected by radar or the naked eye, chilled to the bone, and breathing thin air, and then free-falling to just a few thousand feet was no picnic. Except for Navy SEAL Lieutenant Commander Stan Powczuk and Lieutenant Jennifer Olsen of Naval Intelligence; they actually enjoyed the thrill. Travis Barrett did too, though he was more restrained about showing it. Air Force Captain Hunter Blake, Captain Jacques DuBois, U.S. Marines, and

Sarah Greene accepted it as part of a day's work. Sam Wong liked the HALO insertion about as much as the average person enjoys a good root canal job. But they all had performed this insertion on many training occasions, and on actual missions. They all knew what they were doing, and were expert at it.

They had been flown from their staging area seventy kilometers south of the target to the drop zone twenty-five kilometers to the north of the target. After hurtling through the upper atmosphere and opening their chutes at only 2,000 feet above the drop zone, they landed in rough mountainous terrain.

1930 hours
An apartment in a residential quarter of Ankara, Turkey

A rented green Volkswagen Passat was parked at the curb of a tree-lined street. Very few passersby were present. Two of Lieutenant Commander Bernard Schraer's most trusted bodyguards sat in the front seat, waiting. They were dressed in business suits, a common sight in this neighborhood. The driver, through his rearview mirror, distractedly noticed a man in a sports jacket walking a dog. When he came abreast of the seated passenger, he looked up and down the street, then raised his gloved hand to the level of the passenger's temple and fired his silenced 9mm Beretta twice through the open car window. The driver heard the *pffft pffft* and felt his companion's body lurch against his as his face was sprayed with his dead partner's hot blood, brain matter, and bits of skull bone. The last thing the driver saw was the barrel of the Beretta pointing at a spot between his eyes.

The gunman casually tossed the pistol onto the floor of the car and kept walking the dog. As he strolled along the sidewalk, he nodded to two men in a van belonging to the phone company, parked two car lengths beyond the Volkswagen. These men wore coveralls with the name of the phone company stenciled on them. They climbed out of the van carrying tool cases, walked a few feet, and turned into the entrance of the apartment building.

One of them pushed the buzzer of apartment 3-F. No one answered. They pushed the buzzer of apartment 3-A. No answer. They pushed the buzzer of 3-B. When a woman's voice asked who was there, one of them said, "Phone company." The voice answered, "It must be a mistake. My phone is working." Since there were often problems with the phones in Ankara, they were sure someone would soon buzz them in. The fourth try was a charm; they were buzzed in. Zia took the elevator to the second floor, while Cemal quietly walked up the stairs.

When Zia emerged from the elevator, he saw two men in business suits standing a few feet away from the door to apartment 3-C, one to the right, the other to the left. He nonchalantly strolled toward the men, a bored look on his face. The first man held up his hand, motioning for Zia to stop. He did. The guard patted him down and found nothing. He asked him to open his tool case. The second guard watched the procedure.

Cemal had silently crawled the last few stairs. Keeping low, his head inches from the top stair, he carefully aimed his silenced 9mm Beretta between the shoulder blades of the guard nearest him. The guard speaking to Zia turned to see his partner lurch forward to land on his face. In that split second, Zia struck the guard over the head with his tool chest. As this guard sank to his knees, he struck him again square on the crown of his head. Cemal calmly finished off both guards by putting two bullets through their heads.

Cemal handed a second gun to Zia, who aimed the silenced pistol at the lock and fired. They pushed the door open and rushed inside the apartment. They dashed through the foyer, into the living room, saw that it was empty, and pressed on to the bedroom. They lay on the floor, and pushed the bedroom door open.

They saw a naked man, his back toward them, reaching for a Colt .45mm automatic hanging from the bedpost. An attractive fortyish brunette, equally unclothed, ran for the closet. Cemal jumped up and leaped against the naked man, shoving him off the bed before he could grasp the .45. When the woman began to scream, Zia fired two bullets into her chest. She bounced against the dressing table and slumped to the floor. A gurgling sound emerged from her lungs as she drowned in her own blood.

The naked American was in his late fifties, muscular, and still in good condition. Not as good as the two young Turks, however. The American, lying facedown and pinned by Cemal, jabbed him with his elbow, and then twisted around to face his attacker. He smashed Cemal in the face with his fist and tried to get off the floor to reach the .45, but Zia leapt onto the bed, jumped off on the other side, and landed on top of him. The two Turks punched and choked him. Finally they managed to subdue him enough to pull out a syringe and jab the needle into his arm.

They heard sirens in the street below. Zia looked at Cemal; it was probably the police investigating the Volkswagen containing the two corpses.

Zia walked over to the woman and pumped two 9mm bullets into her forehead, just to be sure. Then they labored to dress the semiconscious Lieutenant Commander Schraer in his civilian clothing.

"What are you sweating so much for," Cemal said to Zia with a laugh. "Are you out of shape?"

Zia frowned and kept working.

They heard more sirens.

"It's our ambulance," Zia said.

They sat Schraer in an easy chair and looked out the window. Three police cars were clustered around the Volkswagen. Uniformed police had cordoned off the area, and a couple of men in civilian clothing were scurrying about, taking notes. An ambulance pulled up in front of the first police car. Two men in white jumped out with stretchers, while a third opened the rear doors. The detectives could see this was an emergency and did not interfere with them. The two men rushed into the building, one of them carrying a rolled-up stretcher.

Less than five minutes later they emerged from the building carrying Lieutenant Commander Schraer on the stretcher. Two detectives looked up at them. One of the ambulance attendants said, "Heart attack."

The detectives nodded and resumed their work.

2035 hours
Outskirts of Kalecik, Turkey

The ambulance had made its way through the suburbs of
Ankara, using its siren. The siren was turned off once the
vehicle was on the highway to the west. Sixty-two kilometers from the capital, three kilometers before the town of
Kalecik, the ambulance pulled off the road onto a dusty
field, as they saw the French-made helicopter descend and
heard the *thwock, thwock, thwock* of the blades. A whirlwind of dust raised by the hovering Aerospatiale Dauphin
chopper blew grit into the eyes of the squinting ambulance
attendants. Their white uniforms were turning tan as they
rushed to open the rear doors.

Lieutenant Commander Bernard Schraer had been
gagged and strapped to the stretcher. His swollen face was
red with rage and he was sweating profusely. The three
attendants lifted him down from the ambulance and carried
him toward the helicopter. Two men in camouflage fatigues
carrying AK-74 assault rifles had jumped out of the chopper and were waiting for the cargo.

One of the men in dirty whites stumbled on a stone. His
hand slipped and he dropped his end of the stretcher. The
naval attaché's head bounced against the ground.

The third attendant, whose hands were free, slapped the
clumsy attendant, saying in Turkish, "Be careful, you idiot.
He's valuable property."

One of the uniformed men shook his AK-74 rifle angrily
at them, "Come on, move it! Hurry!"

Camouflaged men inside the helicopter helped them lift
the stretcher into the chopper and strap it down. The three
men in whites, followed by the two guards, climbed aboard,
and the helicopter whirled up into the dark sky and away.

2330 hours
Kara Kale

The guards heard the chopping sound of helicopter
blades against the chill air. The sound became louder and
soon bright beams of light moved back and forth across the

ground. The guards looked up and moved closer to the spot over which the chopper hovered, their trousers flapping like flags in a stiff wind, dust choking them. They shined their flashlights on the helicopter, and once it had turned off its engines, approached.

Three men jumped out, turned, and waited. Two of them reached up and helped a third man descend. The guards could see that the third man to emerge had his hands bound behind him. Three more men jumped down.

One of the guards mockingly said, "The American Navy has arrived."

One of the guards roughly shoved Lieutenant Commander Schraer toward the open doors of the fortress. Schraer tripped and fell on his face.

"Not so rough," said one of the men who arrived at the helicopter, as he helped the bound man to stand. "This is an important guest. We don't want to damage him."

Seeing the look of disappointment on the other man's face, he smiled and added, "Not yet, anyway."

1530 hours MST
Sangre de Cristo Mountains, New Mexico

Eagle Team had marched the twenty-five kilometers, climbing up and down barren hillsides, when they came within sight of a rise, about half a kilometer to the south, that overlooked the compound. Their Battle Sensor Helmets had skyward communications with a constellation of thirty-six TALON Force dedicated satellites. This straight-up communications component not only afforded each trooper unlimited communications and position location, but digital data transfer regardless of any terrain and line-of-sight obstacles. This capability provided them with continuous, practically unjammable communications and data transfer anywhere on earth. The only obstacles that could degrade or even negate the communications stream would be caves, metal framed buildings, and bunkers.

Using this component of their BSHs, they could see the compound, the razor wire on the perimeter, the position of the entry gate, and the concrete bunker. They saw the guardhouse, but could see no guards. And they spotted what appeared to be metal doors on the west side of the bunker.

Travis said, "There are no personnel visible in the compound. Those that are actually in the compound sure as hell are out of sight and waiting for us."

They viewed the area surrounding the compound and saw men in camouflage dug in on top of the four hillocks surrounding the compound. One to the southeast of the compound, one to the southwest, one to the west, and another to the northeast. This last one was the one directly in front of them. They spotted four Wildcat armored vehicles making the rounds of the area.

Travis said, "All right. Sam and Jack will hike around to the northwestern hill, first turning on the Low Observable Camouflage Suite. Neutralize the two men on the hill. After that, turn the LOCS off. Let yourself be observed, but don't make it obvious. When they send out a force against you, you can use your invisibility capability again. Retreat, leading them further away from the compound, trying to pick them off as you go. The rest of us will stay here. We'll take care of the two men on this northeastern hill. Stan, I want you to become invisible twenty-five minutes from right now, then make your way down to the nearest part of the razor wire fence right opposite us."

"The northeast end of the compound," Stan said.

"Right. Cut a nice opening for us. Jen, at the same time you cut a second opening about halfway down the eastern side of the fence. This way we'll have two or three easy exit possibilities. By this time, the defending force will have sent a party to the northwestern hill where Sam and Jack will be leading them away from the compound, and taking down as many of them as possible. When the openings are cut, the rest of us will turn on our LOCS. Sarah, Hunter, and I will come down, join Stan, and enter the compound from the north opening. Jen, you'll join us from the eastern opening you'll have cut.

"As you know, the invisibility won't be absolutely perfect in broad daylight. Since the other teams are completely familiar with this chameleon camouflage, they'll be extra sensitive to any peculiar shimmering or motion they might see. So keep low, very low, as you move. If there are any

personnel in your path, don't fire. We don't want to alert
them to our presence within the compound. Just go around
them. Naturally, if you see they realize we're there, then
blast them with the stun guns, silencers affixed, of course.

"We'll meet at the bunker doors and set off a noise device. The other team, according to the rules of the game,
will open the doors for us, as if we had blown our way
through. That's when it gets tough."

Sam said, "What do you want Jack and me to do during
your entrance into the bunker."

"Keep the force that's pursuing you busy," Travis commanded. "However, if it looks as though they've gotten
wind of our tactics and realize that the compound's been
entered, they'll probably break off the attack on you, and
try to rush back to help defend the compound. If they do
that, stay hot on their trail, putting out of commission as
many as you can. Meanwhile, you'll be heading back
toward the compound. Then join us." Travis looked around
at his team. "Everyone clear on this?"

1540 hours
Northwest hill

Jack and Sam had just climbed up the northwest hill as
silently as possible. They stayed about eight meters away
from each other. As agreed upon, when Jack got to about
three meters from the troopers on lookout duty, he took
careful aim and fired his laser stun rifle at one of the men.
Sam had kept his sights trained on the left-most of the two
men. When he saw the man on the right bowled over by
the electric charge, he fired his own weapon, knocking
down the other trooper. Two of the enemy officially dead.

They turned off their invisibility component and climbed
to a point just below the crest of the hill.

"Okay, my man," Jack said, "let's play bait. But not
too obviously."

"What do you suggest, big guy?"

"Well, before we show ourselves, let's set up the motion
sensors to tip us off if we can expect company, and from
which direction."

"Okay. I'll climb back down the hill and set up three motion detectors about a hundred yards out. And you can send up an unmanned aerial vehicle to provide advance warning." This aerial vehicle would be able to patrol the area from one to three kilometers between the two Eagle Team members and the compound in a fan-shaped pattern.

"Hmmph . . . Unmanned aerial vehicle," Jack muttered. "Damn, Sammy, when you gon' get used to military short-hand? It's a UAV. Hell of a lot easier."

"Well, Jack, I don't know about you, but I don't find it too difficult to pronounce 'unmanned aerial vehicle.' "

"You don' watch out, I'm goin' unman *your* vehicles, wiseass." The huge black marine flashed Sam a big toothy grin.

Sam laughed and said, "Okay, you're going to use the Hummingbird, right?"

"Shit, no, sucker. That mother's the size of a model air-plane, too damn easy to spot. Besides, we don't need its two-hour flight time. We'll use the Dragonfly; it's only the size of your palm. That's *your* palm, not mine. And its video imaging will be enough. We don't need the Hum-mingbird's video plus thermal imaging. And the thirty-minute flight will do the job. No, the Hummingbird's too easy to spot."

"Exactly."

"Say what?"

Sam said, "We *want* to get detected. Remember?"

Jack shook his head. "Damn, you're right, little buddy." He gave Sam a high five.

Sam monitored the defenders' radio net. After listening to a message, he told Jack, "They've figured we've taken this hill, since they lost communication with the two troop-ers on lookout, and they've directed two Wildcats to at-tack us."

"Okay!" Jack said with satisfaction.

"Wait. And they're sending twelve troopers on foot from the compound."

"Okay. Two Wildcats coming toward us. Two others still patrolling. Twelve troopers coming against us. That's twenty-eight of them drawn away from the compound. That leaves only fourteen defending the compound."

1540 hours
Northeastern perimeter of the compound

Major Travis Barrett, Hunter, Sarah, and Stan, their stealth functions activated, had entered the compound through the opening in the razor wire cut by Stan. They hadn't yet reached the west side of the bunker, but through their imaging capabilities they saw that the heavy metal doors had been opened and that a dozen troopers poured out of the bunker on the double, exited the compound through the gate, and were heading for the northwest hill.

They understood that the breach in the fence had been detected, because stun gun laser fire emanating from the bunker raked the opening and the area between it and the bunker in a fan pattern. The group had been evading the fire by approaching the bunker in a zigzag movement.

Keeping their distance from each other, they worked their way around toward the metal doors. Logically, the troops sent against the hill occupied by Sam and Jack should have been called back to the compound, once the breach was discovered, yet they weren't. They continued toward the hill.

Travis whispered into his transmitter, "Sam must have interfered with their communications."

Hunter reported a peculiar shimmering moving toward them. Then they heard Jen, "Olsen here, three yards in front of the doors."

1545 hours
Northwest hill

Sam had monitored the defenders' command frequency. He heard the orders for the troops to return to the compound to fight the invaders. He copied several transmissions from their leaders, then fabricated several messages in the leaders' own voices saying that the previous orders were a mistake, and that the force sent against the northwest hill should continue the attack and take the hill at all costs. The confusion among the defending forces provided five precious minutes for the rest of Eagle Team.

1547 hours
The compound

Stan tossed the noise-generating grenade at the doors. It went off with a tremendous bang. As agreed upon in the rules of the game, the doors were opened. A withering volley of laser fire greeted them; but they had their stealth still turned on and were on their bellies. In the random firing, Hunter was hit in the shoulder and helmet. His invisibility turned off, and he was officially "dead."

The others carefully singled out their targets and knocked seven of them out of the game. No other defenders were visible, but there had to be seven more in the compound, while, for a brief time twenty were attacking the northwest hill. The latest reports from Sam indicated that he and Jack had knocked out six of the defenders attacking them.

"I'm sending in the Bug," Travis said. He extracted the XM-12 Bug from his cargo pocket and set it into rapid motion. The sensor was a small, almost transparent robot made completely of clear plastic and thin, silver wires. Linked to a microvideo high-frequency transmitter, it not only was the size of a large cockroach, but it crawled along the ground like an insect, reporting movement and visual data directly to team members.

Using their Battle Sensor Devices, the team members saw holographic representations of the main floor of the bunker. They saw offices, and gun positions, all unmanned. The main floor was deserted. They could see there was a stairwell at the rear. Travis received a voice message through his BSD from Sam. "We've put two Wildcats out of commission by frying their engines with our Wristband Radio Frequency Field Generators. And we've made two more kills. But they've broken off the attack and are returning on foot to the compound."

"Follow them. Pick off as many as you can."

Travis and his group rushed to the stairwell and threw an activated Bug down to the second level. The team saw the holographic images of living quarters on one side and holding cells on the other. There were seven defenders all along the entries to the living quarters, laser stun rifles at the ready. The twelve "prisoners" were in four cells, three to a cell.

"Sarah," Travis said, "drop a smoke bomb down there."

"Right, Travis." She tossed a grenade down the stairs, where it gave off a thick white smoke.

"Activate your thermal viewers."

Their Battle Sensor Devices had a thermal viewing capability that allowed each trooper to see in the dark and through smoke and haze. They charged down the stairs and easily neutralized all seven of the defending force.

Then they blasted the locks on the cell doors. "Stan and Jen, stay here to protect the prisoners," Travis ordered. "Sarah, come with me to the lower level to disarm the nuclear devices and destroy the launchers."

The automatic battlefield motion sensor of the battle ensemble detected millimeter wave changes in movement out to seven hundred meters. It was now automatically alerting the team, through a minor electric tingling sensation and voice description, that the compound had been entered by the returning defenders who were on their way to the bunker.

Travis and Sarah disarmed the mock nuclear devices and destroyed the launchers on the bottom level of the bunker. Stan and Jen, seeing through the smoke, picked off the first defenders who showed their heads at the top of the stairs. Jack and Sam, invisibility activated, charged in behind the defenders and knocked them out of the game. The few remaining defenders surrendered, and the game was over. Eagle Team had successfully completed its mission. However, they had lost one of their number.

Chapter 6

Rauf Pasha had taken Mahmoud ibn Hassan el-Badawi by elevator to the third level below ground of Kara Kale. The concrete chamber harbored two sleek and shiny projectiles on individual hydraulic elevators. Several men in white coats, mostly Russians, monitored control panels with switches and flashing lights. A dozen armed guards stood, strolled, or lounged in chairs. They all carried Russian-made AK-74 assault rifles.

As they leisurely strolled through the complex, el-Badawi said, "Has there been a response from the Turkish government, or the Americans, on your offer to give back the American Naval Attaché? Or Ambassador Billings and his wife?"

Rauf Pasha made a sour face. "Not yet. But it is early."

"Early . . . ? They have—what?" he consulted his watch, "about thirty-four hours."

"Yes, Mahmoud, but there must be an immense amount of pressure being exerted by the Americans on the Turkish government to give in to our demands."

"Do you really think so?"

"Oh, there can be no doubt. An important American officer, with military secrets they know without a doubt can be tortured out of him. And he's married to a first cousin of the American president. And their ambassador, who is an old friend of the American president. And Billings's wife, who is connected to a large and influential clan in Texas . . . They must be exerting tremendous pressure on the president. What do *you* think?"

"I suppose, *efendi*."

"Of course, Mahmoud. And, Mahmoud, I have let it be known that we might have some fun with the ambassadorial couple while we wait. Yes, it's just a question of time."

El-Badawi's eyes gleamed. "Have some fun? Yes, I would certainly enjoy having fun with those filthy rich, arrogant representatives of the Great Satan. Are you serious about that, *efendi*, or is that just to shake up the Americans?"

"That depends on what transpires in the near future. We'll see, Mahmoud. We'll see. Meanwhile, I am sure the Americans will capitulate and force the Turkish government to comply with our demands. As I said, it's just a question of time."

Yes, Mahmoud thought, it certainly *is* a question of time. The sands of time are running out.

Rauf Pasha continued speaking. "Unfortunately, democracies need time to make decisions on these matters. It is one of their many defects. A strong leader would simply make a decision and carry it out without concerning himself with electorates, with political maneuvering. What could be more foolish than democracy? What could be more corrupt than catering to the whims of the ignorant people? That is a situation we shall correct in Turkey, when we take the reins. And later, elsewhere." He patted el-Badawi on the arm. "Be patient, my friend. Be patient."

El-Badawi sighed. Rauf Pasha was beginning to get on his nerves. His pretentiousness, his pomposity, his holier-than-thou attitude . . . And his plans for making Kerrie Lopert, that fifteen-year-old beauty, his exclusive property . . .

Rauf Pasha gestured to the missiles. "These beloved creatures are the hornets of God, ready to sting the infidel dogs into submission. The warheads are fully armed, mounted on their hydraulic elevators. They are ready to be launched by my loyal . . ." He chuckled. ". . . my money-hungry Russian scientists and engineers."

El-Badawi kept silent. He was thinking how unpredictable the results of such a catastrophic act were. Who knows how many countries would be dragged into nuclear war, and what would be left of Turkey, of the world, to rule? He hated the Americans with a burning passion, yes. Just as he hated the arrogant Jews and the Christians in general.

He despised the lukewarm Muslims as well. He would heartily delight in beating them all to death with his bare hands, individually, or slitting their throats . . . first raping the women, of course. But Rauf Pasha's way . . . he was beginning to wonder what the end of it all would be, what kind of world would be left to live in afterward. Would he, Mahmoud ibn Hassan el-Badawi, be condemned to live miserably and slowly die a horrible death from radiation poisoning, contaminated food, water, air . . . ?

Rauf Pasha saw the look of concern on el-Badawi's face. He interrupted his lieutenant's thoughts by saying, "Are you afraid, Mahmoud?" Mistake. And he knew it. As soon as the words left his mouth, Rauf Pasha regretted having uttered them.

El-Badawi's face darkened. He turned to his chief and said, "You ask me if I am afraid? I am the son of Hassan el-Badawi, sheikh of the Beni Idris tribe. We are sons of the Libyan desert, and there is no harsher place on earth in which to survive. From time immemorial we have lived by warfare, by attacking caravans, oasis towns, fighting with the other desert tribes. In my land, you fight and win, or you die. There is no other way. You fight for the possession, or at least the use, of wells, the life-giving water, of date palms. You capture black slaves in Chad and Niger and transport them for sale to towns and cities in the more northern areas of Libya. And in this business, we are in competition with the fierce Tuareg tribes, the ones who are always dressed completely in blue, and in which the men cover their faces, but the women do not. And we have to defend ourselves from the other tribes who would kill us to take whatever we have. Including taking our women and our own selves as slaves. And we do the same to them. And we, the Beni Idris, have survived the centuries. Why? Because we are strong, and we are intelligent and skilled in warfare, and, most of all, because we are brave. We are afraid of no one. We fight, give no quarter, and expect no quarter. And if Allah favors us, as he has for centuries, we live, and if not, we die. Everyone dies eventually. What matters is *how* you live. What matters is honor."

Rauf Pasha admired his lieutenant's skill and bravery, but this speech annoyed him. It made him wonder about el-Badawi's loyalty. Not to the Cause, but to him.

Rauf Pasha said, "And your Mu'ammar Qaddafi . . . He too is a son of the Libyan desert, is he not?"

"Of course."

"And he very valiantly stood up to the United States. Training commandos right in his own country to fight the Great Satan. Supplying weapons and money to groups that subverted the whole Western World. Sending people to blow up airplanes, like over Lockerbie . . ."

"Yes . . ."

"But a couple of American bombs from President Reagan, and he's been silent ever since." This was not good, Rauf Pasha thought. Why was he letting his tongue give vent to his private thoughts? Rauf Pasha was feeling irritation and tension because of the failure of the Turkish government to respond to his demands. After all, was this nonresponsiveness not an insult? Had they no respect for him?

El-Badawi stopped in his tracks and looked down at the concrete floor, clenching his jaw muscles.

Rauf Pasha was sick of el-Badawi's talk of the heroism of the Bedouin tribes of the Libyan desert, of his Beni Idris. If they were so powerful, so brave, so expert in warfare, what the hell were they doing living that hand-to-mouth sordid existence out in the desert? Why didn't they conquer Tripoli or Benghazi, which according to el-Badawi are inhabited by effete city people? Why don't el-Badawi's warriors conquer their cities, and even beyond, and live in luxury? But no, his tribesmen were nothing but poor, insignificant wretches struggling with their neighbors merely to stay alive, to subsist.

However, he knew that el-Badawi had been next in line to lead the Beni Idris, but had left that position of honor to his younger brother. Instead, filled with religious zeal, el-Badawi had gone to Afghanistan to fight the Soviets and their Afghan lackeys. He had fought beside the Taliban Militia, who had been trained by the CIA. American fools! Rauf Pasha knew that el-Badawi had fought selflessly and valiantly for Islam, for the Taliban in Afghanistan, and for Rauf Pasha's own as-Saif al-Islam here in Turkey. Truly, he had proved himself over and over again. He was, after all, a valuable man.

Rauf Pasha said, "Friend Mahmoud, I am sorry we have

had cross words. Truly, I am. Will you accept my apologies?"

El-Badawi's eyes misted over with emotion.

"Of course, *efendi*," el-Badawi said, "and I too apologize for my wicked and boastful tongue. Please forgive me, Rauf Pasha." He smiled, faced his chief directly, and spread his arms wide. The two men kissed on the cheek and embraced warmly.

After a moment, Rauf Pasha said, "Mahmoud, my friend, matters will become serious very soon. Why don't you take that young woman to your quarters, and enjoy her."

El-Badawi's heart leaped. "Kerrie Lopert?"

"Isn't she the fifteen-year-old?"

Mahmoud sensed disappointment. "Yes, *efendi*."

"I'm afraid not, Mahmoud, my friend. I want that one brought to *my* quarters. I was referring to the college girl . . ."

"Tracy Licata."

"Well, come now, Mahmoud. Is she not beautiful?"

"Actually, she is, *efendi*, and very desirable . . ." He hesitated.

"Yes . . . ?"

"Well, it's just that she must be nineteen or twenty . . ."

"An older woman, eh?"

"Well, I do prefer them younger . . ."

"So do I, my friend. So if this Kerrie were not here, you'd be very happy with Tracy, is that not so?"

El-Badawi cocked his head to one side. "Yes, that is true."

"So it is all relative."

"I suppose so."

"But, come Mahmoud, it is merely a question of envy. Think: Is it right to covet what rightfully belongs to someone else?"

El-Badawi realized his chief had a point. And Tracy Licata was indeed beautiful. He was being childish. "No, *efendi*, it is not right to covet, but . . ."

"Should not the choicest morsel go to the leader?"

Mahmoud ground his teeth. "Yes, *efendi*. You are absolutely correct."

Rauf Pasha noticed his lieutenant's lingering disappointment. This could be dangerous. He said, "I tell you what,

Mahmoud . . . Today we are going to be very busy. But tonight . . . Ah, tonight, I will have Kerrie for the entire night, and you will have her the following day."

El-Badawi smiled. He seized his chief's right hand and brought it to his lips. "*Shukran, ya rahim. Shukran.*" Thank you, compassionate one. Thank you.

"Yes, this sharing will bring us closer together. The psychologists call this process "bonding" in English. I have studied some psychology, you know, as well as English."

"Listen, *efendi*. Why can we not keep those two women?"

"Mahmoud, you remember what I said about our credibility . . ."

"Yes, of course, my chief. And that is a very wise policy. But why can we not tell them that the girls were so upset by their captivity that they refused to eat? That they went on a hunger strike and died?"

Rauf Pasha pursed his lips and massaged his bearded face. Finally, he said, "I tell you what, my friend. Let me think it over."

"That is all I can ask." El-Badawi paused. "By the way, *efendi*, I have inspected the prison cells recently. These people have had no bath . . ."

"You worry about their comfort, Mahmoud?"

"Those swine? Of course not."

"Then, why are you telling me this?"

"They smell very bad . . ."

Rauf Pasha looked puzzled.

El-Badawi explained, "If we are to enjoy the two women . . ."

The light of recognition lit up on Rauf Pasha's face like the dawn over Lake Van. "Ah, yes. Of course. Have Azzam Hamal take care of that tonight. And have him bring mine to my private quarters, and yours to yours."

"Excellent, idea, *efendi*." He paused. "And our mujahideen, our holy warriors, *efendi*?"

"They will enjoy the other women."

"All our men? There are only five other women, including the ambassador's wife!"

"Well, what can we do? If there are only five, there are only five. Of course, it will have to be arranged in an orderly fashion. We don't want chaos. In fact, we shall arrange this matter so that it will become a lesson in humility."

El-Badawi's eyes glistened. "You mean . . ."

"Yes, of course. The women will be taken outdoors, stripped naked, and violated by all our men. It will be a day-long spectacle. The American men will be forced to watch. Americans are arrogant dogs. This will humble both the women and the men. Humility leads to piety, and piety leads to godliness. In the end, we will be doing them a favor. When they go back to America, they will all be better people."

"How do we do this in an orderly fashion, if you and I are going to be occupied most of the time with our own women?"

"Put Azzam Hamal in charge. Since he's not interested in women, he will be fair in his assigning turns at the women to our holy warriors."

El-Badawi felt as though he overflowed with energy. He trembled as he spoke. "May I start the process now, Rauf Pasha?"

"Certainly. I too am most anxious to taste the fruits of valor and faithfulness."

0920 hours
The Palace of the Holy Revolution, Headquarters of the
Revolutionary Guard, Fourth District, Tehran, Iran

The three-story yellow brick building on a street in downtown Tehran was unimpressive. It was flanked by a grocery store and a vegetable market on one side, and a shoe repair business and barber shop on the other. Four bearded young men in jeans and long-sleeved plaid sport shirts stood watch in front of the building, cradling Kalashnikov assault rifles. Volkswagens, Fords, and various Russian-made cars, many dating from the 1970s, polluted the air with their fumes as they rumbled by. Two women covered from head to foot in black walked rapidly past the guards, who carefully eyed them for any infraction of the dress code. Only the women's eyes were visible, and these shifted nervously from the street in front of them to the guards and their weapons.

Three men in wrinkled double-breasted suits, carrying briefcases, entered the building.

Three other men sat on worn easy chairs in a lounge on the second floor. The mullah Ali Bakhtiari, in black robe and black turban, fingered his long, partially graying beard and looked up at the framed photograph of the late Ayatollah Khomeini, guiding force behind the Islamic Revolution.

The mullah asked, "Have they begun to move out yet?"

The clean-shaven man in the army uniform, medals crowding his chest, knew the question was directed at him. "Yes, Your Holiness. Troops, armored cars, and tanks have left the base at Mahabad," General Mohammad Sephabodi said. "They are moving in a northwesterly direction toward Dazgir at this very moment. A similar detachment has left the base near Tabriz, passed Marand, and turned east. It should reach Khvoy soon."

"Good," Bakhtiari said. "We don't really expect trouble, but it's best to be prepared."

The thirty-two-year-old man in civilian clothes rubbed his closely cropped, sparse beard. He said, "General Sephabodi, have the Turks massed any troops?"

General Sephabodi glanced with obvious disdain at the man, then stared out the window at the commercial buildings across the street. "Mr. Rafsanjani, why would the Turks mass troops at the border of Iran?" He then looked back at the civilian, holding the other man's eyes.

Shahpur Rafsanjani, commander of the Revolutionary Guards, Fourth District of Tehran, hesitated. Then he said, "Well, General, I mean . . . It's just that our friend, Rauf Pasha, has made his demands and is about to use nuclear weapons against allies of the Turkish government . . ."

The mullah stared at Rafsanjani but said nothing.

General Sephabodi answered, "Mr. Rafsanjani, I would not go around calling Rauf Pasha 'our friend.' Nor would I talk freely about the . . . unconventional weapons. His Holiness, of course, knows the facts." He gestured toward Mullah Ali Bakhtiari. "You know them, and I know them. However, my superiors and colleagues of the General Staff know nothing about it. We want to keep it that way."

"But, General, there are only the three of us in this room." Shahpur Rafsanjani sounded offended.

The general smiled, "Of course, that is true. But certain

things become habit with repetition. It would be best not to acquire the bad habit. In the military, we refer to the 'need to know.' Do you understand?''

Bakhtiari said, "Getting back to District Commander Rafsanjani's original question . . . The answer, of course, is that the Turks may suspect that elements in Iran are connected to the situation you referred to, but they don't know it for a fact. And they certainly can't prove it.''

The general added, "And what can they do to that band of Turkish loyal Islamists, anyway? That is, assuming they even know where they are. Sending out an army against them would only precipitate the . . . unconventional attack they wish to avoid.''

The man in black asked, "General, do you think they know where the group is?"

"No, your Holiness. There is absolutely no indication that they do.''

"Then are we indeed foolish for moving our own troops?"

"No. These are not massive troop movements. Anyone observing them would interpret them as modest exercises. Just to keep the troops somewhat alert. Indeed, that is exactly what the commanders of our forces in the field believe.''

"Good," the mullah commented. "We have enough problems here at home. The Reformists have won a majority in Majlis, as you know.''

"Which means," the general said, "that most Iranians seem to want rapprochement with the West, unfortunately.''

"Bah," said District Commander Rafsanjani, "what do the people know?"

"Well, Shahpur," General Sephabodi said, "I believe it was the task of your Revolutionary Guard to educate the people. Was it not?''

"Very well, very well," Mullah Bakhtiari said. "Let us not argue among ourselves. Besides, Rafsanjani and his colleagues are seeing to it that our democracy-loving opponents are being held in check. Traitorous editors and elected officials are being silenced. We still have the power in Iran and we will keep it. Meanwhile, we have troops and armor proceeding to the border area, just in case. Correct, General?"

"Correct."

1120 hours
Iranian armored column on outskirts of Dazgir,
14.4 kilometers east of Kara Kale

The dust hanging over the road marked the area in which the Iranian column came to a halt on a height overlooking the town of Dazgir. Now that the engines were turned off, the sound of birds were again carried on the fragrant air, lulling the soldiers with a pervasive feeling of calm. The late afternoon was brisk but sunny, although they could see gray clouds on the western horizon. There were ten armored troop carriers and five Russian-made T-72 tanks. Soldiers clambered down from the vehicles to stretch their legs. Captain Kermanshahi raised the hatch of his lead T-72 tank and poked his head out to look around, brushing the dust off his uniform.

He extracted his binoculars and scanned the horizon. When his gaze hit upon the mountains to the west, he stopped the movement of his head and lingered on one spot.

Then he climbed completely out of the tank to allow his men to emerge. "Lieutenant Isfahani, come here!"

A thin young man ran up to the captain. "Yes, Captain?"

Handing the lieutenant his binoculars, Captain Kermanshahi said, "Take a look through these, and look over there." He indicated a point to the west. "What do you see?"

The Lieutenant squinted through the binoculars. "Nothing, sir. Ah, wait, yes . . . There is some kind of man-made structure . . ."

"Yes, Lieutenant. Look carefully. Does it look like a private dwelling, an apartment house . . .?"

Lieutenant Isfahani strained to examine it, then, "No, my captain, it looks like some kind of fortified position."

"Yes, I think so too."

"What is it, sir?"

"Damned if I know. I've been in this area many times. In fact, right up to the Turkish border, and I had never noticed that structure before. Unless I was blind in the past and can suddenly see, that structure was not there two years ago."

The lieutenant drew a map from his inside tunic pocket and spread it out on the tank. They both looked at the area in question.

"As you can see, Lieutenant, it's not on the map, either. Pretty soon it's going to disappear."

"How do you mean, sir?"

"Well, those clouds behind it are getting thicker and darker. There may be fog too. If so, it will obscure the view from here."

"Didn't General Sephabodi say anything about it, sir?"

Kermanshahi frowned, "No."

"Is it ours or theirs?"

"From here, Lieutenant, I can't tell if it's on our side of the border or on the Turkish side." He thought for a moment, then, "Lieutenant, get me headquarters."

0935 hours EST
Office of the commander in chief,
Special Operations Command, the Pentagon

Brigadier General Jack Krauss, U.S. Army, was commander of the TALON Joint Task Force. He had just arrived at the office of General Samuel "Buck" Freedman, commander in chief of Special Operations Command (CIN-CSOC). Freedman noticed with satisfaction that Krauss still had the erect carriage of a West Point cadet. He looked at Krauss's weathered face, and at those icy gray eyes that could bore a hole through a man, and thought this Special Forces veteran looked like John Wayne, only harder, more menacing, more convincing. And while the Duke had only been acting, playing a part, Buck Freedman knew that Jack Krauss wasn't. He was the real thing. He'd proved that over and over.

The Marine four-star general said, "Have a seat, Jack."

Krauss said, "Thank you, sir," and sat down. He detected

the strong aroma of freshly brewed coffee in the air. Krauss looked at the marine general and waited for him to speak.

"Coffee, Jack?"

"Thank you, sir."

Freedman swiveled around in his chair, poured the steaming brown liquid into a clean mug, swiveled back toward the Green Beret, and handed him the coffee. The two men had known each other for a long time. While they say that familiarity breeds contempt, for these two seasoned warriors it had bred deep mutual respect and admiration.

Freedman asked, "Eagle Team keeping in touch?"

"Yes, sir. They're on their way to the target now. They should accomplish their mission very soon."

"Barring any serious problems."

"Yes, sir. Barring any serious problems."

"They don't have a lot of time."

"Yes, sir, they don't. But they'll get the job done."

Freedman nodded and then said, almost to himself, "They must. They sure as hell must." Then, he looked at Krauss and said, "Well, Jack, I've got some new data for you that you should forward to your troopers. The U.S. naval attaché to our Embassy in Ankara has been kidnapped."

Krauss narrowed his eyes.

Freedman continued, "We think it's probably this terrorist group your people are dealing with."

"How in hell did they get past security?"

Freedman frowned at his desk. "Schraer kind of helped them on that." He looked up at Krauss and saw the questioning look. "No, no, nothing like that. I mean he had a lady friend he visited, secretly, of course, since he's a married man . . . So he reduced his security to four bodyguards."

"What about them?"

"All dead. Very boldly done. These guys know what they're doing, and, damn it, they've got the guts to do it!"

Krauss asked, "What do they want with him, General? Military secrets?"

"Who the hell knows? What military secrets would they think he has that could help them? Do they give a rat's ass about the disposition of our fleet? Do they have a goddamn navy? No, they probably think we'll pay more attention to an important member of the military than to a bunch of tourists. That's the way those bastards think."

Krauss caught himself rubbing his prosthetic right hand with his left hand again. *Funny,* he thought, *he once read that Cervantes, the author of* Don Quixote, *had lost the use of his left hand in a naval battle with the Turks.* He noticed that his mentor was watching this. As soon as he became aware of what he had unconsciously been doing, he stopped. He looked at the half-empty mug of coffee he had placed on Freedman's desk and then picked it up. He didn't really need any more coffee, but it would keep his left hand occupied and out of trouble.

"By the way . . ." Freedman said.

Kraus never liked to hear a "by the way" from General Freedman. He looked directly at Freedman, waiting for the other shoe to drop.

"Two things, Jack. One: Our satellite reconnaissance has picked up Iranian troop movements."

"Where?"

"Northwestern Iran. They seem to be moving closer to the Turkish border."

"Large scale?"

"No, not at all. But large enough if they happen to cross paths with your troopers."

"Any idea what it's all about?"

"Our sources and our State Department analysts haven't got a clue. Could be routine. Exercises. I'm only mentioning it because, even by accident, your guys might run into them. So they ought to be aware of this."

"Thank you, General. I'll let them know immediately." He looked at Freedman's face and read his thoughts. "And there won't be any international incident."

Freedman smiled, "I know it, Jack."

"Yes, sir. And the second thing . . . ?"

"It concerns Lieutenant Commander Schraer. While there is no specific information these fuckers hope to get out of Schraer, they may apply some pressure . . ."

"Torture."

"Yeah. Thing is, Krauss, Commander Schraer knows something very important."

"Yes . . . ?"

"He knows about Eagle Team's mission."

For a moment, Krauss was speechless.

Freedman continued, "He had a need to know. He was in direct communication with Admiral Zlotchew, commander of the Sixth Fleet, who is standing by to send in our Ospreys to extract your people after their mission is completed, and to lend any other kind of naval support necessary."

Krauss nodded. "So, you're saying under conditions of extreme duress, who knows what he might say."

"Yes. No one can stand torture for too long. I don't care who he is. And a man might give information he thinks his tormenters might appreciate, just so they'll stop torturing him."

"If that information comes out, the element of surprise is destroyed. They'd be ready for Eagle Team."

Chapter 7

Lieutenant Commander Bernard Schraer sat in a wooden chair, his wrists tied to the arms and his ankles to the legs. He had welts, bruises, and cuts on his face from the struggle in the Ankara hotel room. He looked around and saw the bare concrete walls of this small room. The only furniture were the chair he was tied to and two other similar ones, plus a wooden table with various kinds of knives, some sewing needles, a hammer, pliers, wire cutters, and a hacksaw.

He saw Rauf Pasha and Mahmoud el-Badawi sitting opposite him, looking at him the way wolves look at a lamb. And he saw the bald, muscular Azzam Hamal standing close to him. He could actually smell old sweat emanating from Hamal.

Rauf Pasha said, "Commander Schraer, give us some really important information and we will not hurt you."

"Fuck you!"

Rauf Pasha nodded to Hamal, who struck Schraer across the mouth.

Rauf Pasha said, "You should not employ such language, Commander. You should also know that the man who just struck you prefers men to women, and as you might guess, is not one to take no for an answer. Besides, 'Do unto others as you would have them do unto you,' as you infidels are fond of saying."

Schraer stared defiantly at Rauf Pasha.

"Now then, Bernie . . . May I call you Bernie? It seems so much friendlier. Anyway, Bernie, surely the United States is not just sitting on its hands when we are threatening to destroy Athens and Tel Aviv. What, exactly, are they doing about the situation?"

Schraer said nothing. Rauf Pasha nodded to Hamal, who then struck the lieutenant commander viciously in the face and in the stomach. Schraer gasped for breath.

"Come now, Bernie, tell me what your country is doing about the current situation. Surely you know what the U.S. Navy is doing. Is the Sixth Fleet going anywhere they were previously not scheduled for?"

Schraer said nothing. Hamal raised his hand, but Rauf Pasha signaled him to wait.

Rauf Pasha said, "You know, Bernie, my friend, we could do a lot worse than have Hamal knock you around. For example, we could stick a needle through the pupil of your left eye. Do you know what happens if we do that? Well, I am not sure either, since I've never tried it before. And I'm not about to consult with Bashar el-Assad, the opthalmologist who is the new president of Syria. But I imagine it would be excrutiatingly painful, and that . . . how do you say? . . . humours, liquids, in the eye would drain out, resulting in blindness of that eye. Don't you think? And then we would ask you to talk or have the right eye treated in the same manner. Does that sound pleasant?"

Schraer said, "No, it's not pleasant. But, damn it, I don't know what the navy is up to in this matter. I'm the naval attaché to the U.S. Embassy. I don't have a need to know, so they don't advise me."

El-Badawi whispered in Rauf Pasha's ear. Rauf Pasha nodded and said, "You might be telling the truth." He smiled benignly. Then his facial expression became fierce. "On the other hand, it is possible, quite possible, that the U.S. naval attaché in the capital of Turkey *does* have a need to know what his country is doing about something that concerns Turkey. And to coordinate efforts with the Turkish military. Don't you think?" His voice became louder, and he banged his fist on the arm of his chair.

Schraer said, "No. At any rate, I don't know of any unusual movements."

"Well," Rauf Pasha sighed, "maybe we can start out with some harmless, unclassified information to grease the wheels, as you Americans say. Have you ever heard of one Clark M. Zlotchew?"

"Of course."

"Who is he, then?"

"Admiral Zlotchew is the commander of the U.S. Sixth Fleet. Everyone knows that."

"Good, good. That is a start." He paused. "Now, some elements of the Sixth Fleet have been sighted in the Aegean, off the Turkish coast. Do you know why?"

"Of course. Everyone knows why. They're investigating the sinking of the American container vessel."

"Very good. You see . . . ? It is not so difficult to talk to me. What have they found so far?"

"A lot of dead bodies. American seamen machine-gunned by you bastards. They're diving for more evidence."

Rauf Pasha nodded to Hamal, who smacked Schraer in the face. Blood began to trickle from his nose.

Rauf Pasha said, "It is not fitting to use coarse language. Please remain courteous in my presence."

Schraer glared at the Pasha.

"Now, then, just another step further," Rauf Pasha said. "What does Admiral Zlotchew . . . What does *anyone* in the American government—the State Department, the CIA, the Joint Chiefs of Staff, the dog of a president of the United States, anyone—intend to do about the situation?" His voice grew louder.

Schraer said nothing.

Rauf Pasha nodded to Hamal, who punched the naval attaché in the face, sending him and the chair reeling backward. Hamal raised the chair with Schraer in it to its normal position.

"Once more, Bernie, my friend, just what is being done? Surely your people are not just sitting around fornicating with their interns. They must be doing *something* to avoid nuclear destruction. Not to mention to rescue you, Bernie, and the other hostages. And to avenge the sinking of the container ship."

Schraer maintained silence. Hamal raised his fist, but on a signal from Rauf Pasha, lowered it again.

Rauf Pasha thought for a moment, then, "You know, it was very comical how my men machine-gunned those

American seamen in the water. I am told the seamen looked surprised when they were fired upon. Apparently, they thought they were going to be rescued. What idiots you Americans are. Rescued! Indeed. Then they tried to avoid the bullets by diving under the water and holding their breaths. Ha! As if mere water could shield them from bullets. Yes, it was very funny. Very, very funny. You should have been there, Bernie."

"Filthy son of a bitch!"

Rauf Pasha said, "And now, you Americans just sit back and do nothing. You are either stupid or you are cowards. Which is it? Or are you both stupid and cowardly? Hmm? You know who we are because we announced it. But you don't know where we are located, or how strong we are. So much for your CIA and other so-called intelligence services. They are stupid. They know nothing."

Rauf Pasha's keen eyes scrutinized Schraer's face as he spoke and detected a glint in Schraer's eye that suggested that the lieutenant commander knew something. He perceived Schraer clenching his jaw as though he were forcing himself to refrain from saying something to contradict Rauf Pasha. The terrorist leader sensed that the American officer knew something, something important. He felt he had almost gotten him to give up a secret.

Rauf Pasha continued. "Or, if they do know where we are, why do they not, in conjunction with Turkey, with NATO troops, attack us? Are they cowards? Yes, of course, they are cowards." He looked at Schraer to see if his words were having any effect. He could only see Schraer's jaw muscles working.

"Tell me, Bernie, are the Americans all cowards? Are they afraid of us? Are your men really women? Yes, I would wager that even if they knew exactly where to find us, they would do nothing, absolutely nothing. In fact, that is just what they are doing now, isn't it? They send ships off the coast of Turkey to look threatening. Oh, we are trembling. But behind the scenes, they push for the Turkish Intelligence to find us, and the Turkish military to attack us. But the Americans themselves will do nothing. They will not risk any of their precious lives. Your military are effeminate cowards!"

"Bullshit!" Schraer was enraged. He couldn't hold back.

But as soon as he released his anger with that exclamation, he regretted it. He bit his tongue.

Rauf Pasha stared at the American and smiled. "Ah, yes, 'bullshit.' If I understand that quaint American idiom correctly, Bernie, even though it literally refers to manure proceeding from the male of the bovine species, somehow, in the twisted and confused American mind, it refers to falsehoods. So you are saying that my evaluation of the American military is false. That they really are doing something."

Schraer said nothing.

"Which means," Rauf Pasha continued, "that your military is actually taking some kind of action. Doesn't it?"

"I just meant we're not cowards, is all."

"No, no. I think some action, highly secret, no doubt, is being taken. And I am sure you know exactly what it is." Rauf Pasha's face clouded over with rage. He stood up and banged his fist against the table, making the instruments of torture dance. He shouted, "Now, talk, you son of pigs! There is very little time. Talk!"

Schraer remained silent.

El-Badawi stood and whispered into Rauf Pasha's ear again. Rauf Pasha sighed and said, "Just tell us anything important that affects us."

"I don't know anything."

"You are a fool." Then he thought for a moment. "You know, there are other things we could do to you instead of—correction—in *addition* to blinding you with a needle. We could turn you into a eunuch. Without benefit of anesthesia, of course. Would you like that, Bernie my friend?"

Rauf Pasha and Mahmoud el-Badawi laughed heartily.

Then Rauf Pasha said something in Turkish to Azzam Hamal, who then picked up a needle from the table. He held the needle in front of Schraer's face to display it. Then he replaced the needle, picked up the hacksaw and made motions with it as though he were sawing Schraer's leg off. He replaced this tool and picked up the pliers, and by signs showed that he might pull the lieutenant commander's teeth. He replaced that instrument and seized the wire cutter. A broad smile broke out on Azzam Hamal's face. He opened the wire cutter, and with both hands placed it against the American's crotch.

There was no denying it, Schraer felt fear, deep, gut-wrenching fear.

Rauf Pasha said, "Now, Bernie, my friend, we will leave you for a while to rest. And to think. Try to think. Try hard."

1900 hours
The *Selamlik* of Rauf Pasha

Mahmoud el-Badawi leaned back against the multi-colored cushions on the couch, took a long pull on his cigarette, closed his eyes, then allowed the smoke to drift out of his nostrils.

Rauf Pasha, sitting cross-legged on another sofa, sipping coffee, put his cup down on the small table and said, "Very well, Mahmoud, enough small talk. What can I do for you?"

El-Badawi said, "About the prisoners . . ."

"Yes," said Rauf Pasha, smiling. "You see, the Americans, no matter what they say, care more about a handful of their own citizens than about millions of foreigners, like Greeks or Jews. What's more, the Turkish government is sensitive to this fact. So I have made it known to the American government as well as to the Turkish government that these American dogs will be executed if our demands are not met. And, mind you, I have made it clear that it is a slow, horrible death that awaits them. It will take days for them to die once we have started the process. They will beg to be put out of their misery."

"Yes, and now we have Schraer. But Rauf Pasha, all this pressure, and still they have not acceded to our demands. There is very little time left, less than twenty-four hours."

"Don't worry, Mahmoud, the Great Satan will surely pressure the Turkish government to give in to our demands at the last minute. In that way, they will save the American pigs and avert nuclear war. But either way, we win."

"Oh, *efendi*, a favor: I would very much like to at least kill the Zionist pig. What is one Jew in the great scheme of things?"

"Ah yes, Perry Stein, the 'portly Jew.' " He thought for

a moment. "He is not a bad sort, you know, even if he is a Jewish dog. He is an expert in Ottoman history, he is respectful of the Muslim religion, and he speaks Turkish better than you do, if I may say so, Mahmoud. Besides, I too could indulge myself if I wanted to. You see, I would dearly love to dispose of the Armenian son of pigs who has the nerve to set foot in holy Turkey. This Haig Sebouhian.

"But, we must exercise some discipline in the name of the Cause. After all, if we don't keep our pledge, our word will not be respected. And this is important in future dealings. We say we will vaporize Athens and Tel Aviv if we are not handed the government by April six at sunset, then we will do just that. We say we will hand over the hostages if they accede to our demands, then we must do that too. Otherwise, the infidels will have no incentive to meet any further demands. After all, we have our ethics."

"Yes, of course." El-Badawi thought for a moment, then looked up. "But it is always legitimate to kill escaping prisoners, is it not? So, what if they try to escape?"

Rauf Pasha laughed. "You are a crafty devil, Mahmoud ibn Hassan el-Badawi." His face became serious. He looked at the Iranian mullah, who merely shrugged.

Rauf Pasha said, "Let me think about it, my friend."

1700 hours EST
Press Room, the White House, Washington, D.C.

The room was packed with reporters and television cameras. Mary Louise Conti, the President's press secretary, walked briskly to the podium and was inundated with questions. She could see the anger, feel the outrage, the hostility in the room, almost smell it. The reporters frantically shouted to be heard.

"Is it true that Lieutenant Commander Schraer has been kidnapped?"

"Yes, that's true."

"When did it happen?"

"A few hours ago. At about seven thirty P.M., Turkish time. That would be at noon, Eastern Standard Time. It's midnight in Turkey at present."

"Who did it?"

"We have not yet received official word, but we believe it to be the as-Saif al-Islam organization."

"The same group that has the ambassador and those other American hostages?"

"This is what we surmise. But it's not official yet."

"Why Schraer?"

"Well, he *is* the naval attaché to the U.S. Embassy in Ankara."

"Does he have any military secrets?"

"He knows about the disposition of our Sixth Fleet. But this information can't be of much use to this group. They don't have a navy."

Mary Louise called on another reporter, "Okay, Margaret Daley."

A dowdy woman in her fifties rose to her feet and placed her hands on her hips. She spoke very deliberately, very vehemently. "What kind of security do we have for our embassy people that they can be picked up at will by terrorists?"

Mary Louise was about to speak, when Margaret Daley decided to continue speaking. "Oh, another thing. There is no word of exactly what we are doing to free the prisoners. What *are* we doing?"

There was a murmur of agreement among the media people. They were obviously angry with what to them seemed like inaction. *Yes,* Mary Louise thought, *the natives are restless. How much longer can this go on?*

April 6, 0004 hours
High over the Mediterranean Sea,
en route to the Turkish-Iranian border

The seven members of TALON Force Eagle Team were seated in their individual drop capsules on board the specially designed Boeing X-37 Rocketplane. It measured seventy-five feet long, had a twenty-eight foot wingspan, and was twelve feet tall from the bottom of the fuselage to the top of the tail. An L-1011 carrier aircraft had hauled the rocketplane piggyback-style from the 167th Airlift Wing of the West Virginia Air National Guard base in Martinsburg, West Virginia. At 50,000 feet, the X-37 had ignited its two Fastrac rocket engines and separated from the carrier to fly on its own.

As so often before, Captain Sam Wong asked himself what the hell he was doing hurtling through the upper atmosphere, so far above the good old earth's friendly surface, at speeds that scared him when he allowed himself to think about it, in this reusable advanced hypersonic marvel of science. He knew the X-37 could reach altitudes of up to fifty miles above the earth's surface while traveling at a velocity as much as eight times faster than the speed of sound.

This is Buck Rogers stuff, for Pete's sake. It would be a hell of a lot more comfortable watching this on television, stretched out on the couch, like when he was a kid in the Flushing section of Queens, New York, eating popcorn and sipping Mountain Dew while staring at the boob tube. He remembered his mother screaming at him in Mandarin to stop watching the stupid box and do his homework.

But of course, he had already done his homework. Always. He had devoured the material, digested it, made it a part of him. Fast. It was no challenge. He was a fast study; "smart as a whip," the elementary school principal had told his immigrant Chinese parents. Sam smiled thinking about how his father had asked the principal, "What you mean, smart as whip? Whip have no brain, very dumb. My boy dumb?"

Sam Wong was an information management specialist. What the hell was a communications expert like him doing inside a freaking rocket, zipping through the edge of Mother Earth's atmosphere, at speeds that would probably rip your skin off in a second if you were outside the plane? Not to mention being chucked out into the atmosphere inside one of those claustrophobic drop capsules, or "eggshells," as they called the entry packages, so he could land in some God-forsaken hellhole where some not-so-nice people were waiting to make Kung Pao out of his Chinese-American ass.

He always asked himself these questions on the way in, but he knew the answers. He was a patriotic American. He loved his country, the best damn country in the world. He loved his six teammates, and he knew the feeling was mutual. But he knew on some deep level that there was more to it than that. He would sometimes give himself permission to admit, only to himself, that he had this deep-seated need to constantly prove himself. He wasn't satisfied with being a brain, the skinny computer geek who had been pushed around by the jocks in high school. The wedgie king. It wasn't enough to be a genius. He grudgingly admired those high school jocks, so full of confidence, surrounded by beautiful cheerleaders.

In his senior year of high school, he had a revelation: it's not how big or how strong you are that's important. It's what you do with what you have. It's a question of will, of spirit. A hero isn't a guy who's not afraid of anything. Hell, if you're not afraid of anything, you're just an idiot. And if you're the strongest guy in the world, it's really impossible to be considered brave, because you really don't *need* to be afraid of anyone. No, the brave guy is the one who has reason to be afraid, who *is* afraid, but who goes ahead and does what he has to do in spite of that fear. That's bravery. He's the true hero.

So, five-foot-six Sammy Wong had pushed himself to the limits of physical endurance through TALON training and had made it into this, the most elite corps of fighters in the world. This brilliant techno-geek had toughened his skinny body, gained ten pounds, all hard muscle, vastly increased his physical endurance, and learned to handle the most advanced weapons in existence. And the most primitive, like a commando knife. He had gained a great deal of self-confidence in the process. He knew he was not as physically powerful as his teammates, but compared to the average Joe, he felt like Superman.

And he knew that his teammates appreciated him for his spirit as well as his genius, not to mention his wise-ass sense of humor. He knew they loved him the way he loved them. Of course, he felt a special lust for Jennifer Olsen, that gorgeous blonde goddess. And he had a particularly deep friendship with Jack DuBois, that big black man of steel who had been shrewd enough to make a sizable fortune playing the stock market on the Internet. But the whole team was one organism, and they would no sooner abandon one of their number than a man would willingly cut off an arm or a leg. Still, he had to keep proving himself. To himself.

Each member of the team had already been suited in the ultra high-tech TALON Force Battle Ensemble. The BE provided full body armor protection as well as a host of cutting-edge communications devices.

Okay, time for the helmets. Sam knelt down and popped open a pod containing eight dull gray-green helmets stored in racks. These were the lightweight but tough graphite/kevlar helmets, nerve center for the battle equipment, providing not only ballistic protection, but a communication suite, employing voice as well as holographic imaging and computer networking. He handed a helmet to each member of Eagle Team and then clapped one on his own head. They all quickly strapped the camouflage helmets on and extended a wing arm that had been recessed in the side of the helmet shells. This was the Battle Sensor Device. The little arm of the BSD rested at a point just above the eyeline.

Sam sent his fingers rapidly scurrying over the buttons and switches of the panel in the case beneath the helmet rack. Major Travis Barrett's voice was hardly audible as he started to speak.

"Up the volume, Sam, goddamn it!" Stan Powczuk's gravelly voice blasted everyone's eardrums, making them jump.

"I believe he's doing just that, Stan, as we speak," Hunter Blake calmly intoned. The "I believe" boomed, while the other words rapidly decreased in volume until the "Stan, as we speak," came at just the right volume. It sounded to each TALON member as though Hunter were talking in a normal voice right beside them, even though he was speaking barely above a whisper.

"Okay, we're in audio contact." Each member clearly heard Sam's soft-spoken voice. "Let's check out the reception, ladies and gentlemen. Boss?"

"Loud and clear, Sammy."

"Hunter?"

"Roger."

"Sarah?"

"Excellent."

"Stan?"

"You finally got it right."

"Jen?"

"Yes, Sammy, darling." She audibly breathed into her transmitter, ending in a kind of exaggerated whimper.

Sam's eyes widened, and for a moment he lost his concentration.

"Hey girl, you stop messin' with my man's brain." Jack DuBois's low voice smoothly came through. "My little buddy can't afford to have no damn orgasm while wearing his Battle Ensemble. Might short-circuit."

"And he doesn't mean the suit," Hunter said.

Jennifer smiled broadly. "I am woman."

"Ooookay," Sam said. "Major, we're all receiving."

"So I see." Travis Barrett's Texas drawl flowed into their ears as though the major were sitting right beside each one of them. "Well, receive this: Several things have happened. Some you've already been briefed on, others not." Travis filled them in.

"Last, but most certainly not least," Travis said, "they've kidnapped our naval attaché in Ankara."

"Lieutenant Commander Schraer?" Stan asked.

"Afraid so. And Schraer knows about us."

Everyone understood the implications.

Travis said, "Okay, Lieutenant Olsen will fill you in on details. Listen up. Go ahead, Jen."

Lieutenant Jennifer Olsen of Naval Intelligence sailed what looked like a tiny frisby at Sam, who slid the CD-rom into an encrypt/decrypt radio computer he had in a small, black waist pack. He pulled the tiny, almost invisible, antenna up out of the computer body, buckled the durable pack around his waist, pouch in front, and pressed some small buttons inside it.

The team members looked up toward the little monocle-like device of the BSD extended above their left eye. In two seconds, the images of 3-D photographs appeared before them. They were high resolution, so that what they saw was absolutely clear, vivid, and detailed.

Jen explained what they were viewing. "This is a map of Turkey. In the northwest, you see Istanbul, largest city in Turkey. It's an important port and sits astride the Bosphorus Strait, which connects the Black Sea and the Mediterranean. Where it says 'Kara Deniz,' that's Turkish for the Black Sea. As you can see, a ship coming from the east passes from the Black Sea into this narrow channel called the Bosphorus, between European Turkey and the Asian side. From there, it comes out into the Sea of Marmara, then has to pass through another narrow channel between the two continents: the Dardanelles. Once out of this strait it enters the Aegean Sea, between Greece and Turkey, and it's clear sailing to the Med and beyond."

The holographic intra-optical images shifted to display a closer scale aerial photograph of the greater Istanbul area.

Jen continued, "Now, the Bosphorus is not only narrow, but has a lot of tricky twists and turns, including four totally blind curves, one of them at a point that's less than half a mile wide, so that a ship proceeding east might not see a ship coming around a bend toward it until the last minute. This, and the fact that there are some very rapid currents, make navigation difficult. As a result, shipping is restricted and closely watched. It's in a very strategic position. Ship traffic can be choked off very easily. Which has happened.

"As Travis said, the bridges connecting Istanbul to the rest of the country were blown up. So right now, traffic is at a standstill while Turkish Army Engineers, with help from NATO and Israel, are clearing the Strait of debris and trying to recover corpses. It's one hell of a mess."

The image projected on their retinas now changed once more to a smaller scale, taking in Turkey as a whole.

Jen said, "Istanbul is on the European side of the Strait, while most of the country is on the Asian side. That Asian side is called Anatolia, or *Antalya*, as they say in Turkish. You see, slightly west of center, Ankara, the capital. Almost due south of Ankara, slightly east, you'll see Eregli, just before the Taurus Mountain chain and the Mediterranean coast."

"Hey, wait a minute," Sam interrupted. "I see Eregli on the north coast, about one hundred fifty miles due east of Istanbul."

"Yes, I know," Jen said.

"For Chrissake," Stan grumbled, "they got two cities with the same name? They've been whirling their dervishes too much."

Jack said, "Hey, man, we have Portland, Maine, and Portland, Oregon, don't we? And don't get me started on Springfield!"

Travis broke in, "Okay, people, let's allow our intel to finish up. There's not all that much time. Jen?"

Jen continued, "The Eregli in the south is the one that bears on this case. It's a small city of over 30,000 population. This is the town where the councilman was murdered."

"How does that affect us?" Hunter asked.

"Kemal Tarsusu is . . . was . . . a lawyer and city councilman. Not a very important person in the scheme of things. It's just that he was known for his outspoken support of the pro-Western government, and his antipathy to the Islamist movement. He was well liked by the townsfolk. It's important to us only because it's another indication of an anti-American, anti-West movement among Islamists in Turkey. His murder was symbolic."

Stan said, "It scares the shit out of people."

"That's the object of terrorism, by definition," Travis commented.

Jen said, "It sends a message. As does the terrorization of villages in the countryside. The rape and murder of school girls, that kind of thing. The events all seem to be connected." She looked over at Sam Wong. "Now, as to the whereabouts of the hostages. Sammy?"

Sam said, "We knew they were heading for eastern Turkey, toward mountainous territory. But we didn't know exactly where the hostages had disappeared to until just before we boarded the X-37. That's when I received the info."

"Directly from the NSA Top Secret Special Ops Computers at Fort Meade," Travis clarified.

"Those cybernetic implants NSA shoved up your ass are one hell of a time-saver, Sammy my boy," Stan said.

Jack was impatient. "Well, come on, little buddy. Where are they?"

"Our intelligence sources have pinpointed their location. They're being held in the mountains of northwestern Iran . . ."

"What?! Fucking Iran?" Stan burst out. "I thought this was a Turkish deal."

Sam continued, "It is. This place is sixteen kilometers west of Dazgir, Iran, and four point eight kilometers from the Turkish border."

Jen said, "All right, let's zoom in on the area."

The holographic intra-optical images shifted to display a closer scale photograph of the borderlands of southeast Turkey and northwest Iran.

Hunter said, "Mountainous. Damned mountainous."

"That's why we trained in the mountains of New Mexico," Travis commented.

Jen said, "To the west in Turkey, you see Mt. Geliashin, thirteen thousand six hundred seventy-five feet high. You'll notice that just a few kilometers to the south is the border with Iraq. All the way to the east on this image is Lake Urmia, Iran. Now, notice that west of the lake, closer to the Turkish border, is Dazgir, a city of about 32,000 inhabitants. Now between Dazgir and the Turkish border is a wild, practically uninhabited region. The same is true on the Turkish side. All right, Sammy, where does NSA say the hostages are?"

Sam explained, "Okay, now look carefully. Twenty-six kilometers west of Dazgir, and just four point eight kilometers from the Turkish border is that dark smudge. See it? That's the headquarters, or maybe just one of several headquarters, of an extremist Islamic fundamentalist movement led by a former Turkish army officer, Rauf Karahisarli. His men refer to him as Rauf Pasha."

"Shit," rumbled Stan Powzcuk, "I can see why: it's a hell of a lot easier."

"Keep in mind," Sam said, "if you see it written in Turkish, what we're pronouncing *Pasha* is spelled *P-a-ş-a*. No H, but a squiggle under the S."

Sarah asked, "Does the organization have a name?"

Sam said, "Yes. It's called as-Saif al-Islam."

Jen said, "That's Arabic for 'The Sword of Islam.' "

"Why Arabic, if they're Turks?" Hunter asked.

Sam said, "They're militant Islamists. Mostly Turks, yes, but they have a few Iranian volunteer mujahideen, holy warriors, a vicious Libyan America-hater named Mahmoud ibn Hassan el-Badawi, who was trained by our own people in Afghanistan. They have this Iranian cleric, the mullah Najatollah Yazdi; he's the group's spiritual guide. Sixty-nine years old, physically frail.

"So, our sources say that Yazdi speaks Farsi—that's Persian, guys—as well as Arabic and broken Turkish. The Libyan speaks the Libyan dialect of Arabic and a poor but understandable Turkish, the Turks speak Turkish, and the other Iranians speak Persian. So, they use mostly Turkish to communicate. But remember, what binds them together is their holy book, the Quran, written in classical Arabic. So, I'd guess the name as-Saif al-Islam has special resonance for them." Sam looked over at Jen for confirmation.

"Affirmative," Jen said. "How did you know that, you little twerp?"

"Bite me, Brunhilde." Sam said this with a great big smile.

"Hell," said Stan, "it's like our lingo is English, but we use Latin words or phrases in legal matters. American coins all have the motto, '*E pluribus unum*' on them. Like that."

"And lawyers use Latin terms like *habeas corpus* and *corpus delicti*," Sarah said.

Travis said, "Keep in mind, people: we're up against an extremist organization of Islamist terrorists. We're not against Islam. Turkey is almost one hundred percent Muslim, and only a small minority are Islamists who would bring Turkey back to the Middle Ages, while the majority, observant and nonobservant Muslims alike, want to advance into the twenty-first century. There is no real conflict between Islam and modernization. It's just this group of fanatical fundamentalists giving us, and the Turkish nation, a problem. Got that?"

"Hell, Trav," Stan said, "we know that."

Sarah said, "It's something like if the KKK or Neo-Nazis or some similar American racist organization tried to take over the United States government by force. We'd fight them too."

"I'd kick their asses for sure," Jack DuBois rumbled.

Travis nodded, "Just wanted to make sure you all understood the situation. Okay, listen up, boys and girls. We're getting pretty close, so let's wrap it up. Sam?"

"Right, Boss. The as-Saif al-Islam gets funding from several sources. Our old pal, Osama bin-Laden, the Saudi millionaire who's in hiding somewhere, probably Afghanistan, is one important source."

Jen said, "And he's willing and able to shovel money into this kind of organization. He's believed to have engineered the bombings of U.S. embassies in Kenya and Tanzania that killed two hundred twenty-four people. This would fit right in with his endorsement of a statement that

Muslims should kill Americans anywhere they are found. Get that? *Any Americans. Anywhere they're found.* He's being tried in absentia right now in federal court in Manhattan for those African bombings.

"Back in 1990 he formed a terrorist group called al-Qaeda and issued a public declaration of war against the U.S. military in August 1996. The prosecutors say bin-Laden and his followers killed members of the U.S. military in Somalia and Saudi Arabia. He's got his finger in anti-American pies all over the globe. About two years ago he issued a statement called, 'The Nuclear Bomb of Islam' that said, 'It is the duty of the Muslims to prepare as much force as possible to terrorize the enemies of God.' Judging by his anti-American statements and his killings of Americans, he means us."

"Too bad his trial is in absentia," Hunter said.

"Well, he was last seen in Afghanistan, but he's on the FBIs Ten Most Wanted List, and there's a five million dollar reward for his capture and conviction," Jen said.

Sam continued, "He's not the only source of funding for the as-Saif al-Islam. We think they get funds from Iran and Libya too. They sure as hell are being trained in those two countries. We don't know exactly who in the Iranian government apparatus knows about this, if anyone. We're pretty sure that if any of them do know, they sure as hell wouldn't want to admit it.

"The kicker, as you know, is that the Turkish government has, let's see, about fourteen hours left, *fourteen hours*, to allow these terrorists to install an Islamist government."

"Yeah," Jack said, "or they nuke Athens and Tel Aviv. Unbelievable!"

"What's the point?" Hunter asked.

"On one hand," Travis explained, "they'd be destroying a hell of a lot of Greeks, the traditional enemy of Turkey, even though they're both members of NATO, and a lot of Israelis, who, according to the Islamists, had no right to set up a Jewish state in what they consider Muslim territory. Besides, Greece and Israel are geographically the closest representatives of the Western World."

"Okay," Sarah said, "that's on one hand. What's on the other?"

"Such an attack coming from Turkey would invite nuclear retaliation and destroy Turkey. At the very least, it would result in Turkey's being ejected from NATO and from any dealings with the European Union. In self defense, the Turkish people would understandably retreat back into the fold of Islamist nations like Iran. In other words, as-Saif al-Islam's goal would be accomplished. NATO, Europe, and the West, would lose Turkey, which would end up as an extension of Iran threatening the heart of Europe with nuclear weapons, and, of course, gravely endangering U.S. interests in the region. So, if this danger isn't eliminated by tonight at sunset, Turkey turns, one way or another, from a valued ally into a grave danger for the U.S. and the West." He paused and added, "And, of course, if these terrorists take over the government of Turkey, that won't be the end of it."

Hunter commented, "Naturally. Then they'll be in a great position to threaten us directly."

"Today at sunset, you say?" Jack asked. "That's a real tight margin, even for us."

"Yes," Travis answered quietly. "And let's not forget the American prisoners. If it weren't for the presence of the hostages there, Admiral Zlotchew could've launched bunker buster missiles at the target and have done with it. They wouldn't have needed us to go in there. And although we've learned that the hostages were taken to that base, we don't know what the hell they want with them." He paused. "Except, of course, for the naval attaché. They hope to get information from him."

Travis shifted gears, "Okay, y'all. Here's the deal." The Green Beret major's calm Texas drawl flowed into everyone's ears. His deep voice exuded authority. At the same time, it soothed and inspired confidence. "When the time comes, we get shot out of here, we land and come together. The objective is twofold: we rescue the hostages, and we render the nukes harmless. In reverse order. Beyond those objectives, the more of these terrorists we take out, the better.

"Now, you know this is a delicate mission. Speed and secrecy are of the utmost importance. We slip in, do the job, slip back out."

"Surprise is our ace in the hole," Jack said.

"That's for sure," Travis said.

Chapter 8

"How come the Turkish army can't do the job? Or NATO?" Black Jack asked rhetorically. He sighed. "I know, you get an army moving against these guys, they have advance warnings, and they take off and set up again somewhere else. That's the military reason.

"Then there's the diplomatic reason. These turkeys are officially in Iran, not Turkey. A move by Turkey, either alone, or as part of NATO, would produce an international incident. By international law, it would mean a violation of the national sovereignty of Iran.

"But here's the real bitch: they'll nuke Athens and Tel Aviv ahead of schedule if they are attacked."

Travis looked around at each member of his team. "We've got to be fast and neat. No one can know there were Americans there. Not the Iranians, not even the Turks. Our own people can't know. No one can know. Absolutely no one. The Turks would be embarrassed that we had to do the job for them, and the Iranians would bitch to the U.N. We have to do our jobs and get the hell out of there before anyone knows what's happening."

"How many of these dickheads are there?" Stan asked.

Travis nodded at Jen, who said, "The estimate is that they have a total membership of two or three thousand. We think that there are about one hundred fighters, give or take about twenty, at the target location at the present moment."

Hunter snorted. "Fourteen to one. I don't like it."

Travis said, "All right. We've done this kind of thing

before, and we sure as hell can do it again. We must do it, and we will do it."

"We haven't dealt with nukes since the hijacked Russian sub incident," grumbled Stan.

Travis said, "Yeah, and there's something else. I've been reviewing in my mind our tactics. Remember how the eagerness to win, the spirit of competition, the very aggressiveness of those Army Ranger teams were exactly what helped us to win by using that ploy of luring part of their force outside the compound . . . ? That kind of tactical jujitsu we used on them?"

Travis looked around at their expectant faces. "Well, I'm thinking it wouldn't work with Rauf Pasha. He's not going to be eager to have his troops leave the compound, or even the fortress itself. He's not going to know who we are, how many we are, what weapons we're using, what our objectives are . . ."

Stan said, "So he'd be better off in a defensive position, especially at night."

Travis continued. "They're going to hole up. They're going to close up tight as an oyster that knows it has a pearl in it and sees a jeweler looking at it with a damn lupe in his eye. A word of caution: this area is Kurdish territory on both sides of the border. One of the Kurdish factions has been at war with the Turkish government for fifteen years, though things seem quiet for now. That has nothing to do with us. We don't get involved. We stay out of that business completely. Unless, of course, we're attacked."

He looked at Jennifer. "Jen, can we get a close shot of the target?"

"Right, Travis."

The holographic intra-optical images shifted to display a closer scale aerial photograph of the target compound. Travis briefed the Eagle Team on what little was known of the structure of the compound, where they believed the nuclear devices and the prisoners to be, and the basic working game plan they expected to follow.

Sam said, "Wait, we're getting a message from Joint Chiefs of Staff HQ. It's General Krauss."

Everyone listened to the message through the Battle Sensor Device in their helmets. General Krauss said, "Major Barrett, do you receive me?"

"Yes, General. Go ahead."

"Our intelligence sources report that some elements of the Iranian Army have been moving toward the border with Turkey."

Travis said, "Do we know why, General?"

"We have no data on the motivation. It could just be exercises. Or . . ."

"Yes, General . . . ?"

"Well, we know that both Libyan and Iranian funding is behind Rauf Pasha. We know he was trained in Iran, and that his spiritual counselor is an Iranian cleric. Obviously, there are forces within the Iranian government that know of Rauf Pasha's activities, and no doubt the location of his fortress. The possibility exists, then, they might expect a Turkish, or even NATO, crossing of their border to attack Rauf Pasha. Or at least to try to locate him."

Travis said, "It's possible. Are they operating close to our objective?"

"At present, a small force stationed near Mahabad is moving northwest with armored troop carriers and five tanks."

The troopers consulted their holographic maps. Stan said, "The fuckers are moving toward Dazgir. That's only sixteen klicks east of Kara Kale."

Krauss continued. "Another force, from a base near Tabriz, has been moving in a northwesterly direction. It has already passed Marand and has turned east toward Khvoy. In addition to armored troop carriers, they have ten tanks."

"More tanks?" Travis said. "We don't have any anti-tank ammo."

"Yes, I know. You do have the micromines. And, if it comes to that, you can always send for arsenal boxes to be dropped. I don't think it will, though. Those arsenal boxes are voice activated and directed, and can use a brilliant bomblet cluster that'll cover a football-field-sized area with detonations that'll send any personnel and armor in that area straight to hell. But that's a worst-case scenario. You have to make sure it doesn't come to that. We don't want to start a war there. That's all, Major."

"Travis, what do you actually plan to do, then, if Iranian tanks do intervene?" Sarah asked.

"Jack, what was that ancient Chinese military dictum about someone else's hand?"

Jack said, "Sun Tzu wrote, 'Borrow another's hand to kill.' "

"How, specifically, would you accomplish that in this particular case, Trav?" Sarah asked.

"Remember Terrek's Brotherhood, the operation in the Russian Far East and North Korea?"

"Of course. Sam was able to hook us up to the North Korean tank commander's communication link, making it seem like he was sending from inside the Brotherhood's HQ. Even was able to make it sound like Terrek's voice. He got the Korean armored column to attack Terrek."

"Right."

Jen said, "But we don't know Persian."

Travis said, "True. Let's cross that bridge when we get to it. Okay, let's look at our maps."

The troopers consulted the virtual maps. Travis said, "The troops out of Mahabad might be a problem. But the ones out of Tabriz are probably going to make for the border at the Turkish town of Kazim Pasha. Even if they intend to head south to Kara Kale, we should be in and out before they even come close." He paused. "All right . . . These troop movements might mean absolutely nothing. They might be just for practice, or to let Turkey know the hard-liners in Iran are alive and well, in spite of recent elections."

Jen said, "Yes, recent elections put a majority of reformers into the Iranian national legislature, the Majlis. But the Islamists and Revolutionary Guards don't care much about elections. They're closing pro-Western newspapers, threatening editors, kidnapping and even assassinating progressive elected officials . . ."

A seductive female voice came through the helmet audio device. "Ten minutes to exit point."

The team members, in their ceramic drop capsules, pulled their seat harnesses snug.

"Wish there were some other way to exit this craft," Sarah Greene said quietly into her helmet.

"I know, Sarah," Travis Barrett drawled, his voice oozing

confidence, "but there ain't. You've all done this before, and you've done well. You know the drill."

Stan Powczuk growled, "Yeah, yeah, yeah, rapid deceleration when we're crapped out the ass end of the X-37. Blah, blah, blah. Normal ejection at such high speed would shred us into ground beef if it weren't for these eggshells."

Hunter Blake chimed in, "Can it, Stan. Sarah just doesn't feel comfortable doing this."

"Can it yourself, Blake," Stan said. "You're just pissed that the X-37 is one plane you don't know how to fly."

"Hold on, my barnacle-encrusted comrade, we don't know that, now do we? It just happens to be the only plane I've never actually flown. That doesn't mean I don't know *how* to fly it. Or that I couldn't figure out how to do it in a few minutes. I do know that it reaches speeds up to Mach eight—or eight times faster than the speed of sound, for you waterlogged types—and altitudes of up to two hundred fifty thousand feet. In fact, as soon as the X-37 lays its eggs, so to speak, it accelerates to Mach eight, achieves low earth orbit, and returns to a designated runway where it . . ."

". . . lands horizontally," Jen Olsen finished, "as if it were an ordinary airplane. We've heard it before, hotshot."

"Ahh, I do love these drop capsule jumps. It's like being on a ride in the amusement park. But it would really be fun if you and I shared a capsule, Jen."

"Maybe for you, it would," Jen countered. Then she looked over at Sam Wong, who usually felt sick just before ejection time. "Hey Sam, how're you feeling?"

"Fine, Jen. Just fine."

Jack looked at Sam. "Hey, you *look* fine too. You're not kidding."

Sam beamed and nodded.

Stan said, "Well, that's a first. How did you manage that?"

Jack said, "My man has got himself a girlfriend."

"That right?" Hunter said.

Sam blushed and smiled more widely.

Sarah said, "And having a girlfriend produces this kind of effect?" She shook her head. "Amazing."

Sam said, "Well, I just think about her at times like this, and I imagine I'm with her, and . . ."

Hunter said, "Hell, I bet she's some kind of cyber-chick."

Stan said, "More likely he built himself a robot girlfriend."

Jack said, "Hey, I've met the girl. She's hot, lemme tell you. And she hangs all over him no matter where they are. My man's gettin' laid on a regular basis. Everybody knows that puts a guy's stomach at rest. It's scientific, ain't it, Doc?"

"Well . . ."

Jen said, "Sure, I can see that. It's the healing power of woman. Right, Sam?"

Sam said nothing. He just kept smiling.

"Look at the guy," Stan said. He *must* be gettin' it."

Hunter said, "Come on, Sam, tell us about her."

Sam said, "I'd rather remain inscrutable."

Hunter Blake looked over at Jen. "Hey, how about your getting into my drop capsule with me. It would be very Wagnerian."

"How do you mean?"

"You know, the Ring Cycle. Those four operas of Wagner's where these beautiful, blonde, buxom warrior women . . ."

"Yeah, I know, the Valkyries."

"Exactly. Well, you know, these beauties carry warriors slain in battle in their arms up to Valhalla, the Norse paradise."

"But we're going down, not up. And you're not slain, so it's a no go."

"Well, I'm glad to know those are the only reasons."

Jen said, "Anyway, Hunter, five minutes with me in the drop capsule would kill you. I'm too much woman for you."

Stan chimed in, "Listen, hotshot, you want to go to Valhalla, I know a bar at the waterfront in Naples where the broads will . . ."

Now the seductive female voice gently cooed, "Five minutes and counting," in the receiver embedded directly below each team member's right ear.

The usual nervous pre-jump banter suddenly stopped as each team member began to perform a final equipment check.

Travis thought about the amazing technology that allowed TALON Force to make pinpoint insertions into hostile territory. Just before reaching the target area, the X-37 would decelerate just enough to permit the drop capsules to be shot out of the rear of the aircraft. The capsules would fly through the atmosphere, computerized fins guiding them to their destination. The capsules were treated with a chemical that would be activated as soon as they were ejected, and the chemically treated shells would break up into fragments so small they couldn't be detected by radar, and would leave no tell-tale evidence on the ground. From that point, they would free-fall to the target area and open their parachutes at low altitude.

Suddenly they sensed the steady vibration of the Fastrac engines as they decelerated. Travis knew it was almost time. He swiftly cast an experienced eye over each member of Eagle Team. Hunter Blake, as usual, looked cool, almost bored. Stan Powczuk nodded confidently, and Jack DuBois looked alert, ready, and self-assured. Jen Olsen's eyes sparkled with excitement; Travis thought she looked like his kids opening a present on Christmas morning. Sarah Greene, a tight smile on her face, gave Travis a thumbs up. Travis looked at Sam Wong. He still looked good. *His girlfriend must be somethin' else; his biosensors aren't going to have to activate any Dramamine injection this time,* Travis thought.

The Eagle Team commander quickly accessed his people's vital signs. Everyone's pulse was elevated to some extent, except for Hunter, but Sarah's was considerably higher.

"One minute to jump," the female voice languidly announced over the communications network. Hunter thought the tone would have gone better with the statement: *let me slip into something more comfortable.*

Travis's soothing baritone calmly gave the command, "All right, prepare to drop."

Each team member locked down the protective drop capsule covering by pulling a handle. A flight technician came back from the cockpit to check the connections on each of the seven eggshells. When he came to the seventh, he told Travis, "A-okay and ready to go, sir." He added, "Go get 'em."

The Major said, "We will." Then he pulled down the cover and sealed his capsule.

Thank God for our scientists and technicians, Travis

thought. There's no way anyone could survive that kind of pressure without these special gravity-rack suspension belts to counteract it.

Travis took a deep breath, then contacted the pilot over his comm net. "Pilot. Eagle Team, ready for drop."

"Let's go for it!" Stan growled.

"Safe home, all of us," Sarah added.

Travis kept his eyes trained on the battle sensor screen. He saw a green light flash across the screen and immediately felt tremendous pressure as the X-37 launched his capsule into the thin atmosphere. He felt the lurching and bobbing of the capsule as it hurtled toward the ground, swiftly dropping from thinner to thicker air. He was aware of the capsule having been frigid initially and its present warming from the increasing friction of the upper atmosphere. The buffeting became more severe.

Travis said, "Listen up. Sam, how are you doin'?"

"Fine, Boss. I'd still rather be on the ground."

"You will be, pretty damn soon. Sarah, how about you?"

Her voice sounded a bit shaky. "Oh, I'm doing fine, Trav."

"Jen?"

"Having a ball, big daddy."

"Stan, you?"

"Loving it, Trav."

"Jack?"

"Ready to rock and roll."

"Hunter?"

"Everything's cool."

Travis drawled, "Okay, folks, see you on the ground."

His capsule had begun to feel uncomfortably warm and to shake violently. It began to break up at the designated altitude. The rush of cold, fresh air in his free fall was like a bugle playing reveille in his ear.

0025 hours
Prison cells, second level below ground, Kara Kale

It was a corridor with a concrete floor, concrete ceiling, and one long concrete wall. Across from this wall was a series of cells. At one end of the corridor was another concrete wall. At the other end was the metal door that separated this chamber from the guard's room and the staircase. The area smelled of sweat, urine, feces, and fear.

There were three cells. Each cell, measuring ten feet by ten feet, contained two double-decker beds bolted to the wall, floor, and ceiling. There was no other furniture. Each prisoner was given a bowl in which to deposit bodily waste, and a second one for receiving food and water. The waste products were collected once a day, at approximately 0800 hours. At that same hour, breakfast was handed out: a cup of water and a chunk of stale bread. The main meal, the only other meal, was served at 1600 hours: sardines and rice, or a watery soup that probably contained some element of chicken, with a half handful of rice in it. The guards, of course, were not always punctual in the serving of food or the removal of waste. They weren't overly concerned with washing their hands, either.

Clara Billings, Mary Cavanaugh, Carol Snyder, Ruth Johnson, Tracy Licata, Kathy Lopert, and her fifteen-year-old daughter, Kerrie, were crowded into one cell and had to share the four bunk beds as best they could. Kathy, of course was glad, if any one in this situation could be said to be glad, to be in the same cell with her daughter, with whom she shared a bed.

Ambassador Billings, Haig "Harry" Sebouhian, Dr. Perry Stein, Otto Dierkes, and Bob Cavanaugh were in the next cell. Mark McCain, Henry Snyder, the Reverend David Juhl, Dave Lopert, and his ten-year-old son Billy were in the third cell. Dave Lopert chose to sleep on the concrete floor so Billy could use the bed. Lieutenant Commander Schraer had a private cell near the interrogation room.

The prisoners' conversations were interrupted by the sound of boots clomping along the concrete floor and echoing along the corridor. The sound caused consternation. They had already been given "dinner," so why were their captors coming to visit?

Three men came over to the women's cell. The tall, thin man with the keys at his belt was Kemal, referred to as "Camel" by the prisoners, because of his stooping posture and smell as well as his name. He guarded the cells from

1600 hours to 2400 hours from his office behind the steel door. The prisoners didn't know the other two. One was short and had a closely clipped beard and shaved head. The other was of average height and clean-shaven.

The newcomers looked into the cell and spoke among themselves and to the guard. They peered into the cell, and when the bald man's gaze fell on the blonde teenager, he muttered something to the guard. Sensing that she was the object of discussion, Kerri Lopert shrank against her mother in fear, while Kathy protectively pressed her daughter to her.

The clean-shaven man's eyes lingered on the slender figure and long dark hair of a young woman several years older than Kerrie. Twenty-year-old Tracy Licata, despondently staring at the concrete floor, didn't even notice that she was the object of attention. The man nodded to the guard, who inserted the key in the lock, turned it, and opened the cell door.

0045 hours
The shower rooms of Kara Kale

The shower rooms of the fortress of Kara Kale looked like the shower rooms in an old-fashioned American high school gymnasium. There were ten showerheads along one wall and ten more on the opposite wall. There were drains in the concrete floor. The ceilings and walls were also of concrete. The long room just before the shower room contained lockers against the walls and two lines of benches. Today there were scrub brushes, sponges, towels, and two terry cloth robes on the benches.

When the guards brought Tracy Licata and Kerri Lopert to the dressing rooms and left them with Azzam Hamal, one of the guards told the girls in broken English, "No afraid. Azzam no like ladies."

This statement only succeeded in making the girls even more afraid, since they interpreted it to mean "he hates women."

Azzam Hamal, in his late forties, was short and squat. Thickly muscled, he gave the appearance of an ox. The beads of perspiration on his shaved head glistened under the sixty-watt bulb, and his leer exposed a golden tooth. His pockmarked face bore the imprint of an old scar that ran from the corner of his right eye to below his cheekbone.

He said something to the English-speaking guard in Turkish. The guard smiled and translated, "Off clothing. Off clothing." Then he stared expectantly at the girls.

The girls looked at each other in horror, but did nothing.

Azzam spoke again, sounding angry. The guard, in an angry tone, said, "Off clothing. Off clothing. Now! Yes, now!"

Tears began to run down Kerrie's cheeks. Seeing no action, Azzam said something else. The guard translated in a softer tone, "For bathing. Only for bathing." He pointed to the showerheads in the adjoining room.

Azzam said something. The guard translated, "No afraid. He not want you."

Tracy was accustomed to college life and had lived in a co-ed dorm, so the idea of undressing in front of men and taking a shower was not totally foreign to her. She didn't like the looks of Azzam, but since he wasn't interested in women, what the hell. She started to strip off her sticky clothes. Then she looked at the two guards whose eyes were burning a hole through her garments and stopped. She looked at Azzam and pointed at the guards. Then she waved her hands as though she were pushing them away.

Azzam understood. He said something to the guards. They grumbled, and he said something else. Within that Turkish sentence, the girls recognized the names Rauf Pasha and el-Badawi. Tracy supposed that orders had been given to treat them better than the others. The guards frowned, turned, and walked off, grumbling. Their booted footsteps echoed on the concrete. When Azzam heard the metal door slam shut, he gestured for the girls to continue the procedure.

Tracy unbuttoned her blouse but saw that Kerrie was frozen, tears spilling from her eyes.

Azzam yelled at Kerri. No reaction.

Tracy said, "C'mon, Kerrie. It's okay. We need a shower, and this mad Turk is gay or something. Get undressed before he really gets mad."

Kerrie just stood in place.

Tracy had already removed her bra. Azzam glanced at her firm breasts with distaste. Then he took three strides over to Kerrie. He was fed up with her behavior. He didn't want to keep Rauf Pasha waiting for his prize. He felt like smacking Kerri around to get her moving, but he knew his chief wanted her in good condition. He grabbed Kerrie by the shoulders and shook her. He yelled in her face. Nothing. Then he grabbed her by the hair with his left hand and began to pull her clothing off with the other hand.

These stupid girls were going to be cleaned up and delivered to his bosses one way or another. And soon. Even if he had to scrub this one down himself. Of course, that meant he would have to take off his own clothes and get in the shower with her, so his clothes wouldn't get wet. He shuddered at the thought, since he had already had his monthly shower, but duty came first, and he would do what he had to do.

Chapter 9

Hunter Blake was one of the seven human beings dropping precipitously through the atmosphere high over the wild mountains below. He was in the plastic capsule with no control over his movements, at the mercy of gravity and winds. When the eggshell broke apart, he knew he would be falling through the air, wind searing his face, making breathing difficult, until finally he could open his chute and have some direction over his movements. He was accustomed to the HALO drop, even enjoyed it at times, the way a kid enjoys the roller coaster. But he preferred having more control over his movements through the air. Like in the cockpit of a jet fighter.

In an airplane you feel free. You have the feeling you're free of everything. You're the master of your own fate. You're in control. If it's a fighter plane, there's danger, yes, but that's what tests your nerve, your ability to make split-second life-and-death decisions, your skills, your ability to remain cool in extreme situations. It's freedom and it's living to the fullest.

As the capsule began to break apart, Hunter thought of that time in 1991 over the skies of Kuwait and Iraq during the Gulf War. He was only a kid, actually, just graduated from the Air Force Academy in Colorado Springs. He was flying an F-117 Nighthawk stealth fighter/bomber. He didn't find that exciting enough. It was too easy. You flew in at night undetected, evading stray antiaircraft fire, dropped your load, and flew back to base. One day he volunteered to fly a swing-wing F-15 jet fighter in a daytime raid over

Baghdad. That way, the enemy could see you, and it was all up to you what the result would be. It was one on one.

He remembered the thrill of his first combat mission in the F-15, the anticipation. Practice was one thing, but combat was something else. He climbed the ladder into the cockpit of the jet and dropped into the front seat. He scanned the hundreds of buttons, levers, radios, and mini-computers in the cockpit with satisfaction. A flight technician helped him strap in. Each leg was attached to three buckles, then a belt was applied to his waist, and another one across his stomach and then two shoulder harnesses.

He put on his helmet with the attached oxygen mask. He pulled the plastic bubble canopy down and then went through the checklist: AIC, VTR, radio, radar, and the rest of it. This was routine for him, but it was somehow different now. He felt a surge of adrenalin as the engines responded and roared to life. Hunter then performed his preliminary checks, after which he headed down the tarmac toward the runway. The hissing of the radio and the high-pitched whine of the turbojets were somehow more stimulating than during practice.

He pulled up to the "parking lot" and turned the handle clockwise that armed the ejection seat. He taxied out and then raced down the runway with the afterburners blasting and smoothly zoomed off into the clear blue sky of Saudia Arabia. When the afterburners cut off, he had the peculiar false sensation that he was slowing down. Then he pulled left, feeling the first Gs of this flight, and headed for Baghdad.

Later, after having dropped his bombs over Baghdad, encountering no enemy fighters, but merely evading antiaircraft fire, Hunter was flying back to the Saudi base at an altitude of 18,000 feet. He was wired. And yet, strangely tranquil now that he was homeward bound. He looked up through the plastic bubble of his canopy and saw a glorious blue sky. His wingman, Lieutenant Robert Karski, flew Turkey Hawk 92, the F-15 on his left and 500 feet higher. They had done their job and were cruising home at 310 knots. Hunter banked Turkey Hawk 98 slightly to look at the expanse of sand and the shimmering blue of the Persian Gulf in the distance. A voice crackled on the intercom. From the backseat, Chuck Whalen, his radar officer said,

"Ninety-eight has contact. One-eighty at sixty." This gave Hunter the contact's bearing in degrees and its range in miles.

Whalen immediately reported, "Contact's climbing. Now he's at twenty thousand feet. Sharply accelerating. Coming straight this way at five hundred fifty knots."

"Karski," Hunter told his wingman, "I'm climbing to twenty thousand feet. Let's move into a loose combat spread."

"Roger." Karski climbed to twenty-eight thousand feet and to a point two miles off Hunter's left wing.

From the backseat, Whalen told Hunter to come left twenty degrees. This was the start of a long slow circle that would position him behind the Iraqi plane. Then the bogey changed course and headed directly for Turkey Hawk 98. Whalen told Hunter to come forty degrees right. The Iraqi jet once more changed course. It was still closing on Turkey Hawk 98. Hunter figured the radar apparatus at An-Nasiriya was tracking him, and forwarding the information to the Iraqi pilot.

Hunter and Karski pushed their throttles forward to 600 knots. Hunter was going to hold the bogey's attention by heading directly at it, while Karski would be the "shooter," and circle until reaching a position from which he would have a clear path to aim his heat-seeking Sidewinder missiles at the enemy's exhaust.

Whalen saw that what he had thought on first contact was one single blip on the radar scope now split into two blips. They were two jets flying so closely in a "welded wing" formation that they had first appeared to be just one plane. Hunter was now able to identify the enemy aircraft as French-built Mirages. The F-15s accelerated to 700 knots. The combined speed of the F-15s and Mirages closing on each other was now 1,250 knots, meaning that the closure rate was fourteen miles per minute. Hunter's reaction time to events had to be excellent; it would soon be tested. This was the moment he had been trained for and had been waiting for.

Karski banked Turkey Hawk 92 hard right, starting to make a tight turn that would position him behind the Mirages. His G-suit inflated to squeeze his legs and stomach as though he were being crushed by a giant fist. The pres-

sure exerted by the G-suit forced the blood back up to his
brain and vital organs to prevent him from blacking out
as his body was gripped by a force seven times the pull
of gravity.

Karski now saw the Iraqi Mirages. The lead enemy plane
was 1,000 feet in front of Hunter's Turkey Hawk 98, and
500 feet below him. Suddenly, Karski saw the entire right
side of the Iraqi leader turn bright, as though some kind
of fire or explosion had occurred. When he saw the missile
flying from its rail under the Mirage's wing, he realized
what was happening.

"Blake, he just shot at you!"

Hunter had seen it and climbed 500 feet. He saw the
Iraqi missile come off the Mirage's wing and then slide
under him. The missile shot crazily across the sky below
him, leaving a white trail, its sensors trying to locate a heat
source that did not exist. Finally the rocket motor exhausted its fuel and flamed out.

Hunter broke right, his Turkey Hawk 98 practically on
top of the Mirage. He and Karski were in a right-hand turn
when Hunter called Karski. He said, "I'm going for the guy
who fired at us. You take the wingman."

"Roger."

The lead Mirage zoomed into a right-hand turn as it
climbed. His wingman made a level turn to the left, turning
tail to fly toward his home base. But the lead Mirage kept
coming. Hunter's Turkey Hawk 98 rolled in toward the
wingman's tailpipe. Hunter shot his missile from a distance
of one mile. He saw the Sidewinder hit the Mirage's tail.
Having lost control of the plane, the Iraqi pilot ejected
within a few seconds of being hit. When Hunter last saw
him, he was swaying from his parachute.

Karski in Turkey Hawk 92 was on the tail of the retreating wingman. In what appeared to be a sudden reversal
of attitude, the Mirage accelerated and soared to a height
3,000 feet above Karski's F-15, and then steeply dived and
fired both missiles. One sailed past Karski, finally flamed
out, and thudded into the desert below. The other one
smashed directly into Karski's cockpit. The plane exploded,
split in two, and fell through the air.

There was no time to think or feel emotion. Hunter accelerated his F-15 and pushed down on the stick. He dived

until he was 2,000 feet under the leader, then pulled back
sharply on the stick to come up under him, accelerating.
As he climbed at seven times the force of gravity, the
G-suit exerted tremendous pressure on his legs and stomach. He saw the Mirage above him and fired a Sidewinder.
The Mirage banked and steeply climbed, but his maneuver
exposed its exhaust to the Sidewinder. Hunter saw the missile track upward at twice the speed of sound and shoot
right into the Mirage's tailpipe. Hunter saw the enemy jet
explode in a ball of fire. Then he saw the debris falling
toward him and realized that he was right in the path of
the falling debris.

"Christ, did I just kill myself?" he asked himself, thinking
of what would happen if that material struck his engine.

He pushed down on the stick until his F-15 was hori-
zontal and shot straight forward at seven Gs and out of the
path of the falling pieces of Mirage. Then he pulled the
stick to him and climbed. Once clear, Hunter knocked the
stick all the way to the left and flipped upside down to see
what had happened to the Mirage. He saw the Mirage
below him tumbling end over end. Both the engine and the
tail were completely missing. Hunter saw the canopy being
jettisoned, then the ejection seat. The pilot started to fall,
and the chute opened. The whole thing took no more than
a minute.

Hunter righted the plane and just to let off steam, did
some negative Gs by flipping around and pushing the stick
all the way down. He felt his F-15 drop as though he were
on a roller coaster. His harness went loose, and he felt
himself defying gravity, floating in the cockpit. His helmet
hit the canopy. When he came down to 18,000 feet, he
leveled off.

Hunter set his jet on autopilot to allow it to fly itself
while he calmed down. This was his first for-real dogfight,
and the first time he had seen two buddies wiped from the
face of the earth; Bob Karski and his radar officer, Mike
Levy, were gone. He clearly remembered their faces, the
sound of their voices, Karski's boisterous laughter at Levy's
wise-ass sense of humor. They had been there, real as could
be, and in one second disappeared into nothing.

As he coasted along, the normally supercool Hunter
Blake suddenly realized he was shaking. An extremely

skilled pilot, even at that tender age, he missed the first two approaches before he actually managed to land on the runway. His reactions to the next few combat engagements weren't very different from those of his first. Talking with other fighter pilots over a few beers, he would find that this was absolutely normal. The tremendous amount of adrenalin injected into a jet fighter pilot's system in combat doesn't just dissipate immediately after the engagement. After many more missions, his reactions became somewhat less severe.

But Hunter Blake loved every minute of it, the whole thing. The speed, the chance to test what he thought of as his nerves of steel. He loved pitting his nerve and skills against those of the enemy in a life-and-death contest. Most of all, he enjoyed the sense of being completely free and in control of his own fate.

This was not the feeling he had at the present moment, falling through the atmosphere, his chute not yet opened, the mountains of Turkey, Iran, and Iraq surging up to meet him with surprising speed. Still, it was a thrill ride, no doubt about it. And soon he would open the chute and be able to direct it.

0048 hours
A mountain valley in southeastern Turkey,
near the Iranian and Iraqi borders

It was a fine evening. The moon and stars shone bright in the clear sky. The elevation produced a briskness in the air, so that it felt more like late October than April. The seven members of TALON Force Eagle Team stood in a high meadow surrounded by mountains. They knew that in the distance to the northeast loomed the snow-capped summit of Mt. Geliashin, 13,675 feet high, even though they couldn't see it. No traces of human habitation could be seen with their thermal viewers. The air was still. There was no need to use the communications suite of the Battle Sensor Helmets they wore; they could speak directly to one other.

Major Travis Barrett checked on the status of each member of the team gathered around him before proceeding to business.

Sam Wong would be embarrassed to bring it up again, since he had raved about it so many times in the past, but he couldn't help thinking of that classic Akira Kurosawa film *The Seven Samurai*. Seven well-trained and disciplined samurai warriors defended villagers from bandits in sixteenth-century Japan. They fought as a team, a well-oiled machine, just like the seven troopers of TALON Force Eagle Team. Both groups of seven were effective, not solely because of bravery, skill, devotion to duty, cutting-edge equipment, constant training, and discipline, but also because of teamwork. There were no prima donnas going out on their own. Sam thought of this now because Major Barrett always checked on the status of each member of his group, before and after an action. This is exactly what Kanbei, leader of the seven samurai, did. Sam loved that movie, and its star, that tough old bird, at least on screen, Toshiro Mifune. He knew that his buddy Jack DuBois did too; they'd had quite a few discussions about it.

"Okay, troopers, status report."

This procedure, after so many missions completely routine for the team, was a backup to any possible loss of their networked stream of information. Each trooper answered in turn.

Jack started, "DuBois, all systems internal green. One XM-29 rifle. Ten 20mm rounds of airburst ammo, two hundred 5.56mm rounds. One silenced OHWS. 45 caliber pistol, forty-nine rounds. Three command-detonated micromines. Three Bugs. One knife. One NLG. One water pouch with one emergency field ration."

The XM-29 combat rifle combined a 20mm grenade launcher with a 5.56mm rifle, which was aimed by a smart fire control system. This system included an accurate laser range finder, ballistic computer, direct view optics, video camera, electronic compass, thermal mode, and automatic target tracker. The Offensive Handgun Weapon System consisted of a .45 caliber semiautomatic pistol, a laser aiming module, and a silencer. It held a seven-round clip and was effective up to fifty meters.

The NLG was the Nonlethal Generator, used to incapacitate temporarily, rather than to kill.

"Blake. All systems internal green. One XM-29. Six 20mm rounds, one hundred and twelve 5.56mm rounds. One silenced OHWS .45 caliber pistol, twenty-eight rounds. One command-detonated micromine. One Dragonfly UAV. One knife. One water pouch with one emergency field ration."

"Powczuk. Green. One XM-29. Five 20mm rounds, two hundred and twelve 5.56mm rounds. One OHWS .45 caliber pistol, twenty-eight rounds. Four command-detonated micromines. One Dragonfly UAV, and one Bug. Three knives. Two water pouches with one emergency field ration."

Travis ordered, "Turn on the voice transmitters." Then he touched Powczuk and DuBois on the shoulder in succession. "Stan, Jack, post security."

Stan and Jack nodded, moved fifty meters to the north and south respectively, charged their XM-29 rifles, and lay prone to cover the approaches to the meadow.

Travis said, "Greene?"

"Systems green." Sarah smiled and shrugged. "One XM-29, one 20mm round, twelve 5.56 rounds. One 9mm Beretta pistol, thirty rounds. One Nonlethal Generator. One surgical kit. Two water pouches with one emergency field ration."

"Wong. Green. One XM-29, one 20mm round, twelve 5.56 rounds. One silenced 9mm Beretta, forty-five rounds. One special communications pack. One Hummingbird UAV. One knife. One water pouch, and one emergency field ration."

"Olsen. Green. One XM-29, six 20mm rounds, thirty 5.56 rounds, one 9mm Beretta, sixty rounds. Four command-detonated micromines. One Hummingbird UAV. One knife. Two water pouches with one emergency field ration."

Then Travis answered for himself. "Barrett. Internal systems green. One XM-29. Ten 20mm rounds, one hundred 5.56mm rounds. One command-detonated micromine. One Dragonfly UAV. One knife. One water pouch with one emergency field ration.

"Okay, team, listen up," Travis commanded. "We're one point six kilometers into Iran. Turkey's back there." He pointed west. "Iraq is about eight klicks to the south."

"Shit," Stan said, "Fucking Iran and Iraq."

"Scylla and Charibdis," Jack commented.

"What?" Stan said.

Sarah smiled, "He means we're between a rock and a hard place."

"More like *Iraq* and a hard place," Sam said. Everyone groaned.

"All right," Travis said, "let's cut the crap. We're just a little over three klicks from our target. When we get to the crest of that ridge," he pointed northeast, "we'll be able to see the target with the naked eye."

Chapter 10

Eagle Team climbed and descended hills in mountainous terrain for forty minutes. They came to the lip of a ridge and halted. In that brief time the weather had changed. The night had become darker and colder.

"Great," Sam Wong complained, "fog and rain."

"Hey, little man," Hunter said, "don't complain. We'll be glad if it keeps up. Especially if the fog thickens. We can see through all that with our BSDs up to three thousand meters."

"Our stealth capability will be even more effective," Sarah said. "If that's possible, considering it's nighttime."

Sam smiled, "I know, I know. I just get my kicks complaining."

Jen said, "If that's how you get your kicks, Sammy, then you've really got to get out more."

Jack smiled and said, "It ain't *out* he's needin', Jenny girl. It's *in*. Then out. Then in. Then out. Then . . ."

Sam turned and gave Jack the finger. Jack laughed uproariously.

Travis said, "Let's stick to business, troopers."

Travis's second in command, Lieutenant Commander Stan Powczuk, said, "What's the plan, Travis?"

"Okay," Travis said, "let's take a good look at the layout."

They brought their Battle Sensor Devices, with night vision capability, down over their left eye and studied the fortress of Kara Kale. Travis gave an oral rundown on what they were seeing, to make sure everyone was observing the same items.

"The outer perimeter fence is circular razor wire . . ."

"Always a pleasure," Stan commented wryly.

Travis continued, "The perimeter itself is circular. Then there's an inner perimeter fence, rectangular. Seems to be made of the same material as the outer fence. The fortress itself seems to be made out of stone. Or maybe concrete."

Travis studied the view carefully. "There is a guard shack at the gate. There are two men in it. Four guard towers around the outer perimeter each equipped with a searchlight and a machine gun. Three men in each tower, the gunner, the ammo belt handler, and the searchlight operator. He's equipped with, hmm, perhaps a sniper rifle.

"Look at the building itself. One story high, probably has a floor or two below as a bunker. A tower on the southeast corner." He stared hard. "See those huge doors taking up about half the eastern end of the roof?"

Stan said, "Must be over the missiles!"

"Looks like it," Travis said. He continued. "There are two, no, three helicopters parked just north of the building. Looks like they're Aerospatiale Dauphins."

Hunter commented, "Yeah. The French'll sell to anyone."

"Travis, what if Schraer's been forced to give us away?" Sarah asked.

"In that case, our job will be a little harder. But I don't believe that would happen. After all, they don't know about our existence, so their questions won't elicit that kind of information."

Stan said, "He wouldn't talk even if they asked the right questions."

Sam said, "They don't exactly respect the Geneva Convention, you know."

Sarah said, "Anyone will talk, finally, under torture. No matter how brave the man is, he's only flesh and blood."

The others looked at the ground in silence. Everyone knew this was true.

"Look," Travis said, "it's much easier to make a person answer very specific questions, like 'What direction will they be coming from,' or 'When are they to begin the attack.' But they don't have any specific questions to ask."

Sam said, "That's true. That's the good news. But what if they just torture him, asking for any information at all that bears on this situation? Info that could help them. If he's in enough pain, the poor bastard has to give them something. Something reasonable. Something that sounds convincing. He might blurt out something too close to the truth. He might have already done so."

"Yeah," Travis conceded, "he might have."

"Then they would just be waiting for us. And whatever we're looking at would just be a set-up."

"Okay, now look," Travis said. "All this is a possibility. But it's only that: a possibility. And even if it turns out to be fact, we're soldiers, damn it! Even if we've lost the advantage of surprise, which we don't know to be true, we still have the tremendous advantage of our training and cutting-edge weaponry."

"Not to mention invisibility," Jen said. "And that's one hell of an advantage. Come on guys, no matter what, we're going to clean those bastards' clocks and get the job done."

"Yeah, fuckin' A," Jack said.

Travis knew the job would be a hell of a lot more dangerous if the element of surprise had been snatched from them, but was glad to hear all of them make noises that showed their confidence and determination.

Sarah said, "We've got to get all of those hostages out of there."

"We will, Sarah," Travis said, "but remember, the most important item on our list is not to rescue the hostages. It's to prevent nuclear war and save the lives of millions of people, because once it starts, no one knows how it will end."

Sarah said, "You mean we're just going to ignore whatever they're going to do to those people and move on to the nuclear weapons?"

Travis slowly said, "Now, Sarah. Think about it. What do you think? Eighteen people, or the possibility of millions of men, women, and children, ultimately including American men, women, and children, being vaporized . . ." He looked at her. "And those who don't die immediately, suffering a horrible lingering death. And then, the planet itself . . . Nuclear contamination . . . Well, Sarah, you of all people know better than any of us."

Sarah sighed and nodded. "I know, Travis, you're right."

0138 hours
Private quarters of Rauf Pasha, Kara Kale

Kerrie Lopert, clad only in the terry cloth bathrobe, was thrust into Rauf Pasha's quarters by the two guards. They closed the door behind her and waited outside. She pressed her back against the closed door and stared at Rauf Pasha, who was clad in a green silk dressing gown. He smiled as he gazed at her pretty face, her blonde hair still damp from the shower, and her frightened childlike face. He smelled the aroma of soap emanating from her scrubbed body.

This was much more pleasant than working with the American naval attaché. Hamal, of course, would not agree. He laughed. *Ah, well, one cannot argue with tastes.* After he enjoyed himself with this fine piece of young American womanhood, Rauf Pasha would be better prepared to deal with Schraer. And deal with him he would. He would squeeze every drop of information out of him that he had. Schraer would beg to be allowed to tell all. And then he would plead for them to kill him. Rauf Pasha now gave his full attention to Kerrie.

"Come in, my dear," he cajoled. "Do not be afraid." The way in which he said this last sentence reminded her of the way in which Count Dracula, in the old Universal movie, pronounced the identical sentence. She shuddered.

0139 hours
Quarters of Mahmoud el-Badawi, Kara Kale

Her long dark hair spilling over her bathrobe, Tracy Licata stood by the door of Mahmoud el-Badawi's private quarters, her arms folded, looking down at the rugs on the floor.

El-Badawi wore a khaki T-shirt and shorts. He said, "Ah, an American beauty. Enter."

Tracy looked up at him and said, "You don't like Americans, do you?"

El-Badawi spoke with the gentleness of one who is secure in his power, like the cat with the mouse. "No, my dear, in fact I . . . what is the word? . . . ah, yes, I *despise* them with all my heart." He smiled.

"Then why am I here? And what's all that "dear" stuff?"

El-Badawi looked puzzled. He thought for a moment and then understood. Ah, the mysterious ways the American mind works. "You mean, if I hate Americans, why am I going to make love to you?"

Tracy raised her eyebrows.

"What a peculiar question," el-Badawi said. "What connection is there between the two concepts? You are only a woman. When I say I hate Americans, I refer to the men. Women are of no consequence, not important enough to be hated. Women are not fully people. They are possessions of their men, like horses, cattle, houses, furniture. Can I hate a cow, a chair . . . ? So I do not hate you. No, I want to possess you, just like I desire any of my enemy's possessions. You are my booty. I take you from my American enemies, the way I would take any of their possessions to use for my own pleasure. This way, I enjoy . . . what is the word, yes, *victory*, over my enemies."

"You filthy pig!" she couldn't help screaming.

El-Badawi reddened and smacked her across the face, sending her sprawling onto the bed. He said, "I don't hate you, my little colt, but I will be severe if I have to, just as I would to break a wild horse."

0145 hours
At the entrance to Kara Kale

Eagle Team had advanced to the outer gate, the Low Observable Camouflage Suite of their Battle Ensemble in operation. Stan and Travis had the sheaths of their silenced Colt .45 caliber pistols plugged into the LOCSs as well, so that the weapons were invisible. The rain and darkness ensured their invisibility, while the rain and occasional thunder cloaked any sound their footsteps might have made. It even washed away their footprints. They couldn't help wonder if Lieutenant Commander Schraer had given the plan away. If so, they were walking into a trap. They pushed that thought from their minds and forged on with their operation.

When they reached the guard shack, Stan, as prearranged, aimed his silenced Colt .45 at the head of one of the guards, while Travis aimed his at the other's head. Travis whispered "Stan, now," into his transmitter. It came through Stan's receiver as clearly as if Travis had been talking in a normal voice. Stan and Travis each fired once. The two guards were hurled against the opposite side of the shack and slumped to the floor, blood and brain matter spattering the walls and chairs. The skull of one of the guards crashed through the glass window. Neither the *pffft* of the silenced weapons nor the crash and tinkle of broken glass could be heard above the storm.

Sarah entered the shack. She glanced at the bodies only for a moment and then found the correct button. She pushed it, and the gate swung open.

The team advanced up the road on the double toward the two guards standing at the gate of the inner perimeter fence. When they were within four yards of the guards, Sarah's foot splashed water as she stepped into a puddle. Jack's feet did the same.

The guards stared at the puddles in disbelief. They raised their AK-74s. Travis whispered into his transmitter, "Scatter fast." After a moment he said, "Jack, shoot your man."

Jack didn't have to ask which one. He shot the man nearest him. The .45 caliber bullet tore through one guard's heart, knocking him back against the razor wire fence, making a small hole as it entered his chest and a larger one as it exited his back. The other guard gaped in amazement and horror. He raised his Kalashnikov, but Travis shot him, making his skull explode.

0146 hours
Rauf Pasha's private quarters, Kara Kale

Rauf Pasha had removed Kerrie Lopert's bathrobe. She stood there, looking down at the Persian rug under her feet, tears running down her face, practically hyperventilating. Rauf Pasha slowly walked around her, leisurely admiring her: her blonde hair and blue eyes, her round, firm breasts and pink nipples. As he circled behind her he admired her sturdy thighs and fondled the silken skin of her perfectly round buttocks. He pressed his body against her back, his manhood throbbing.

Rauf Pasha began to breath more rapidly. She shuddered and sobbed more loudly. He forced himself to pull away and continue his inspection. Having made a full circle, he now faced her. He pulled off his silk dressing gown and tossed it on the floor. He took a step toward Kerrie and pressed against her, his arms around her, his hands stroking her buttocks.

"Do not be afraid, little dove, I will be good to you."

0146 hours
Private quarters of Mahmoud el-Badawi, Kara Kale

Mahmoud el-Badawi thrust his fingers up through Tracy's dark hair and made a fist. Having her firmly in hand, he used his left hand to roughly pull off her bathrobe. Then he threw her back down on the bed.

"Enough of this, American bitch," el-Badawi growled. "Prepare to be broken like a young camel." He looked down at her and said, "Oh, and I want you to know that when I've had my fill of you, you'll go to Rauf Pasha." He chuckled. "Yes, he'll have my leavings."

Tracy, now completely unclothed, was in a fetal position, her hands covering her face.

El-Badawi was enjoying the conversation. It was his foreplay. He added, "And when he tires of you, guess what? Go ahead. Guess."

Seeing she was not going to play the game, he supplied the answer. "You might become the baggage of all our brave warriors. *All* of them." Still seeing no reaction, he went on, "Or, if you find favor in my eyes, you could become my exclusive property. It all depends on your behavior. So, my darling Tracy," he pronounced the word "darling" with mock tenderness, "let's not waste any more time."

0148 hours
Communications Center, Kara Kale

The man at the control panels heard the buzzing and noticed the red light that indicated the outer perimeter gate had been opened. He tried to communicate with the guard shack. No answer. He kept trying. Two minutes later another buzzer sounded, and another red light went on signaling that the gate to the inner perimeter had been opened. *What the hell?* He tried to communicate with the inner perimeter guards. No response. Getting close to two o'clock in the morning, his boss in bed with his new "girlfriend," and he had to disturb him. He hesitated, but then made up his mind. He pressed the general alarm button and a loud klaxon began honking throughout the fortress.

0150 hours
Rauf Pasha's quarters,
First level below ground, Kara Kale

Rauf Pasha had his arms around Kerri Lopert when he heard the sound. The raucous honk of the klaxon shook him out of his amorous mood. He turned and raced back to the phone to contact the Communications Center.

"What the hell is going on?"

"We are being invaded, Rauf Pasha."

"Invaded . . . ? By whom?"

The voice on the other end did not respond immediately. "We do not know, *efendi*."

"What do you mean, you don't know?!"

"All we know so far is that both the outer and inner perimeters have been breached. We cannot contact the guards at either gate. But no one has seen anyone yet."

Rauf Pasha cursed effusively. He looked long and hard at Kerrie, who was still standing there, a nude statue, frozen with fear.

"You idiots! I'll be right there."

Rauf Pasha threw on his black camouflage uniform, seized his AK-74 and his Colt .45, locked Kerrie in his quarters, and rushed to the Communications Center.

0150 hours
Mahmoud el-Badawi's private quarters
First level below ground, Kara Kale

Tracy Licata was in the fetal position on the bed, unclothed, her hands covering her face. Mahmoud el-Badawi
glared at her, then stripped off his T-shirt, when the klaxon
blasted. *"Airi b'teezak, ibn sharmuta!"* he cursed. *What the
hell is going on?!* He pulled his T-shirt back on, looked at
Tracy lying naked on the bed, and knocked a lamp off the
night table with a backward swipe of his hand. Next he
picked up a chair and flung it across the room, smashing it
to bits. Then he hurriedly donned his black uniform,
grabbed his weapons, and made for the door.

"I'll be back!" he yelled at Tracy as he locked the door.

0150 hours
Second level below ground,
the entrance to the prison cells, Kara Kale

The short, squat man with the gold tooth had told the
guard to open the door to the corridor off which the prisoners' cells were located. Behind him, the first ten men chosen
were lined up, eagerly awaiting entrance. They were sleepy
and still chilled from the rain, but they were anxious to get
at the women.

The sleepy guard had some trouble with the key, but
finally opened the door. The klaxon jolted the men. They
froze in their tracks.

Azzam Hamal held the first man back who was about to
enter the corridor. He restrained him with a hand on his
chest. "Damn it! Everyone to his post! Immediately!"

The men were motionless, glaring at him. Azzam Hamal
smacked the first man across the face.

"You are mujahideen," Hamal roared. "God is watching
you. Remember what we're here for. Go! Now!"

They snapped out of their mood of rage and frustration,
turned and moved to their posts on the double.

0150 hours
Kara Kale Compound

The men on the guard towers were shaken out of their
lethargy by the blast of the klaxons. They switched on the
searchlights and played them around the entire compound.
They prepared the 12.7mm heavy machine guns for firing
and followed the searchlights with their eyes, seeking out
intruders, nervously fingering the triggers.

The machine gunner on the southwest tower shouted to
the man on the searchlight, "Leave it there, right there!"

He fired a round.

"What did you shoot at?"

The gunner wrinkled his brow. "I . . . I don't know. I
thought I saw something funny."

"Funny?" the ammo handler asked. "How do you
mean?"

"I don't know exactly. Someone, something, seemed to
move."

The other two men in the tower eyed him suspiciously,
but the searchlight operator kept playing his light over the
ground. Then they heard a burst of machine-gun fire from
the northwest guard tower. This sound was immediately
followed by a scream of pain.

Chapter 11

The searchlights were playing all over the compound, searching for the intruders. Machine guns in the guard towers were sporadically firing short bursts. Men in camouflage fatigues ran back and forth in confusion, pointing their AK-74 assault rifles from side to side, seeking a target. The 12.7mm machine-gun bullets stitched lines of dust sometimes too close for comfort as the Eagle Team troopers raced toward the steel doors, stealth-sheathed XM-29 combat rifles in their gloved hands.

A scream of agony pierced the night air as a machine gun fired off a blast. Travis heard the rapid thumping of the gun followed by the scream and turned his head in the direction of the sounds. He saw green tracers from the northwest guard tower rip up one of the terrorists and dash him facedown to the dusty ground. In the confusion, he had been shot by his own men. Friendly fire.

Travis said into his transmitter, "We've got to neutralize those machine guns. They could hit us by accident. And when the hostages come out . . . Hunter, take the southwest. Sam, the northwest. Jack, take the northeast. Jen, the southeast."

The XM-29 combat rifle combines a 5.56mm rifle, aimed by a smart fire control system, with a 20mm grenade launcher. The ammo casings for the 5.56mm rounds and the grenades disintegrate after firing. In this way, no brass is ejected from the weapon, yet another stealth feature.

The four assigned to the towers quickly judged the distance to their respective targets and set the miniature electronic fuse to air burst at the correct target range. When each one squeezed the trigger, there was a plop, followed by a loud bang and a flash of light close to the target as the high explosive round went off. The visual impression given by the four launches was almost like a show of fireworks. The physical effect was not the same. Men and machine guns were ripped apart and blown from the wrecked towers.

Travis said, "Sam, get me an FM radio link to Rauf Pasha's communications. If we get lucky, he'll use English for some messages. He has a mixed-nationality crew and probably Russian technicians. I want to know what he's doing."

"Right on it, Boss."

Stan said, "Trav, think they'll open the doors to let their troops out to fight?"

"No. I'm betting they'll stay holed up inside, the better to keep us out. They don't know how many we are. The SOB is probably going to start the process of arming the two missiles right now to blast them on their way to Armageddon."

Stan said, "Demolition?"

"You got it. But first . . ."

Four terrorists carried two RPK 7.62mm machine guns and placed them on either side of the doors. They were wild-eyed, frantically searching for the unseen enemy. They were accompanied by two guards carrying AK-74 assault rifles.

Travis said, "Jack, Sam, Jen, move around the corner of the building to the north side; keep out of the way of the machine guns. Hunter and Sarah, same thing to the south. Stan, you work your way around the guard on our left. I'll do the same with the one on our right. You first."

Stan ran to a point three yards directly to the right of the guards. He steadied himself on the corner of the building and aimed the XM-29 rifle. He didn't need to use the laser range finder, ballistic computer, or video camera. He used the direct view optics and fired. The 5.56mm bullet blasted through his man's temples. The man slumped over onto the nearest machine gunner crouched below him. Stan, without hesitation, then shot down at the startled machine gunner, who fell to his left side.

Travis had been peering from around the corner of the south side of the building. The moment Stan's machine gunner fell over, Travis stepped around the corner to the front of the building. The guard near him turned to his right to witness his fellows being shot by something he couldn't see and pointed his assault rifle in Hunter's general direction. Travis squeezed off a round, sending the man falling on top of his machine gunner, who, totally confused and terrified, stood up and started to run. Not soon enough. Travis put a bullet between the man's shoulder blades, as Hunter put one through his head. The man fell forward onto his face.

Travis spoke into his transmitter, "We're going to pull these RPKs back with us, out of range of the blast, and turn them around to face the doors. Hunter and Jen, the one on the left. Jack and Sam, the other one. Stan, go for it!" Then he said, "Sam, you got that FM link yet?"

"Not yet, Boss. Any second now."

They moved the RPK 7.62s to positions twenty yards in front of the doors. Stan was about to place the Semtex charge at a critical point on the doors when a man in a camouflage outfit passed him, then stopped suddenly because he caught a glimpse of the very visible plastique floating to the door as a searchlight beam passed by. The man pointed his Kalashnikov assault rifle at the unknown floating object.

Shit! Here I am with a load of plastic explosives in my left hand, my rifle on my shoulder, and now this clown . . . Stan shot his free right hand into the terrorist's abdomen, being very careful not to jar the Semtex in his left hand. The man doubled over, gasping for breath. Stan then chopped at the back of his neck, and the man fell to the ground. Then he kicked the man in the head. When he saw that the man lay still, Stan extracted his forty-five, placed it against the base of the terrorist's skull, and fired, still holding the Semtex steady in his left hand.

Then he kneaded the wad of Semtex between his hands as though it were dough until it formed a four-foot-long bread stick. He then extracted a roll of duct tape from one of his pockets and securely taped the claylike explosive along the line at which the two doors met.

He was conscious of the sound of boots scraping rapidly through the gravel, voices shouting commands or uttering curses—he couldn't understand the language—and bright lights sweeping past him and on him, temporarily blinding him at times. But he never lost his concentration.

Then he extracted an electronic detonator containing

semiconductors and computer chips, stuck it into the Semtex, and ran back to where he knew, by the location of the machine guns, the team was lying pressed to the ground. In his dash, he crashed on top of Sarah, since he couldn't see any of his invisible colleagues. He knew it was Sarah because he recognized her voice when she groaned.

"Sorry, Doc."

"And you didn't even take me to dinner first, ya big gorilla," she said. After a brief moment, she said, "Uh, Stan, you can get off me now."

He rolled off next to her. "So was it good for you too, huh?"

Sam said, "Major, I've got the link. We can receive and send."

"Okay," Travis said.

Stan spoke the voice-activation signal into his transmitter, which was linked to the detonator. "Kaboom," he whispered.

Kaboom they heard. They saw a flash of light followed by a cloud of dark smoke, and heard a loud crash. Even before the smoke cleared, their thermal viewers allowed them to see that the iron doors had been blown open and into the building, and that some dazed men were staggering around near the entrance, while others were lying on the ground. Several yards behind, twenty other men in camouflage came rushing toward the entrance, brandishing AK-74s, some with grenades in their hands. They began firing their assault rifles into the darkness. The darkness in which Eagle Team waited.

0155 hours
Communications Center
Second level below ground, Kara Kale

Rauf Pasha and Mahmoud el-Badawi stood among the TV screens, switches, buttons, microphones, and lights of the Communications Center. They scanned the closed-circuit television screens, but could see nothing but their own men running chaotically around the compound, in and out of the searchlights sweeping the area.

"Wait!" Rauf Pasha cried. "Look!" He pointed at the screen that showed the area in front of the doors.

"What the hell . . . ?"

What they saw, as the searchlights swept by, was a pair of RPK 7.62mm machine guns that seemed to float from one position to another. Rauf Pasha and Mahmoud el-Badawi looked at each other in horrified incomprehension.

El-Badawi said, "They must be wearing black camouflage, whoever they are. So we couldn't see them in all that darkness. Especially on a TV screen."

"Even when the searchlight swept across the machine guns?"

El-Badawi shrugged. "These things can happen."

"Who the hell can they be?" Rauf Pasha said, to no one in particular.

El-Badawi said, "Turkish Special Forces?"

"I doubt it, here on the Iranian side."

"Iranians?"

"What the hell would the Iranians be attacking us for?"

El-Badawi said, "No use wondering who they are. Let's kill the infidels, whoever they are!"

"Wait!" Rauf Pasha said. "We don't yet know how many invaders there are, or what weapons they have. Let the men on the outside take care of themselves. For now, keep the doors closed. We don't want our men rushing outside to be slaughtered. We need to protect this building, the missiles, the hostages . . . ourselves.

"Mahmoud, get to work and organize the men. Each one to his station, until further orders." He looked at the TV screen showing the entrance hallway on the ground level. He saw about thirty of his men moving toward the doors.

"Idiots!" Rauf Pasha yelled. "No one gave them orders to move to the entrance. They should be at their posts, awaiting orders. What the hell are they doing?" He turned to el-Badawi, "Mahmoud, get them organized!"

Just then they felt a tremor. They looked at each other. El-Badawi pointed to the screen covering the entrance hall. They saw the doors fly in and apart, crushing several men, leaving others dazedly wandering about. They saw twenty of their men, further back in the hallway, rush toward the smoke-filled entrance.

Rauf Pasha told the communications clerk to hook him up on the special network to Revolutionary Guard Headquarters in Tehran.

After a moment, "Well . . . ?!" Rauf Pasha asked, impatience in his voice.

The clerk, without turning from the microphone, said, "They haven't answered yet, *efendi*."

"What?! Where the hell are they?"

"Rauf Pasha, it *is* two o'clock in the morning, *efendi*."

Rauf Pasha looked at the clerk as though he were looking at a dead cat being devoured by maggots. In a low, menacing voice, he said, "I am aware of the time. Get those Iranian bastards to answer."

The clerk turned pale and said, "I am trying, *efendi*."

"Let me know when they answer," Rauf Pasha commanded. Then he ran over to the red telephone on the wall. He put it to his ear and pushed two buttons. "Rauf Pasha here. Is the missile set on the correct coordinates for the target? Good. Prepare for launching." He paused, his eyes blazing. Then, "Yes, you fool, you heard me correctly! Prepare for launching. Fast!"

0202 hours

As the group of twenty terrorists came rushing toward the open entrance to the fortress, Travis ordered, "Sam and Jen, on the left-hand machine gun. Jen, gunner, Sam, ammo handler. Hunter and Sarah, the right-hand one. Hunter, gunner, Sarah, ammo. Wait till I give the word to fire."

"Aaagh!"

"What happened?" Travis asked.

"Hunter here. I've been hit."

0202 hours
Communications Center

"*Efendi*, I have them."

Rauf Pasha strode over to the clerk's station, tore the microphone from his hand, and in Persian said, "Who is this?"

A sleepy voice answered, "Revolutionary Guards, Fourth District of Tehran."

Rauf Pasha was even more irritated by the yawn he detected in the man's answer. "Are you the man on duty?"

"Yes, sir, I am. Who is this?"

"This is Rauf Pasha." He paused. "You do know my name, don't you?"

The voice on the other end suddenly sounded more alert. "Oh, yes, sir. Of course, I do. *Ch'tori*, Rauf Pasha?"

"What, you waste time to ask me how I am?" Then without giving the Revolutionary Guard time to respond, "We are shitty, that's how we are. We are being invaded. We need assistance. How far away is the nearest Iranian military unit?"

"Just a moment, please."

"Come on, come on, man." Rauf Pasha clenched his fist.

Finally, "Rauf Pasha, Captain Kermanshahi is in command of ten armored troop carriers and five T-72 tanks. They are located at Dazgir, sixteen kilometers from your location."

"Good. Tell them to proceed here at once."

"But they are to be deployed only in case of an emergency, sir."

"Son of a pig! What the hell do you think *this* is? Never mind, I'll tell you. *This* is an emergency. We are not here arresting little old ladies for showing too much of their flabby arms in public, like you Revolutionary Guards! This is war! *Jihad*, Holy War, you imbecile! Send the troops!"

"I'm sorry, Rauf Pasha. I don't have the authority to give orders to military personnel."

"Then why in God's name am I talking to you?"

"I can't answer that question, sir. You called me."

Rauf Pasha bit his lip in frustration until the blood came. "You ignorant piece of shit! Damn you to hell!" He glanced at the wall clock, then his wristwatch, and made a supreme effort to calm himself. "Who has the authority to move this particular unit?"

"That would be General Mohammad Sephabodi."

Forcing himself to speak politely, Rauf Pasha said, "Are you able to communicate with General Sephabodi?"

A pause. "Well . . ."

"Can you or can you not?"

"I can, theoretically."

"Theoretically!" Rauf Pasha thundered. "What are you, a professor of philosophy?"

"Not exactly, not yet, but I'm taking courses in *Sufi* philosophy, and . . ."

"Enough!" Rauf Pasha had been sarcastic, but now he realized that the young man on the other end of the line was serious. "Listen to me, you stinking camel turd. Contact General Sephabodi, and . . ."

"But, sir, it is five minutes after two o'clock in the morning . . ."

"I am aware of the time, damn your eyes!"

The voice on the other end was becoming shaky. ". . . and, the general would be asleep . . ."

"Wake him, you fool, wake him! He will thank you. Your mullah, Ali Bakhtiari, will thank you, even your supreme leader, Ali Khamenei, will thank you. You'll receive material rewards from one and eternal blessings from the other. And if you don't act *immediately*, I will cut your balls off personally and shove them up your philosophical ass. Understood?"

"Yes, sir." The man's voice quavered. "What shall I say?"

"Listen carefully. Tell the general we are being attacked by an as yet unidentified force. Are you taking this down? Tell him to send the nearest military units here immediately. Time is of the essence. Do you understand? Time. And, listen carefully now, have him supply me with the proper code to be in direct communication with the tank commander . . . What was his name again?"

"Ah . . . That would be Captain Kermanshahi, sir."

"Yes, and have Kermanshahi understand that I have authority to command him. Clear?"

"Yes, sir. I shall deliver the message. Then, it's up to General . . ."

"Yes, yes, yes. Very well. Now, get right on it! Hurry!"

0203 hours

Travis said, "Hunter, where were you hit, and how bad?"

"Left upper arm. I don't think it hit a bone. I think the bullet went clean through."

Sam said, "Major, Rauf Pasha's talking English to someone."

"English? Must be dealing with non-Turkish engineers

and scientists. Probably Russians. Since he doesn't know Russian, their common language must be English. Convenient for us. What's he saying?"

"Hold on, Major." Sam listened for a bit, and then, a hint of panic in his voice, "He just ordered them to start the process of launching the missile."

"Did you say 'the missile?' Singular?"

"That's what he said, Trav."

Travis looked puzzled, but concentrated on the matter at hand. "Then we better start moving our collective asses!"

The twenty terrorists were at the entrance, firing wildly. Bullets were whizzing through the air over Eagle Team's heads, some too close for comfort, and Hunter had already been wounded.

Travis commanded, "Fire the machine guns!"

The RPK 7.62mm guns opened up, chattering loudly, throwing green tracers through the air and into the entranceway. The frontmost terrorists were knocked backward, their torsos stitched with holes. Almost cut in half, they fell, one after the other, like dominoes. The others turned to run, but were cut down as well before they could reach the first doorway off the corridor.

Travis said, "Jack, send in a Dragonfly."

Jack reached into a deep pocket and brought out what looked like a palm-sized model airplane. It was an unmanned aerial vehicle (UAV) with a delta wing and rear-mounted prop. It carried a microelectronics payload that provided video imaging and could fly for as much as thirty minutes. He sent it into the building, directing it by voice control.

All team members lowered their Battle Sensor Devices to just above the left eye to view what the Dragonfly was picking up. They saw offices to the right and to the left, camouflage-clad men, some with AK-74s, others, clerks, they figured, grasping pistols. Halfway down the hall was a staircase. Directly forward the Dragonfly entered what appeared to be barracks containing double-decker beds that could sleep one hundred men. As the UAV circled around the room, they counted eight men on the floor holding their weapons trained on the doorway.

Jack directed the Dragonfly back to the staircase and down to the first level below ground. He turned the UAV to the left and they saw the Communications Center to the right.

Among the electronic equipment were fifteen armed men. To the left they viewed a room with the door closed and a plaque reading EL-BADAWI. Beyond that was an office with five armed men in it. Jack turned the UAV in the other direction. It passed the staircase and came to a closed door.

"Well," Travis said, "can't expect all doors to be open. Jack, take it downstairs."

They saw the stairs leading down. Then they saw an iron door.

"That's all we're going to see for now, I guess," Travis said. "But it's practically a sure thing, judging from what we saw of the outside, that the east end of the building has the shaft for the missiles to launch through those doors on the roof we saw before. The missile must be on the bottom level."

Sam said, "Travis, the Pasha is having a long conversation. The coordinates, I'd say, point to Tehran."

"What's he saying?"

"I don't know. It must be Turkish. Or maybe Persian."

"Jen," Travis said, "you've been studying Arabic. How close is Persian or Turkish to Arabic?"

"Not. Except for some borrowed vocab. Sorry, Travis."

Sarah said, "Travis, what about Hunter?"

"Hunter, how're you doin'?" Travis asked.

"Not bad, Trav. The ATMP is doing its job." In Hunter's case, it had directed the immediate closure of the flesh wound. Directed by the sensors, the brilliant electro-designated contraction fibers of the Low Observable Camouflage outfit had been issued computer-generated instructions. The outermost fibers joined together to close the hole in the tough material itself. Then the innermost fibers had separated from the outermost ones and pressed tightly into and against the wound, acting as a suture, closing the wound and stopping the flow of blood from it. Based on the bio-chip readings, the ATMP had then injected Hunter with the correct amount of fluids to make up for blood loss, and antibiotics to prevent infection.

"How bad is the pain?" Travis said. He added, "And don't be cool, Hunter. I need to know."

"Okay, Travis. It feels like one bitch of a red-hot poker has pushed its way through my upper arm, and it's still lying there, throbbing away."

Sarah said, "Remember, Hunter, you can call in anesthetics by voice control, as you need it."

"Thanks, Sarah, I know. But I'd rather keep a clear head during this operation. If I need some, I'll take some. But, for now, I can take the pain."

Travis said, "But you can't fire your XM-29 rifle, right?"

"No, damn it, Travis. Can't use the left arm."

"All right, here it is. We have to move fast now. The element of surprise is gone. And the clock is ticking for nuclear catastrophe. We're going to move down the whole ground level, completely neutralizing it." He paused. "Not you Hunter. I want you to stay right outside the building while we clean up the main floor."

"But, Travis, I can use my .45 with my right hand."

"I know it, Hunter. That's exactly what I want you to do. I'll tell you when the ground level is clear. Then you come in, go into the nearest office. Then, keeping your cammo on, leave your rifle strapped to your shoulder, take cover, but keep your .45 in your right hand to cover our backs if need be."

"But, Trav . . ."

"Hunter, I need you on the ground floor." His tone left no room for discussion. "That's an order."

Hunter sighed. "Roger, sir."

"Stan," Travis commanded, "I want these machine guns to be destroyed after we leave them here."

"Way ahead of you, Trav. I already placed the charges."

"All right," Travis said. "Our objective is to reach the third level. That is, the second level below ground. And the eastern end of the building. That's where the missiles are, and that's where they're being directed from. Now, invisible or not, keep low. Don't bunch up. Don't forget to disengage the night-vision capability when we're in lighted areas. You know the drill. Let's get 'em."

0212 hours
Zero Level of Kara Kale

Hunter pressed against the wall around the north corner, grasping his .45 caliber pistol, and watched the sector between the west and north of the building, including the entranceway. The rest of the team, keeping low, walking quietly and swiftly, proceeded to their assigned positions. Travis went to the second doorway to the left. Jen and Jack proceeded to the doorway straight ahead at the rear, the general sleeping quarters. Sam and Sarah took the first doorway to the offices on the left. Stan took the room on the right-hand side of the corridor. He whispered, "Kaboom," voice-detonating the fuse on the Semtex affixed to the two machine guns left behind. He looked back down the corridor to the entranceway, heard the explosion, and saw the flash of light.

Travis waited until each trooper reported he or she was in position. They already knew how many terrorists were in each room, as well as their positions by having just seen the images projected by the Dragonfly onto their BSDs. Since his troopers were invisible, Travis couldn't see them, but knew they were in place by their whispering their names to him on the transmitter. Sam had adjusted the volume so that the quietest of whispers would come through clearly. In the present scenario, "in position" meant they had actually entered the room, walking very slowly and quietly, to the most advantageous positions with relation to the targets. All this while the terrorists had their weapons trained on the doorway.

Because they were in stealth mode, they would probably not be detected if they made absolutely no noise. "Probably," because there was always the possibility in daylight or in artificially lighted areas that someone might notice some kind of shimmering or ghostly outline and fire at it.

Although the corridor lights were on, the rooms were in darkness. In this way, the defenders of Kara Kale hoped to camouflage themselves while silhouetting the outlines of the invaders. It would also take invaders coming from lighted areas to a darkened one a few precious seconds to adjust to the darkness, whereas the defenders had already adjusted. A sound yet low-tech procedure. However, not when the invaders were TALON Force troopers.

When each trooper had reported, Travis said, "Go!"

All hell broke loose.

Chapter 12

Sam and Sarah, in positions that would allow them maximum coverage of the targets, but avoiding their firing at each other, used the thermal mode and very accurate laser range finder of their XM-29 rifles to aim at their targets. They would line the green dot, visible only to them through the XM-29 scope, on the most vulnerable point of their targets and squeeze the trigger.

Between them, Sarah and Sam had neutralized six of the confused enemy before they could react. The terrorists were stunned and started firing wildly at the doorway into the corridor, where they expected the attack to come from. Six more were killed before the remaining three defenders in this office realized that they were being fired on from the rear and the flank.

The three turned to fire wildly in the general direction of the two troopers. Sam felt wind from the bullets whizzing past his cheek. He carefully aimed and immediately put two bullets through the head of the man who had gotten too close. Then he squatted and swung his rifle until the green dot alighted on the forehead of a man sheltering beneath a desk and fired. A hole appeared above the man's nose, and his head snapped back against the wall. Sarah drilled the last man through the chest.

Travis had entered the second office on the left and circled around behind the six defenders. In rapid succession, he shot one, then two, then three. The other three squirmed to be in position to shoot at the source of firing. As they turned, Travis killed the fourth and fifth. The sixth panicked. He stood up and ran for the corridor. Travis picked him off.

0213 hours
Zero Level, Office Number Two

Because there were eight men in the office to the right of the corridor, and only one of him, Stan extracted a DEFTEC No. 25 grenade from a pocket. This "flashbang" device was intended to frighten and temporarily blind and deafen the victims. He pulled the pin, holding the spoon down with his thumb, and tossed the flashbang into the office. The 1.5-second fuse didn't leave much time to move away, so as soon as he tossed it in, he sprinted as far from the office door as he could.

Even with his hands clapped over his ears, the tremendous bang produced by the explosion was uncomfortably loud. For the men in the room, the approximately 175 decibels were terrifying and rendered them temporarily deaf. The flash was equivalent to 2.42 candlepower, temporarily blinding them as well.

Stan rushed back to the door and entered. The eight men were holding their heads and looking completely disoriented. Stan knew this condition wouldn't last very long. He picked off one after the other with his XM-29 rifle.

0213 hours
Zero Level, the barracks

At the rear of Zero Level were the barracks. It could accommodate one hundred men in twenty-five double-decker bunk beds on the left, and twenty-five on the right, with an aisle down the middle from the doorway to the far wall. Yet, only eight defenders happened to take cover there.

Jack peered into the room and saw that the men were still in the positions they had seen on the Dragonfly imaging. Three had taken cover along the far wall, behind the insufficient cover of beds, their weapons aimed directly at the doorway. Three others were along the wall to Eagle Team's left, and two were to the right. Somehow they hadn't seen it on the Dragonfly imaging, but through their thermal viewing now saw clearly that two of the men against the far wall were manning an RPK 7.62mm machine gun.

"Jen, ease in toward the right," Jack whispered. "I'll take the left. I'll ice the machine gunner. You take the ammo handler. After they go down, we'd better both take out the third man against the wall, in case he tries to get on the machine gun. Tell me when you're in place."

Four seconds later, Jen whispered, "Aiming."

Jack fired several bursts at the same time Jen did. The gunner and the ammo handler bounced against the walls and were still. Five other men immediately began firing their Kalashnikovs at the doorway. Neither Jen nor Jack were there. The third man at the wall did make a lunge for the machine gun. The automatic target tracker on Jen's XM-29 caught him in motion, and he sprawled out face-down a foot away from the gun.

Jen lined a green laser dot against the forehead of one of the men to the right. She squeezed the trigger. He fell against the wall. Then she moved the dot to the second man and fired.

Jack had crawled to a point three feet from the nearest man on the left. He held his breath, but the man must have noticed something, because he turned in Jack's direction, his AK-74 practically in Jack's face. Jack knocked the man's weapon away and fired twice at the terrorist's heart and a third time at his forehead, at point-blank range. The next man looked at his dead companion, confused. Jack shot him through the head. At the same time, the next man oversaw his dead companions and swung his weapon in Jack's direction, but was hit by fire coming from Jen's rifle across the room.

"Thanks, Jen," Jack said, "I owe you one."

When the firing stopped, Travis waited a moment, then whispered into his transmitter, "Status report. Sam?"

"Fine, Boss. Target neutralized."

"Sarah?"

"I'm all right, Trav. Target neutralized."

"Stan?"

"Asses have been kicked."

Suddenly, the sound of gunshots interrupted the status report. It seemed to come from near the entrance.

0215 hours
Communications Center

"I'm sorry, *efendi*, we've lost communication with the ground level."

Rauf Pasha was livid. "What the hell is going on? Who are the invaders?"

"The last thing we heard from ground level was that they had still not seen the invader clearly."

Rauf Pasha rubbed his close-cut beard while he pondered the situation.

The communications clerk said, "Rauf Pasha, we have General Mohammad Sephabodi. He wants to . . ."

"Yes, yes, give me the microphone." Switching from Turkish to Persian, Rauf Pasha said, "General, I . . ."

"What in the name of Allah are you getting me out of bed for at this ungodly hour?"

"We are being invaded."

"We? What do you mean, 'we'?"

"Kara Kale is being invaded, and it stands on Iranian territory, does it not, General?"

Pause. "All right, who is invading? Turkey? Iraq? Who?"

"I don't know, General, but . . ."

"What do you mean, you don't know?"

"It is nighttime . . ."

"I'm well aware of that."

"The attack was sudden. Without warning."

"The best kind of attack, militarily, is it not?"

Rauf Pasha was turning red. "General, whoever is attacking us is attacking our party, as-Saif al-Islam . . ."

"Your thing, not mine."

"I think your Supreme Leader, Ali Khamenei, would disagree. As well as other powerful people in Iran."

There was a moment of silence. Finally, "Very well, Rauf

Pasha." General Sephabodi pronounced his title sarcastically. "How can I help you?"

"You have troops, armored vehicles, tanks only sixteen kilometers from here. I understand that they are there precisely for such a contingency. You yourself, and the ayatollah, and the Revolutionary Guard . . ."

"*Elements* of the Revolutionary Guard," the general corrected.

". . . placed them there to help my . . . our cause."

"Yes," the general sighed, "you are correct." As a professional soldier, he felt distaste for this terrorist, who to date had never fought army to army, but had only engaged in hit-and-run guerrilla operations of no consequence. *This is a man who thought he was serving God by raping and killing young girls. But, if he convinced my superiors that he can deliver Turkey to us on a silver platter . . . then who am I to refuse him help?*

He said, "I am just a bit sleepy and irritable right now . . ."

"Ah, I am sorry to have disturbed you. You must be with your Afghan mistress . . ."

"If you don't mind, Rauf Pasha, let's keep this on a professional level."

"Will you send the troops?"

"Yes, Rauf Pasha. I will contact Captain Kermanshahi immediately and tell him to proceed with all speed to Kara Kale. Since I don't know what the hell is going on . . . Since you don't know who is invading Iranian territory, or why, or with how many troops and what kind of equipment, I will give you his code and inform him to take orders directly from you."

"When do you think they will arrive? This is urgent. We are being overwhelmed by what must be superior forces."

"Well, Kara Kale is not on the map—at your insistence, I might add—and it's dark out . . . I will instruct him on how to proceed. He should be there in ten to twelve minutes from when I call him. Which I will do immediately."

"Rauf Pasha," Mahmoud el-Badawi yelled, "there is no word from the ground level, we heard gunfire . . . They'll be coming down here next . . ."

"Yes, yes. Be ready at the staircase with your weapons. And you two," he said, pointing to two men, "set up a machine gun at the bottom of the staircase." He paused, starting to wonder about the efficiency of his men, and added, "Have it aiming *upward*, at anyone coming down the stairs."

Rauf Pasha then contacted the missile room on the second level below ground. "Well, are you ready to launch?"

A Russian-accented voice answered in English. "We have started the procedure. The rooftop doors are already open, and . . ."

"Spare me the details. How long till launch?"

"Hmmm . . . I would say . . ."

"Come on you Russian money grubber. Do I not pay you handsomely?"

"Not for being in a war zone, Rauf Pasha."

"Damn your infidel ass! How many fucking minutes?"

"Launch time is precisely . . . 0036 Greenwich Mean Time."

"What? What the hell is wrong with you? Don't you know what time it is right here?"

"Of course, Comrade . . . excuse me, old habits . . . Rauf Pasha. Launch time is 0236 hours."

0217 hours
Corridor of Zero Level

They turned toward the shots and saw the bodies of two terrorists at the entrance. Travis said, "Hunter, status?"

"I've just used my .45 on two of Rauf Pasha's men. They were heading back into the building."

"Good, now just take up a position in the first office on the left, as you come in. We're going below. You watch our backs."

"Roger."

Travis continued the status check. "Jen?"

"Fine."

"Jack?"

"No problem."

"Boss!" Sam said. "Conversation in English between Rauf Pasha and someone who must be the chief engineer or something."

"Yeah . . . ?"

"Launch will take place at 0236 hours!"

"My God! Nineteen minutes!" Sarah breathed.

Sam continued, "Another conversation between Rauf Pasha and someone in Tehran. Not in English. Wait a minute . . ." Sam paused. "Message from HQ."

Everyone waited impatiently.

Sam said, "HQ says that satellite intel shows an Iranian force of five T-72 tanks and ten armored troop carriers moving from Dazgir in this direction. Judging by distance and the columns' speed, they should be here by 0230 hours."

0218 hours
Communications Center

Rauf Pasha shouted, "Azzam Hamal, get all the prisoners down here at once!"

"Here to the Communications Center, *efendi*?"

"Yes, exactly."

"The two girls too? They're already on this level."

He stared at Hamal's bare scalp, shining under the bright lights, and rubbed his beard, thinking. He was torn between military tactics and desire. Then Mahmoud el-Badawi caught his eye. The Libyan's look was threatening. This would be a poor time for internal disputes. Besides, he himself was not sure. Rauf Pasha said, "No, leave the two girls where they are. Now go. Hurry!"

"Yes, *efendi*."

Azzam Hamal slung his Kalashnikov over his shoulder and rushed down the staircase to the second level below ground, which contained the prison cells, the arsenal, and the missile room.

Jen had swiftly and silently gone down the staircase to the landing. Peeking over the railing, she saw two men setting up a machine gun at the foot of the stairs.

"Travis," she whispered into her transmitter, "they're setting up a machine gun. And we can assume the room is full of armed men. Shall I throw some Bugs down?"

The XM-12 Bug was a robot sensor that resembled an insect. Linked to a microvideo high-frequency transmitter, it was a small, practically transparent robot made of clear plastic and thin, silver wires that would crawl along a surface and send video images. As it crawled along, the troopers would receive clear images of what the Bug was "seeing." If they used it in this case, they would know what was in the Communications Center: the equipment, the number of men, and what they were doing. Several Bugs could be used at once, providing direct visual data in different areas. The team would know exactly what it was getting into.

Travis checked his watch. "Negative, Jen. Negative. No time. Use an antipersonnel grenade, and get back up here."

Jen pulled the pin, counted two seconds, and then tossed it underhand in a low arc to a spot one yard behind the machine gun. Then she sprinted up the stairs and joined the others around the corner.

Rauf Pasha and his men heard the clunk and metalic rolling sound. They saw the dark oval-shaped object bounce and roll.

Rauf Pasha screamed, "Down!" as he flung himself to the floor. The two gun handlers and five men who happened to be closest to them didn't have a chance. As they dove for cover, the explosion sent shards of steel flying in all directions. The impact blew the seven men to pieces, sending those pieces flying, bouncing off the concrete walls, as the shrapnel sliced through them. El-Badawi and several others were knocked down by the blast. Half the men had hot shards of steel imbedded in their flesh and were bleeding. Rauf Pasha, dazed, heard groaning around him, and saw bodies and parts of bodies around the area of the Communications Center nearest the stairs. The machine gun was unusable.

Rauf Pasha pulled himself together. "To the missile room. Everyone!"

There were seven corpses in the Communications Center. Six men were too severely wounded to move. Rauf Pasha, el-Badawi, and seven of their followers hurried to the staircase and headed down, just as they heard footsteps rushing down the staircase from Level Zero.

Eagle Team set foot on the first level below ground just

as Rauf Pasha and his men reached the second level below ground. They surveyed the Communications Center at a glance, the corpses, the wounded . . . Then they broke into the adjoining rooms. Jen found Tracy Licata in el-Badawi's quarters. She checked with Travis, who told her to tell Tracy to stay put for the time being. They burst into Rauf Pasha's luxurious reception hall, the *selamlik*, and wondered at the oriental rugs and cushion-covered couches. Then they blasted the lock on the steel door to Rauf Pasha's private quarters, just off the *selamlik*, and found Kerri Lopert sitting on a chair, her eyes wide with fright, her arms hugging her knees, holding her bathrobe tightly around her. Travis explained, very rapidly, that they were going to get her out of there. When everyone reported that his or her sector was secure, Travis said, "It's 0222. We have no more than fourteen minutes."

When they reached the second level below ground, they saw a space in front of them barely large enough for the desk and chair in it. To the left was a steel door. To the right, another steel door. Standing halfway down the staircase, Travis let loose a burst from his XM-29 rifle to blast the lock mechanism of the door on the left. There was a corridor with a blank wall to the right and prison cells on the left. The cells were empty, the doors left open.

"What have they done with the hostages?" Sarah said.

"I'm afraid we're about to find out," Travis answered.

Once more halfway back up the staircase, they blasted the lock on the second door. Staying behind the doorjamb, Stan opened it. A hail of fire from AK-74 assault rifles and submachine guns was directed from the room to the right straight at the doorway. The bullets flew through the corridor of the prison block, ricocheting against the wall at the end, bouncing off concrete walls and metal bars, creating a deafening noise of guns firing and bullets pinging. After twenty seconds of intense fire, the shooting halted.

Travis wondered why Rauf Pasha's men were not right at the doorway, where they could angle their fire up the staircase as well as straight ahead. Then he saw why. Now that the metal door was open, the troopers could see into the room by means of their Battle Sensor Devices. They saw that the room on the right was the arsenal. There were assault rifles, submachine guns, .45 caliber pistols, knives, cases of TNT, Semtex, and artificial fertilizer that could be turned into explosives. There were even mortars, antitank rockets, and shoulder-held rocket launchers.

Halfway back in the arsenal, the troopers viewed a group of disheveled, weary men and women lined up as a barrier. They had to be the hostages, standing as human shields in front of Rauf Pasha's men.

Sam whispered into his transmitter, "Boss, they're using the hostages as shields, and they're armed to the teeth."

Sarah said, "We can't attack them!"

"We have to get through to the missile room beyond them. Jack, get that NLG off your back, set it, and push it in front of the doorway."

The Non Lethal Generator was the size of a wastepaper basket. It would emit a powerful low-frequency radio wave that would severely upset the nervous systems of humans and animals. As a directional device, people close to it but not targeted, would feel only a temporary ringing in their ears and fluttering of eyelids. But the unprotected humans it was aimed at, within a range of 600 meters, would become uncontrollably sick within seconds. Travis figured the hostages would rather be temporarily sick than permanently dead.

Jack turned a black plastic knob to set the controls for direction and intensity, and, shielding himself behind the iron door, carefully placed it in the entranceway to the arsenal. Then he flicked the switch and moved back up the stairs.

Through their BSDs the team watched as both hostages and terrorists, all the way through the arsenal and into the missile room beyond, doubled over, buckled at the knees, and began to vomit. The team saw them sinking prostrate to the ground, weapons falling from hands and clattering to the concrete floor. They heard groaning, punctuated by the barking sound of retching. They noticed dark spots grow on trousers. The smell of vomit, urine, and fecal matter wafted out to the staircase.

"Turn it off," Travis commanded after ten seconds. "Kill the terrorists except for the three men in white coats back there." Then he said, "Sam, you come with me to stop the launch and disarm the missiles. We can disengage the stealth feature now. Sarah, take care of the hostages. Come on, Sam, we have ten minutes!"

As the terrorists in the arsenal were being finished off, Travis and Sam rushed beyond them to the missile room. There they found banks of closed-circuit TV screens, dials, switches, lights of various colors and two shiny, awesome missiles, one lying in its rack, the other pointed upward at the blackness of the open sky. On the floor were twelve men in pools of vomit and urine, groaning. Three wore lab coats. The rest were clad in camouflage fatigues and lay near their AK-74s. They quickly put the uniformed men out of their misery with well-aimed shots.

In perfect Russian, Travis said, "Who's chief engineer here?"

No answer.

He kicked the nearest man in the arm and continued in Russian, baring his teeth and placing his XM-29 against the technician's head. "There's no time to fuck around, *sukan sinch*. Who's the chief engineer?"

"I am in charge." He sounded weak. Travis knew he damn well had to be weak. But he could think and he could talk.

"Ochin kharasho. Very well. I swear to God I'm going to jam this rifle up your ass and pull the trigger if you don't tell us how to stop the launch. And *fast*! If that missile blasts off, so does your ass! Cooperate and you live. Now, we have enough knowledge so we can figure out how to disarm this thing, but it'll cost us precious time. You know exactly how to do it. I know you communicated with Rauf Pasha in English. Instruct me and this man here in English," pointing to Sam. "We have nine goddamn minutes before launch time."

Suddenly, Travis heard Hunter's voice on his BSD. "Trav, we have company. There are tanks and armored cars coming down the road."

Travis spoke rapidly to the chief technician. "If someone here doesn't speak Persian, we may be in a battle with Iranian forces. If we're interrupted from stopping the launch, you're a dead man, so . . ."

"That man," the chief technician indicated the young, dark-haired technician, "is Iranian. He speaks his language and mine."

Travis spoke very rapidly, but very clearly, in Russian to the Iranian. "If you deliver my message in Farsi, convincingly, you live. That's not a threat. That's just the way it is. If we're attacked by Iranian forces, we all might be killed. If we are not killed, but the interruption causes the missile to launch, then I kill all three of you. Fact is, I don't want a fight with the Iranians. I don't want to kill any of them, and I don't want them to kill any of us. But most of all, I want to stop the missile launch."

The Iranian looked at Travis and knew he was not joking. He nodded.

Travis added, "When we get hooked up to the tank commander, my friend here," he jerked his thumb at Sam, "will hand you his helmet. Put it on and say what I tell you."

"*Khoob.*" Very well, the Iranian said.

Everyone but Sarah, who was treating the hostages, was now in the missile room.

"Sam," Travis said, "get us a link with the tank commander. Let me know when you get it."

"Already working on it, Boss. Should have it very soon."

"Good. Jen, help me. Sam's busy. The chief technician is going to tell us how to stop the launch." Looking at the white-coated technician, now able to sit up, Travis said, "Start."

The technician said, "You see the metal flap about three inches below your eye level on the opposite side of the missile?"

Travis and Jen walked around to the other side of the missile. Travis said, "Yes, I see it."

"Here, the key to open it is in my labcoat pocket." He extended the key.

Jennifer took a few steps, bent down and took the key. Travis nodded, and Jennifer inserted the key and twisted it to the right. Nothing happened. She turned it to the left, and heard a faint click. She placed her fingers under the edge of the flap and lifted. Inside there was a panel with two dials and a digital clock.

Jen said, "We have eight minutes and thirty-nine seconds. Thirty-eight seconds."

"Okay," Travis said to the technician, "go on."

"First, you need to remove the panel. Underneath is the timer and the wires connecting it to the ignition."

"They're small Phillips head screws. Where's the correct screwdriver?"

As Travis stared at the seconds sliding away on the digital display, he heard only silence from the technician. He looked over and saw the man had fallen back against the floor into a supine position.

"Stan," he commanded, looking over at him, "check him out."

Stan ran over to the man, felt the pulse in his neck, listened for breathing, and rapidly looked him over. "Trav, he's alive, not having a heart attack. He's fainted."

"Shit! Get Sarah in here. Have her revive him, pronto!"

Stan called to Sarah who came running in on the double. As Stan explained the problem and Sarah went over to the technician, Jack had been searching all the surfaces in the room. He found a red metal box. On opening it, he found a set of screwdrivers of various types and sizes.

"I've got the screwdrivers, Trav."

Travis, staring at the countdown rate, saw a reading of 07:02 shift to 07:01. He was about to tell Jack to bring it over, when Jack dropped down beside him with the open box. Jack extracted one of the Phillips head screwdrivers and said, "Here, try this one."

Travis grabbed it and tried to fit it into the screw head. Too big.

"Smaller one," he said.

Jack handed him the next size down. Travis took the screwdriver and fitted it into the grooves. He began to turn the screw. After several turns, he removed it. There were seven more to go. Sweat was beginning to run down his brow and temples. The indicator read 06:55.

"Jen, you take over."

Jen took the screwdriver from Travis and worked swiftly. Travis called over to Sarah, "How's he coming?"

"I think he's starting to come around."

"Keep at it, Sarah."

When the indicator showed 06:34, Jen said, "Okay, the screws are out, Trav."

Travis looked at the technician and saw he was not yet in a condition to tell him what to do next.

"Remove the panel, Jen."

Jen placed her fingernails under the brass panel and

lifted it away. She carefully arranged it so that while it was dangling from its black wires, she could still read the digital display. Underneath was another surface on which was an inch-square raised cube with a tiny dial that was turning almost imperceptibly. Three wires—a red one, a green one, and a blue one—ran from the cube two inches to connect with a metallic cylinder.

Travis said, "The dial must be the timer. The cylinder's the ignition."

Jen nodded, "Must be. Now, what are the *three* wires here for? All you need is one." She had already taken a wire cutter from one of her pockets.

Jack said, "There's probably an extra one that will set the device off if it's cut before the correct one is severed. The third must be a dummy, just to confuse anyone trying to stop the process."

Stan said, "How do we know that two of them won't set the thing off if severed?"

"We don't," Travis said, anxiously glancing at the technician, who seemed to be coming around. "Sarah, ask him which wires to cut in what order! We have six and a half minutes."

Sarah said, "I asked him, but he seems disoriented. He's babbling in Russian."

Travis rushed over to hear what the technician was saying, but heard only indistinct and confused mumblings. "Son of a bitch!" Travis said very quietly. Then he slapped the technician sharply several times. The technician opened his eyes wide and looked around him.

In Russian, Travis said, "There are three wires: red, green, and blue. Which do we cut first. Come on!"

The technician looked up at Travis. He shook his head as if to clear it. "Uh, first the blue . . . Then the red . . . No, no . . . First the red, and then the blue . . ."

"Are you sure?"

"Yes, I am pretty sure . . ."

"*Pretty* sure?! You'd better be *damn* sure or it's your ass!"

"My what?"

"Let me put it this way: be accurate or be dead!" He looked over at Jen. "Jen, how much time?"

"Five minutes, one second. Five minutes . . ."

"Once more, which wires in what order?"

The technician looked more alert now. "First, the red wire. Second the blue one."

"Green one last?" Travis said.

"Yes."

"Did you get that, Jen?"

"Yeah, Trav. I'm on it."

Sam said, "Boss, I'm in communication with the Iranian tank commander."

Travis interrupted the procedure just long enough to nod to Sam to hand the Iranian the helmet and to tell the Iranian what to say.

After receiving instructions, the Iranian said, "Captain Kermanshahi, I am an Iranian technician working at this establishment. We were invaded by an unidentified force. Everyone but myself and two other technicians have been killed. You must turn back, repeat, turn back. The invaders are gone, but they have arranged for this place to produce a nuclear explosion that will rain death on millions of people in western Iran if we don't correct it." The lie was for the purpose of chasing the Iranians away from the scene.

"We are working on that right now. Even if we manage to prevent that catastrophe, there may still be radiation leaks that will kill us, and anything living within a five kilometer diameter. Since you can be of no help now, you should take your men as far away as possible from here as you can. I must get back to work now. We have only . . ." He looked at Travis, and pointed to his wristwatch, shrugging his shoulders.

Travis held up ten fingers and then five. He exaggerated the time period because he wanted the tank commander to feel he had a good chance of getting away.

"We have only fifteen minutes. I am signing off."

Turning back to the chief technician, beads of sweat on his forehead, he said, "We only have three more minutes. Keep talking."

Sam spoke into his helmet transmitter. "Hunter, what's happening up there? What are the Iranian troops doing?"

"They came to a halt a little while ago. They're just standing there, engines running. Wait, wait . . . They seem to be . . . Yes, they are turning around." He paused to watch. After a few moments, he said, "Sam, they're taking off. Rapidly. Very rapidly. You were expecting this, weren't you, you little techno-weenie?"

"I'll explain later, bird boy."

Meanwhile, Jen had applied the wire cutter to the red wire. "Let's hope this guy's mind isn't too messed up by the NLG to remember accurately," she mumbled. "Okay," she said under her breath, "here goes."

She held her breath, closed her eyes, and cut the red wire. Nothing. So far so good.

"Second wire is blue, right, Trav?"

"Affirmative, Jen."

"Let's hope he isn't lying either." She placed the wire cutter blades around the blue wire, sweat running down her face. All eyes were following her every motion.

The technician said something to Travis, who then called across to Jen, as calmly as he could, "Oh, Jen . . . Be careful not to sweat onto the wiring. He says the Russian workmanship is a little sloppy sometimes, and there might be a tiny section of the wires exposed. A drop of sweat might set it off."

"Jesus Christ!" Jen murmured between clenched teeth. She removed the wire cutter from the blue wire, leaned back slowly, taking care not to make too sudden a movement, which might shake a bead of sweat off onto the wires. Sarah ran over and mopped her brow and face with a gauze pad.

Jen replaced the wire cutter on the blue wire, said, "Here we go," and cut. Then she glanced at the digital display on the panel hanging by the black wires. It showed 02:05.

Sarah stood by her, mopping her brow. Jen placed the cutter blades around the green wire, closed her eyes, and silently prayed. Then she cut.

Chapter 13

When the launch mechanism had stopped at 0234 hours and 30 seconds, just one and a half minutes before zero hour, Jen had sighed, sat on the floor, leaning back against the console, and closed her eyes. The others just stared at her silently for a full ten seconds. Then they yelled and cheered and jumped up and down and hugged each other. The tension built up for so long, and with such a narrow margin of error, had to be released. After a minute of jubilation, they began to calm down.

Travis said, "All right, troops, let's finish up." He looked around at them and said, "Great job, guys. Really great. I'm proud to work with you all." Then he contacted Hunter through his Battle Sensor Helmet. "Hunter, relax. Everything's secure. How's it goin' up there?"

"Fine, Trav. No sign of a living thing up here or anywhere on the compound. The ones on the surface who survived must have taken off when they saw how things were going."

"They might've been more worried by what they didn't see than what they did see. What about the Iranian troops?"

"Took off. Just turned around and took off as though they were afraid of a nuclear explosion or something."

"They were."

"What?"

"Explain later."

"That's what Sam said."

"Hunter, we're coming up with the hostages and three prisoners, the nuke technicians."

Sarah had treated the hostages first, and then the three technicians. Both sets of people were still wobbly on their feet and had queasy stomachs, but were gradually improving.

Travis spotted, among the hostages, a graying but robust man in his fifties who seemed to exhibit a military bearing in spite of the ordeal. "Lieutenant Commander Schraer?"

"Yes. And you are . . . ?"

Travis saluted and said, "Major Travis Barrett, U.S. Army, sir. You're safe now, Commander."

Returning the salute, Schraer said, "Not exactly."

Travis looked alarmed. "How do you mean, sir?"

"Well . . . The conditions under which I was kidnapped. . . . And then there's my wife . . ."

Stan broke in, "Yeah, I know what you mean, sir!"

Travis gave Stan a disapproving look, but the Lieutenant Commander smiled and asked, "Are you complaining, son . . . ? Or are you bragging?"

Sam, in the arsenal, called out, "Travis, I don't see Rauf Pasha here."

Travis went into the arsenal and inspected the faces of the dead terrorists. Because of the photographs they had viewed electronically, he would be able to recognize the two top men of as-Saif al-Islam.

He nudged the body of a clean-shaven man with a hole drilled through his forehead and another through his chest. "Mahmoud ibn Hassan el-Badawi," Travis confirmed. "Murderer, rapist, torturer . . ."

He looked carefully at each body. No Rauf Pasha. "Where the hell did he get to?"

Jack pointed to the wall and said, "Hey, those mortars are just lyin' all over the place, like turds in a pigpen. Everything else in here is neat as can be."

Jennifer walked over to the pile of mortars and inspected the wall behind them. "Travis, c'mere."

Travis joined her and stared at the wall. "Isn't that . . .?"

"Sure looks like it." Looking closely, he noticed an almost imperceptible line on the wall in the shape of a door. He pushed it, and it opened. "Son of gun!"

"A secret escape hatch?"

"Looks like it," Travis assented. Recessed about five feet

into the tunnel, he saw a metal ladder. "There's room for only one person at a time to climb it," he said.

"Let me handle it." As so often before, Stan volunteered for the most dangerous mission.

"You've got it, with Jen as backup. But let's set this up right. I'm going to alert Hunter topside."

Travis spoke into his transmitter, "Hunter."

"Yeah, Trav."

"Turn on your stealth mode again. Rauf Pasha's missing. We're looking for him on the subterranean levels. Now, I'm sending Sarah up to join you, so stay in constant communication with her till she arrives."

Travis turned to the others, "Stealth on. Jack, Sam, come with me up to the first level underground. Sarah, you come with us, but keep going to join Hunter. Stan, Jen, don't do anything till I tell you we've secured the next level up. Okay, let's go."

As they turned to dash up the staircase, Travis saw that the three technicians were shakily getting to their feet and heading for chairs. In Russian, he called out, "You three. Just stay there until I send for you."

When Travis, Jack, and Sam reached the first underground level, they found the wrecked Communications Center empty. Same situation for el-Badawi's office. In his private quarters next door, they found Tracy Licata glumly sitting on the bed where they had left her. Travis gently said, "It's us, darlin'. Just stay here a little while longer. We'll be back for you before you know it." She smiled.

This time the thick iron door to the *selamlik* was closed. Travis tried it: locked. He spoke into his transmitter, "Stan, Jen, everything west of that fancy living room is secured. But that fancy living room or parlor or whatever the hell it is, is locked. Sarah, where are you?"

"Hunter and I have searched the entire ground level. All secure up here."

"Hunter, how're you doin'?"

"Let's go surfin', dude!"

"Travis, I gave him a painkiller," said Sarah.

Travis nodded and said, "Stan, Jen, go ahead. Be very careful. We're going in through the door."

Travis shot the locking apparatus and pushed the door open as the three of them lay flat on the ground. They saw

Kerrie Lopert in her terry cloth robe, facing them at the far end of the *selamlik* with some apparatus strapped around the upper part of her body. She sat there sobbing.

"What the fuck . . . ?" Jack murmured.

Directly to Kerrie's left the door to Rauf Pasha's private quarters was ajar. Rauf Pasha couldn't be seen, but his voice called out, "Welcome, barbarian dogs! Listen carefully. Strapped to the girl you will see a bomb that is capable of blowing this whole establishment to bits. I don't know, because I've never tested the theory, and I'm no scientist, but who's to say it wouldn't also detonate the nuclear material?"

"Kerrie, honey," Travis called in to her, "take it easy. You're going to be all right." His deep voice and Texas drawl had a soothing effect on the girl.

Rauf Pasha called out, "Listen, you American pigs, very carefully. If you kill me, we're all dead. The bomb is set to go off in ten . . . No, nine minutes from now. If you all leave immediately, I will stop it from detonating. Otherwise, we all die. But first, make yourselves visible."

"Sam," Travis whispered, "do you think the HERF can fry that particular mechanism?"

Sam looked carefully at the bomb. "Absolutely. The device is electronic."

"Okay, go ahead."

The HERF was the wristband High Energy Radio Frequency transmitter that would shoot a short, intense burst of directed radio frequency energy to disable electronic devices. This RF Field Generator was woven into the Battle Ensemble.

Sam aimed the HERF gun by pointing his left arm at the bomb and using a voice command. The electromagnetic pulse bursts fired at the bomb overloaded its circuits and put it out of commission.

"Stan, what's up?" Travis asked.

Stan whispered in the transmitter, "There's this hatch I've got to lift. Hold on."

Stan then said, "He must've locked it from above. It won't push open. I'll have to blast it."

"Okay. The bomb's fried. Don't worry about that. Just watch out for yourself. We're crawling toward him."

Stan, the demolitions expert, extracted a ball of Semtex

from a pocket, pinched off a piece the size of a marble, jammed the detonator into it, and said, "Jen, back down to the arsenal. Trav, we're going to the arsenal and closing the door down there. The fuse is set for seventy seconds from right now."

Travis, Sam, and Jack had been slowly and quietly crawling toward Kerrie and the door to Rauf Pasha's quarters. They could see the end of the AK-74 assault rifle protruding from behind the door.

"Stan, Jen, when it goes off we're going to blast him. Don't get in the line of fire."

Travis was now an arm's length away from the barrel of Rauf Pasha's Kalashnikov. He didn't know if the metal door was too thick for their bullets, and he worried that when Rauf Pasha heard the blast, his reflexes might make him fire at Kerrie, rather than immediately turn toward the sound. He couldn't take the chance. There were still forty seconds to go.

Travis turned off his stealth capability, so his team members could see him. He had no intention of being hit by friendly fire, no matter how friendly, he told himself. Now plainly visible to his teammates, but hidden from Rauf Pasha by the door, Travis set his XM-29 down, got to his knees, lunged forward, seized the Kalashnikov barrel with both hands, and pushed it firmly down. A long burst raked the floor a foot and a half in front of Kerrie's feet. Sam and Jack stood up and rushed toward Travis and the gun barrel.

Travis pressed the barrel against the floor and kept it in place. Rauf Pasha let go of the rifle, rose from a prone position to his knees, and pulled a .45 caliber pistol out of his holster. Before he could point it at Travis, they all heard what sounded like a cherry bomb and the dull thud of the hatch landing on a carpeted floor. Rauf Pasha instinctively turned his head toward the sound. In that split second, Travis, still kneeling, lunged at the terrorist chief and jammed his knuckles into his Adam's apple, forcing Rauf Pasha to gasp for breath. At the same time, Jack came down hard with his boot on the terrorist's wrist, while aiming his XM-29 at him. He fired a burst into his face. Blood, bone, and brain matter splattered.

Stan emerged from the hatchway, followed by Jen. Surveying the scene, Jen said, "Sorry we didn't make it to your barbecue, Trav."

Travis just sat there for a couple of seconds, calming down.

Stan rushed over to Kerrie and said, "Take it easy, kid. You're okay now. I'm just going to get this damn contraption off you."

The demolitions expert knelt in front of Kerrie, took some tools out of a pocket, and began to delicately disconnect wires and switches. In two minutes he looked up at her face and said, "Okay, kid. The bomb is now completely and permanently dead."

Kerrie smiled at Stan with gratitude on her tear-streaked face. Then she bent over and hugged him.

When she released him, he said, "Okay, I'll just get you out of that harness now."

"That's okay, Stan," Jen said, "I'll do that."

0304 hours

They went up to the ground level to join Hunter and Sarah with all the hostages and the three technicians. They had turned off their stealth capability once they had killed Rauf Pasha. Sarah inspected Hunter's wound, then examined the hostages and treated them, as needed, for exhaustion, anxiety, dehydration, and some minor cuts and abrasions. Then they proceeded outdoors.

Travis said, "We've got to do something about the arsenal down there without taking the chance of setting off any nuclear reaction. We've got to neutralize that nuclear material as well."

"How do you destroy that shit without spewing it all over the place?" Jack asked.

"Not with my explosives," Stan said.

"Not with any conventional explosive weapons either," Travis said.

"Right," Stan said.

"Bunker Buster?" Sarah asked.

Travis nodded. The Hard and/or Deeply Buried Target Defeat Capability weapons not only penetrated deeply to completely destroy underground facilities, but had agent neutralization as their key aspect, whether nuclear, biological, or chemical. The Bunker Buster would vaporize weapons of mass destruction with minimal collateral damage.

Hunter asked groggily, "Are we going to have it launched from Incirlik Air Base in Turkey?"

"No," Travis said, "we'd rather do it from out at sea, in international waters, rather than involve our base in Turkey."

"Sixth Fleet?" Stan asked.

"Right. Admiral Zlotchew has a couple of Bunker Busters standing by on the USS Oregon fifteen miles out to sea due west of Iskenderun."

Travis turned to Sam, "Sam, we're going to need you to communicate with HQ to tell them to forward the order to launch the Bunker Buster. Not now. When we're out of here."

"I'm already in contact with them, Boss. They're just waiting for my signal."

Turning to Hunter, Travis said, "We want to get away from here ASAP, so we can call in the Bunker Busters fast. But the hostages aren't fit to hike. Hunter, can you fly one of those choppers with your bum arm?"

Hunter looked at him slyly and said, "No, but I can fly it with my good arm."

"You're sure?"

"Have faith, Travis, have faith."

"Sarah . . . ?" Travis said. "Can you sober him up and get him flight ready?"

"It'll be a pleasure, Travis. Hunter, come here. Please drop trou and bend over." A long hypodermic awaited, hidden from Hunter's field of vision.

"Sarah, I thought you'd never ask. Ow!"

"Okay, let's get in the first chopper and start it up. Stan, place some explosives charges on the other two. I want them destroyed."

"Aye, aye. Boss."

0311 hours
The hills above Kara Kale

They were approaching the spot that Travis chose to land and wait for the Ospreys. They swept their light beams around the area and caught six men down below. Caught in the beam of light, the men looked startled. Several of them shot up at the chopper.

"Grenade, Trav?" Stan said, already switching his XM-29 to the grenade setting, setting the electronic fuse, and leaning out the door.

"Affirmative."

The air burst over the terrorists' heads knocked them flat against the ground while sending shrapnel tearing through them.

"Enemy neutralized," Stan said.

"All right. We'll land now. Sam, ask HQ for a direct link to Admiral Zlotchew so you . . ."

"Already did that, Boss."

Travis shook his head and smiled. "Okay, give the admiral the coordinates for the Bunker Buster. And give him our present coordinates so he can send a V-22 Super Osprey for us."

Jack said, "Yeah, little buddy, but make sure the Busters go out *there*, and the Osprey comes down *here*, not the other way around."

"Good thing you told me that, Jackoff, my man."

Jack laughed long and loud, the tension easing off him.

As he maneuvered, Hunter, now chemically alert, said, "That is one sweet flying machine, Trav. Combines the attributes of a helicopter with those of a high-speed turboprop. They're damned fast, they're reliable unless Marines are flying them, and they're so stealthy that they can get past most radars undetected."

"Which means, we're just about on our way out of here." Sam sounded happy.

Stan said, "What's the hurry, Sam I am?"

Sam muttered something in Mandarin, which of course, no one else in the helicopter understood.

Stan laughed and said, "Well, as they say in Vietnamese, *phok yu tu*, little guy."

Sarah said, only half jokingly, "Hey, stop picking on Sam. At least he knows that 'interface' has nothing to do with lap dancing."

"It doesn't?" Stan said.

Eagle Team was unwinding, having a good time. But Travis looked worried.

Sarah said, "What's the matter, Trav?"

"I was just wondering . . . Why the hell was only one missile set for launching?"

She thought for a moment. "Maybe they were going to take out one city and then see what reactions there would be. Maybe they figured if they actually did that, the U.S., Europe, everyone else would force the Turkish government to hand over the reins."

"Maybe . . ." He didn't sound totally convinced.

0630 hours
Aboard the V-22 Super Osprey over Iskenderun
and the Gulf of Alexandretta

Behind them the horizon was turning from gray to red and purple. In front of them, the black sky and sea lightened to gray. Travis could barely make out where the border between land and sea lay. He knew they were passing over the ancient city of Iskenderun, named for Alexander the Great of Macedon, and that within minutes they would be landing on the deck of the carrier Antietam. He looked around at his Eagle Team, some of whom were dozing, and pride in their abilities and dedication warmed his innards. In front of him were the three engineers, their hands in plastic cuffs behind their backs.

However, a dark misgiving had been welling up in Travis's mind ever since they finished putting the missile out of commission. Now that the immediate emergency was taken care of, this doubt had turned into suspicion, and finally took concrete form in his consciousness. It was as though a star had burst in his mind. If he believed in astrology, he would have thought it was an unlucky star.

"Holy shit!" he said, smacking his forehead. Then he yelled in Russian above the sound of the chopper's engines, "Granovsky, get back here!"

Travis noticed that the Russian looked worried, very worried. "Da . . . ?"

"I have a problem, Granovsky. Come over here."

The engineer raised himself, turned, squeezed himself between the two other engineers, and lurched toward Travis. Travis helped him sit down beside him.

"Why was only one missile armed?" Travis asked.

"At first," Granovsky said, glancing nervously at the Iranian technician, "I was afraid to tell you . . ."

"Afraid . . . ?"

"*Da!*" He would have liked to whisper, but he had to shout in order to be heard above the roar of the Osprey's engines. He jutted his chin in the direction of the Iranian engineer. "Please speak quietly, Major."

Travis saw what Granovsky was afraid of. "Does that one understand English?"

"Who the hell knows?" Granovsky said.

"Okay. Go on in English. Fast."

"The reason you found only one missile ready for launch instead of two . . ."

"Yes . . . ?"

"The missile you disarmed was aimed at Tel Aviv. The other nuclear device is being delivered by hand."

Travis stared at the Russian.

The engineer continued, "One of their 'martyrs' is delivering it to Athens, where he will set it off. Rauf Pasha would have done the same for Tel Aviv. It is more dependable. But security is too tight in Israel, while in Greece . . ." He shrugged. "Just last year, the British military attaché was murdered, Brigadier Stephen Saunders had . . ."

Travis interrupted, "For God's sake!" He paused for a moment, then, "When is it going to be detonated?"

"The missile was to be launched first. Rauf Pasha thought that the horrifying destruction in Israel would make the West relent and force the Turkish government to surrender to his organization. Athens was to be destroyed at one minute to midnight of April sixth if the martyr did not receive word to the contrary."

Travis made a quick calculation. "At 2359 hours today. That's about eighteen hours from now!"

"I did my job for pay. But I have no personal interest in seeing nuclear war."

"Then what the hell were you waiting for?!"

"I told you. I was afraid." He glanced at the Iranian.

Travis said, "Sam, contact Admiral Zlotchew. Tell him we should be landing in about ten or fifteen minutes. Say we're dropping Hunter for medical treatment, and three prisoners, engineers, to hold for questioning. Tell him to be ready to refuel the Osprey, or give us one that's already fueled up, whichever's faster."

The engineer at Travis's side looked worried. He said, "Major . . ." He shot a glance at the other two engineers.

Travis followed his eyes and added, "And Sam, tell them to keep the engineers strictly separated from each other. Separate compartments."

"*Spasiba*," the engineer thanked Travis with a sigh of relief.

Chapter 14

Travis strained to look at the horizon, which he could now clearly see. The sun had turned the sky behind him to yellow and orange. Looking forward, Travis saw the dark gray sea clearly distinguished from the lighter gray of the sky. He also detected the dark shapes that he knew were elements of the Sixth Fleet. The rising sun was behind them, but he saw the reflection it cast before them as an orange highway cutting through the sea to lead them to the fleet.

Above the roaring of the Osprey's engines, Travis shouted into the Russian engineer's ear, "Granovsky, how many men in the team?"

"Three. The 'martyr,' who will be carrying the bomb, and two others. They were to drive from Istanbul to the border near Edirne, then cross into northern Greece at Orestiás. Greek security is notoriously lax, you know. They were to behave as tourists on a holiday. From Orestiás they were to drive to Athens."

"But there might be others already in place in Athens?"

"Who knows?" Granovsky shrugged.

"When did these three leave Istanbul?"

"March thirtieth."

"Eight days ago. Then they've been in Athens for some time now."

"No doubt. They were to wait for the nuclear blast to take place in Israel, and if they had no further orders from Rauf Pasha . . ."

"Detonate the bomb in Athens." Travis finished Granovsky's sentence for him.

The Russian nodded.

"But now that no missile has exploded in Israel, and the Turkish government has not been taken over by Rauf Pasha, and, obviously, there's no communication between these three men and their late leader . . ."

Granovsky shrugged.

Travis switched from Russian to English and called out to his troopers, "Eagle Team, I want to talk to you through your BSHs."

They looked surprised at the need for using the Battle Sensor Helmets for communication at this point. When Travis saw they were wearing their helmets, he spoke in a low voice, but was heard clearly by all members of the team. He summed up the situation as he knew it, then he said, "People, we're going to Athens. Except for you, Hunter. You'll have your wound taken care of on shipboard."

"But, Trav . . ."

"That's an order, Hunter. Sam . . ."

"You want General Krauss," Sam said.

"Right."

"Trav, it's almost midnight in Washington. He won't be at NSA HQ."

"Get whoever's on duty and tell them to get hold of him, no matter where he is, on the double."

Travis heard the difference in the sound of the motors, and felt the deceleration of the plane and the change in vibration as the Osprey tilted the huge rotors on its wingtips into the upright position and began to descend like a helicopter. Below was the flight deck of U.S.S. Antietam, and, on that deck, a second Osprey.

0015 hours EST
National Security Agency, Eastern COMCTR,
Classified Specific Grid, Ft. Meade, Maryland

Brigadier General Jack Krauss, Commander of the TALON Joint Task Force, rushed down the hall, buttoning his shirt, his necktie uncharacteristically untied. Once inside the communications center, he was handed the mike and earphones.

"Sam. Krauss here. Report."

Krauss listened, then he said, "Major Barrett did the right thing. We have no TALON Force teams that can get to Athens faster than you people." He paused to listen, then, "Yes, you must stop these people at all costs.

"Now, keep in mind, the Greeks are our allies in NATO, like the Turks, but we would rather they didn't know about this. First of all, there's no time for them to evacuate such a highly populated area. There would be panic, and the mobs would get in the way of any attempt to get to the terrorists. Not to mention that this would warn the bombers that their presence is known. They would probably detonate the bomb as soon as they knew they had been found out. Besides, you're better equipped than the Greek security forces to handle this."

He paused to listen to Sam, then responded. "Yes, I know: you don't know Athens. Listen, there is a man in Athens who can help you locate the terrorists. He's a private detective who worked in Los Angeles for eight years and has helped the CIA for several years now. He's absolutely dependable. His name is Stavros Vardakis. He has good friends on the Athens Police Force and on the border Gendarmerie. In the underworld as well. I'm going to tell you how to contact him before I sign off. Immediately after we finish this conversation, I'm going to contact Vardakis and ask him to see what he can find out about a car of Turkish registry, with three Turks in it, that entered Greece at Orestiás eight days ago. And I'm going to ready a street map of Athens for you to call up on your Battle Sensor Devices whenever you need to." He paused. "Where are you now?"

Krauss pushed a button and a map of Greece and western Turkey appeared on the screen before him. "Over Korkudeli? Good. This isn't going to be easy, but I know you're going to come through. You've got to."

0840 hours
Aboard the Osprey, above the Greek island of Andros

Major Barrett briefed Eagle Team. "General Krauss arranged with the Greek government for us to land at a

NATO resort on the Greek coast about forty-two miles from Athens. We should be landing in ten to fifteen minutes. The story is that we're just another bunch of U.S. military officers serving with NATO, and we're coming in for some R and R. Commander Nelson Preswick-MacPhee, Royal British Navy, is in charge of the base. Now, we can't bring any weapons into Greece or into the NATO compound if we're not on duty there."

Stan said, "Well, we're not expected to use our bare hands, are we, Trav?"

Travis said, "Krauss has assured us that our contact, Stavros Vardakis, has buried a weapons cache three miles from the NATO base. I have the exact coordinates."

Jen said, "What kind of weapons?"

Travis grimaced, "Five Heckler & Koch HK P9S 9mm pistols, and two CZ 75 Compact 9mm pistols."

There was a moment of silence. Then Jack said, "That's it?"

"No, there will be seven combat knives as well." He paused. "Look," Travis soothingly intoned, "we're going to be operating in a large, cosmopolitan city, in a friendly country. In broad daylight. And we're operating in secret. Now, I know the Greeks aren't exactly the most security-conscious fellas in the world, but come on. We're not going to be lugging any mortars with us, or elephant guns, or even assault rifles or submachine guns." He paused. "And you can be sure this Stavros Vardakis doesn't have access to our TALON Force weaponry."

"What about our Battle Ensemble?" Sarah asked.

"Oh, yeah. Definitely."

0940 hours
Three miles down the coastal road from
the NATO resort base, Greece

The Osprey had landed at the NATO resort, and Eagle Team had checked in with Commander Preswick-MacPhee's security section. They had been assigned air-conditioned stucco cabins, whitewashed to resemble homes in the Greek islands. Attired in sports clothes, but carrying the Battle Ensembles in backpacks and gym bags, they had checked out of the base in two Renault Twingos, a blue one and a red one. They pulled the tiny cars off the road three miles from the base near a billboard picturing a beautiful young woman in a bikini. She was looking wistfully at the bottle of Ouzo Kallipygos perched on an umbrella table occupied by a leering and mustached young man.

Three hundred yards away were men in Speedos and women in thong bikinis lying on the beach, splashing through the surf, swimming beyond in the sparkling blue water. Others were sitting on the beach, drinking coffee from thermos bottles, eating croissants, or simply lying on blankets in the sand, pressed up against each other. Many of the female bathers, tall, blonde, full-breasted Scandinavians, wore only the bottoms of their bikinis. Children were constructing sand castles or digging in the sand.

Stan and Jack were digging as well. Shielded from the road by the billboard, and surrounded on three sides by two Renault Twingos and five Eagle Team members behaving as though they were having a picnic, they uncovered the handguns, holsters, ammunition, and sheathed knives planted by Stavros Vardakis.

Travis took one of the CZ 75s and gave the other to Jack. He distributed the five HK P9Ss to the rest of the team. Each team member received a combat knife.

As they strapped the weapons on inside the cars, Sarah breathed deeply, smiled, and said, "Mmmm . . . a beautiful sunny, warm day, the shushing of the surf, the smell of salt in the air . . . It feels as though we should be on vacation now."

Sam said, "Hold that thought, Doc."

1045 hours
Downtown Athens, Greece

They had checked into the Herculeum Hotel on Pireos Avenue, a block southwest of Omonia Square and plugged their Battle Ensembles into currency converters to recharge the batteries. From there they drove down Athinas Street in the direction of Monastiraki, and parked the Renaults across the street from each other, around the corner from the meeting place at the Athens Market. Looking like tourists, they leisurely strolled in pairs on opposite sides of the street, taking in the crowds of sightseers and local businessmen and shoppers. The traffic was heavy with all types of vehicles, with drivers swearing at each other adding to the noise of automobile engines, honking horns, and the cries of street vendors, some selling newspapers, some hawking ice cream, others lemonade. The sound of bouzouki music clashed with the blare of Greek rock blasting from car windows. The air was thick with the smell of exhaust fumes mixed with the aroma of strong coffee drifting out of doorways.

"Look!" Sarah said to Travis. He looked up toward where she was pointing and saw it in the distance through a light haze: sun shining on the pillared ruins of the Parthenon atop the Acropolis. Rising right out of the center of this modern, vibrant, noisy city, this gleaming marble temple seemed to hover in the clear blue sky like a celestial vision. In its serene beauty it seemed to be above the turmoil of daily life below.

"Yup." He nodded and continued walking.

They looked across the street and saw the fruits and vegetables market, turned left, and passed through the meat market that surrounds the fish market on three sides.

Sam said, "What's that big wooly animal? It looks like a giant wild boar or a mastadon."

Travis smiled, "I believe that's called a sheep, Sam."

"Right."

They passed from the meat market to the fish market. The pavement was slippery beneath their feet with pungent fishy water. They saw a vast variety of seafood: cod, hake, sardines, octopus, squid, crabs . . . The air was thick with the aroma of sea creatures. They heard the merchants' voices competing with each other in volume as they called out their prices. *Dódeka drachmata! Triskadeka drachmata!*

As he passed one of the stalls, Jack said, "Hey, those are pigs' feet, aren't they?"

Sarah said, "How the heck would I know? Probably."

"Then what in hell are they doing in the fish section?"

Sarah shrugged.

They turned the corner and saw the umbrella-shaded tables and chairs on the crowded street in front of the Café Demetrios. As they came closer they saw Stavros Vardakis sitting at a table close to the plate-glass window reading the *Times* of London. He looked to be in his late thirties. Somewhat stocky, he had dark brown hair and a mustache and was wearing khaki Dockers, a red-and-white striped T-shirt, and a brass-buttoned navy blue blazer. The final touch, fitting the pre-arranged description, was the white carnation in his buttonhole.

Travis and Sarah approached his table and Travis said, "Excuse me. Are these seats taken?"

The man looked up at Travis, cast an admiring eye at Sarah from head to toe, smiled, and said, "No, no. Please sit."

Travis and Sarah sat down and saw that Sam had sat three tables from them. Jack and Jen seemed to be peering into shop windows nearby, while Stan had crossed the street and sat down at the sidewalk table of the Café Thalia across the street.

As prearranged, Travis asked if the man had awakened early that day, "*Xipnises proí?*"

The man smiled and told him he did wake up early, but only because his wife kicked him out of bed.

Travis then asked after the man's health. "*Ti kanis?*"

"*Kalá, evkharistó.*" He told him he was well and thanked him for inquiring. Asking Travis what he wanted, the Greek said, "*Ti thelis?*"

"*Thelo nafao.*" Travis informed him he wanted to eat. Then switching to English, "Do they have good food here?"

"Much better than Denny's, I assure you." It was the correct answer.

"Do you come here often?" Travis asked.

Sticking to the script, the Greek said, "Well, that depends on how busy I am, and if I'm gaining too much weight." He patted his stomach.

Perfect. Travis knew this was Stavros Vardakis. "Good to meet you," he said. "What have you found out?"

Vardakis opened the *Times* to the financial section, and pointed to paragraphs in it as he spoke, as though he were referring to the news items. He said, "My friends on the border patrol tell me that there were three Turkish men who crossed the border at Orestiás eight days ago. They were traveling in a green Fiat Punto, Turkish license plates AG 5210-C."

"How is it that these men were noticed?"

"After they had passed through customs, one of the guards reported to his officer that something had bothered him about these men, but he hadn't known what it was until later."

"Yes . . . ?"

"In the first place, not many Turkish tourists pass from Edirne to Orestiás. Mostly there is commercial traffic from Turkey. Usually in trailer trucks. Most Turks, if they want to visit Greece, will fly to Athens or take a cruise to the Islands. Besides, these men did not look like the vacationing kind."

"How do you mean?"

"They were wearing sports clothes, but they didn't look at ease in them. They didn't look natural."

Travis nodded.

Vardakis continued, "The border patrol develops a sixth sense about these things. Nothing supernatural, it just comes with experience. It's the same when you go from Canada to the U.S. I know this from personal experience. Anyway, when the guard thought about it, he could pin down a few more things."

The waiter approached and asked if he could be of service. Travis ordered two eggs, once over, sausage, coffee and pita bread. Sarah ordered a Greek omelette with feta cheese and tomatoes, coffee, and a croissant.

When the waiter left, Travis said, "What kind of things?"

"For one thing, they never smiled."

"What does that mean?"

"Well, people on vacation usually smile when they are talking to the guards. Even joke and laugh. Even the ones not on vacation, like the truck drivers, usually joke with the guards, too. Not these men. They looked serious. Very serious. They looked like they were not accustomed to laughing or smiling, according to the guards."

"Anything else?"

"Yes. The men's faces. They were lighter skinned around the lower jaw and lips than from the nose up."

Sarah said, "Ah, of course. They had recently shaved off beards and mustaches."

"Yes," Vardakis said, smiling at her. "Now, we know that it is typical of Islamists to wear beards and mustaches. Okay. But all three of these men to have recently shaved . . . ? What for?"

"To not look like Islamists, people who would not likely be traveling as tourists," Sarah said.

"Exactly."

"Clever," Travis said.

"Not clever enough," Vardakis said. "If they had any brains, they would have started to shave longer ago and would have exposed their faces to the weather before making the journey. Or one or two of them would have kept a mustache, so they wouldn't look uniform. No, not the sharpest knives in the drawer, as they say in America."

"I meant it was clever of the guards to notice." Travis resisted the temptation to add, "Too bad they weren't sharp enough to spot it right away and search the car."

"Yes."

"Why haven't the police picked them up? Didn't they put out an APB on them?"

Vardakis smiled and shook his head slowly. "An all-points-bulletin? I'm afraid not."

"But why?"

Vardakis laughed. "Look, the guard reported it to the officer in charge of his station. That officer reported it to his superior here in Athens. From that point on, the report seems to have disappeared into thin air. The only reason I know about it is because that officer is a friend of mine. He owes me. So when I ask, he tells me. Besides, I always make it worth his while, just as your friends make it worth my while."

Vardakis noticed the look in the Americans' eyes. He added, "Look, I love your country almost as much as I love mine. Fortunately, they are allies. What's good for one is good for the other. But . . . A man has to live, no?"

Travis nodded. "Of course. All right. We don't have a hell of a lot of time. Do you know where these boys are now?"

"My network of colleagues tells me that men of their description, riding in a green Fiat Punto, same license plates, stayed at a motel outside of Thessaloníki the night they entered Greece. I had my local people check on second- and third-class hotels and motels in the Athens area, as well as on car rental agencies."

"What did they find?"

"The following evening, that is, seven days ago, three men answering the right description dropped off the Fiat in question to the Hertz Car Rental Agency at twelve Synglou Avenue. From there my people followed them. They took a bus toward the downtown Plaka area. They got off at Ermou Street and Syntagma Square. Ten minutes later they were picked up by a man in a yellow Volkswagen Passat."

"Do you have the license plate number?"

"Yes. Chi Lambda 7264 Alpha."

Sarah said, "Chi is an X, Lambda looks like an upside-down V, and Alpha is the same as our letter A. Right?"

"Exactly." He gave Sarah a big smile.

"Where did they end up?" Travis said.

"Luckily, while one man was on the bus with them, another had followed the bus by automobile. He then followed the Volkswagen."

"And . . . ?"

"They checked into a family-type hotel on Amerikis Street just around the corner from Panepistimiou Avenue. It's on the same street as the Tourist Information Center. Don't be confused if someone refers to Panepistimiou as Venizelou. That's the old name for it."

"You have the exact location. That's great work, Vardakis, really."

"Thank you. I have good people." He smiled. "Oh, the name of the hotel is the Paradissos. No doubt the owners have a sense of humor. Oh, and it caters especially to visitors from the Middle East."

"Do you have the room number?"

"Two of the newly arrived Turks are in room twenty-two. The third one shares room twenty-three across the hall with one of the men who picked them up here in Athens. The passenger in the Volkswagen that picked them up is in room twenty-one with another man. Two more men, who seemed to be in their group, are in room twenty-four."

"How do you know they belong to their group?"

"They were in the welcoming committee when they arrived at the hotel. And who knows, more of them may be in other rooms." Vardakis paused. "Listen, the guy with the device strapped to him . . . He's not the only one who is to be a 'martyr.' The others, I would think, have to stay with him until zero hour to protect him. To make sure no one interferes."

"Makes sense," Travis said. "They're all suicide bombers."

"Right. And every evening they bring in women."

"It's the least they can do," Travis said. "They're probably keeping on a permanent high too with some kind of chemical substance." He thought for a moment. "The women they bring. What kind do they have a hankerin' for?"

"Pardon?"

"Do they like 'em big, small, brunette, blonde . . . ?"

"Ah, now that you mention it, my men commented that usually there seems to be a definite preference for well-endowed blondes."

Sarah looked at her watch. "Travis, we don't have much time. Zero hour is 2359 hours today. It's now 1120 hours."

Vardakis said, "Look, if you go to the Paradissos, you're going to stick out like sore thumbs. You don't look anything like Middle Easterners. Tell you what . . . I will take you to the Paradissos. You will be a bunch of tourists, stingy tourists, I might add, to use that hotel instead of one of the luxury hotels. What languages do you and your people speak? I mean really speak."

"Forget it. We've already checked into a different hotel. And once we get to the Paradissos, we can handle it ourselves."

"But your appearance."

"Trust me, Stavros. We appreciate all you've done, and we sincerely thank you for offering to help us further. But, believe me, we have a way of getting in and out without even being seen. It's part of our equipment. You don't have that advantage, so . . ."

"Without being seen!?"

"Trust me."

Vardakis said, "A lot is hanging on your success, you know?" He sounded worried.

Travis spoke as soothingly as possible. "Believe me, I

don't want to see Athens wiped off the map. I don't want nuclear war to break out. And I don't particularly feel like being vaporized myself. Have confidence, my friend." Travis stood up, followed by Sarah. He then said to Vardakis, "Oh, Stavros. You can help us out a little bit more."

"Yes? Tell me what you want."

"I want you to come with us and direct us to a boutique. You know, where they sell sexy women's clothes."

Vardakis and Sarah stared at Travis.

"Did you say 'sexy women's clothes'?" Sarah said.

"Let me re-phrase that, women's sexy clothes."

Sarah said, "Travis, what . . . ?"

Vardakis said, "Ah, I believe I understand." He leered at Sarah.

"Not just for her. For that blonde over there too." He jutted his jaw in the direction of Jen, who was strolling along the sidewalk with Jack, peering into store windows.

Vardakis paused to admire her and then said, "Do they speak Greek or Turkish?"

"No."

"Then you need me to bring them in and introduce them. I shall be delighted to play the part of procurer. But first, I'll have to head off two of the women they scheduled for tonight and their pimps."

"You know them?"

"Of course."

Travis rubbed his chin thoughtfully for a moment. "You're on, Stavros. But that's as far as it goes. Once they've been introduced, you leave."

"Fair enough. By the way, I'll say she's from Sweden. They'll really like that."

Travis said, "At what time of day do they bring the prostitutes?"

"They started by bringing them at around ten at night, and they stay for a couple of hours. But they've been advancing the hour each day, and prolonging the time with the women."

"Makes sense. As the time gets closer, they're more and more nervous. What was the timing last night?"

"Yesterday they brought them in at about seven o'clock in the evening. The women stayed until two in the morning."

Travis said, "You better find out when they're scheduled for tonight. I bet they plan to have the women with them right up to the end."

Vardakis nodded. "Okay. I'll take the two women to the Aphrodite Boutique for their fancy clothing, then I'll go find the pimps and deal with them."

As they walked to their cars, Sarah quietly said, "It *is* going to be in broad daylight, Trav. And the weapons we'll be using aren't ours, so we won't be able to conceal them with our Battle Ensemble sheaths. When we pull a gun out, it will be visible."

"Well, then," he drawled, "we won't pull the guns out too soon and wave them around, now will we, Sarah darlin'? Besides, we might not even need them for the main event."

Chapter 15

Stavros Vardakis had helped Jen and Sarah purchase the proper attire for the evening's activities. He was now in an *ouzerie-cafeneon* upstairs from the vegetable market. Workmen on afternoon break were at the bar or sitting at tables smoking and chatting, some drinking the clear anise-flavored 80-proof ouzo, others imbibing Metaxa brandy. Still others sipped their thick, syrupy coffee from demi-tasse cups.

Vardakis spotted the man at a corner table in the depths of the smoke-filled room. The man, in his early thirties, had a shaved head, a handlebar mustache, several small gold rings in his ear, and a gold stud in his nose.

Vardakis walked to the man's table, said, "*Yasu*," and sat down.

The other man looked at him quizzically and nodded.

Vardakis said, "*Ti kanis?*"

"*Kalá*," the man replied wearily.

"Just having breakfast so late in the day, Evstratios, my friend?"

Evstratios Pappas took a drag on his Turkish cigarette and unhurriedly let the smoke flow out of his mouth and nostrils. Then he turned to Vardakis. "To what do I owe the honor, Stavros?"

"Listen to me Evstratios. This is very important. A matter of life and death."

"Please . . ." He sneered. "Life and death my ass. Give me a break, Stavros."

"Evstratios, listen to me. I am not exaggerating. I said life and death, and I meant it."

Pappas stared at Vardakis's face for a moment and saw that he was dead serious. "Whose life or death?"

"Yours."

Pappas glanced at the holstered Colt .45 under Vardakis's jacket. "*Skatá*! Are you threatening me!?"

"No, Evstratios. I am definitely not threatening you. I am telling you that if you don't do me a favor, then both you and I, and a lot of other people are going to die. Very soon."

"What the hell are you talking about, Vardakis?"

"Look, those men at the Paradissos . . . How many of the women do you supply?"

"I bring them four. The other four are supplied by two other guys. But, what . . . ?"

"We don't have a lot of time. Listen carefully. I need you to bring only two tonight. I will bring two women myself."

"What . . . !? You are going into my business?"

"No, Evstratios, I am not going to compete with you. The women I am going to bring are not really prostitutes. I just want them to seem so."

"I don't know what the hell is going on, but I'll be losing money."

"Don't worry about that. I'll pay you. I'm telling you, Evstratios, it is a matter of life and death. For you, for me, for a lot of people."

"Could you explain this to me?"

Vardakis sighed. "No, my friend. I'm afraid I really cannot explain it. Not yet, anyway."

"But . . ."

"Believe me, Evstratios. I absolutely cannot explain it at this time. But it is vital that you do me this favor. This is no joking matter."

Pappas thought for a moment, then said, "Stavros, I have known you for a long time. You are a nosy bastard and one stiff pain in the ass. You can be a real prick." Pappas saw Stavros open his mouth to speak but cut him off. "However," Pappas said, "however, I know you to be an honest man, a man of your word. So I have no choice but to believe what you say. You have never lied to me, and it wouldn't make sense for you to want to play pimp unless you had a good reason."

"Then . . . ?"

"Yes, damn it."

"Wonderful, Evstratios, my good friend!" Vardakis slapped Pappas on the back. "Oh, and listen, there will be no need for you to bring the other two women either. They would only be in danger."

Vardakis stood, bent over, and in a low voice added, "Oh, and Evstratios . . . Please don't warn these fellows. Because if you do, there's a very good chance that you and I and the rest of Athens will die if they are successful. But if you should warn them, and they still are not successful, then I will come and kill you myself. That *is* a threat. And you know I honor my word."

1315 hours
The Herculeum Hotel, Athens, Greece

The members of the Eagle Team were gathered in Travis's room. Travis said, "Okay, Sarah, we bought those small syringes in a medical supply store, a mortar and pestle, and a small bottle of cough syrup in a pharmacy . . ."

"Guaifenecin with dextromethorphan," Sarah said.

Travis continued, ". . . a bottle of aspirin in a second pharmacy, some chemical in a pest-control supply house, and some olive oil in a grocery store."

"Sounds real healthful," Sam wryly commented.

"Except maybe for the pest control shit," Jack said.

"If you're going to use a hypodermic, wouldn't it be simpler to use hydrogen cyanide," Sam asked.

"Yes," Sarah said, "It's even more potent than phosgene, and would be the perfect blood agent for individual assassination. But we don't happen to have any with us, since we weren't expecting this kind of scenario, and I certainly wouldn't try to acquire any here in Greece. It would attract attention."

"What about simply injecting an air bubble into the bloodstream?" Travis said.

"Yes, but you'd have to be sure you inserted it into a blood vessel. Victims tend to be uncooperative in their own assassination, you know, and not hold still long enough for us to accurately get the needle into the right spot. This material I'm going to whip up can be stuck anywhere in the flesh, and it'll work. Even a scratch that breaks the skin will do it." Sarah paused. "God, how I hate this method of fighting."

Stan said, "You mean by injection?"

"Yes, there's just something so . . . so sinister about it. But not only that. Using sex to kill a man . . ."

Travis said, "Yes, Sarah, I know. But don't forget who we're dealing with: rapists, mass murderers of innocent men, women, and children. And, as we speak, they're ready to set off a nuclear device in the heart of a huge city. You, more than anyone else, know what the effects of that would be."

"Of course, Travis, I understand all that. And don't worry, I'll do it."

"I know you will." He looked at the boxes and bottles on the tables. "Okay, Sarah, now what do you do with all those ingredients?" Travis asked.

"Watch," she said.

Sarah took a handful of aspirin and placed them in the mortar. Then, using the pestle, she crushed the aspirin into a fine powder. She poured a teaspoonful of the red cough remedy into the mortar and stirred this combination until the aspirin dissolved completely in the thick red liquid, turning it pink.

"Hand me the packet of Lethosias, Stan," Sarah said.

She saw he looked puzzled, so she clarified, "That Greek pest-control stuff."

Stan handed her the packet, and she poured two teaspoonfuls of the powder into the mortar. Then she stirred slowly until it was absorbed into the mixture.

"Okay," she said, "now, the olive oil . . ."

She reached for the small bottle of Korinthos Olive Oil and poured two teaspoonfuls into the mortar. Once more she stirred until the ingredients were thoroughly blended.

Jen said, "Looks disgusting. Makes you want to puke."

"Vomiting would be the thing to do if you swallowed this stuff, Jen. But no one's going to have to take it orally. Stan, could you get me a glass of tap water?"

When Stan brought the water, Sarah poured a quarter of the glass into the mortar and mixed thoroughly. Then she reached into her pack and extracted a tiny glass vial containing a purple liquid.

"What the hell is that?" Jack asked.

"It's my own mixture. I make it out of several herbs that grow wild in the Pyrenees. Perfectly harmless in itself, some of them are used in making a Basque brandy. But when I add a couple of drops to this mixture . . ."

She poured the purple liquid into the mortar. There was a hissing sound, tiny bubbles appeared on the surface of the mixture, and a puff of vapor rose from the mortar. She looked at Jen and said, "All right, Jen, let's load the syringes."

Jen said, "Travis, when do we have to get into our slut costumes?"

"Vardakis said that the pimp said they were to get the women there at 1800 hours."

"It's a shame to have to kill so much time," Stan said.

Travis said, "Yeah, I know. But we can't go in blasting away in a frontal attack. He'd be sure to push the button before we got to him. But this way, with the women, is the easiest way, and the surest way to neutralize these bastards and prevent a catastrophe. And they just won't be expecting the women before that time, so we can't go too much earlier."

Jack said, "Okay, Trav, let's go over the plan again."

Travis nodded. "Right. Vardakis, acting as pimp, shows up at the Paradissos Hotel with Jen and Sarah. Jen goes with the bomb carrier, and Sarah with any of the other eight . . ."

Sam interrupted, "Trav, how do we arrange it so Jen goes with the bomb carrier? Suppose someone else wants her."

"Vardakis said that the bomb carrier seems to be given first choice, and . . ."

"Hey," Sarah said. "What am I, chopped liver?"

"What?"

"I mean, how do you know he won't pick me?"

Travis looked down at the floor for a moment. Then, "Well, Vardakis said they seem to prefer them big and blonde. I guess it's a novelty for them. And you're damn sexy, Sarah, but you're petite and brunette."

Stan said, "I'd pick you, Sarah. No offense, Jen, but I like 'em small and dark."

"Anyway, if the bomber picks Sarah," Travis said, "that's no problem either. It doesn't matter which one of the two offs the man. Just as long as one of them is picked."

"Suppose the bomber picks one of the four other women?" Sam said.

"That's why we're going to get there a half hour before time."

Stan said, "Okay, Trav, we get there at 1730 hours."

"Right. Then Jen and Sarah go to their rooms with the two men. They'll be separate rooms. They like their privacy. No kinky orgies or stuff like that."

Jack said, "According to Vardakis, they take turns, right? I mean, only two men are with the women at any given time."

"Right. Three men are in the hallway outside the rooms, and three of them are down near the reception desk. Vardakis thinks they must be packing heat, like we are."

Sam said, "We're using our Battle Ensemble . . ."

"Yes. Here's the tricky part. We can't ride around Athens in those uniforms, and we sure as hell can't ride around while invisible. Either way it would be sure to attract attention."

"Then . . . ?" Jack said.

"Right next door to the hotel is a greasy spoon, according to Vardakis. It has bathrooms. We walk in, go straight to the men's room and change into our BEs. And activate the stealth mode immediately."

"Won't the customers think it's strange to see the men's room door open and close with no one going through?" Jen said.

Travis shrugged and said, "We can't worry about that."

"All five of us dudes can't go in at the same time," Jack said. "The locals might think we're havin' some kind of party in there."

Travis smiled. "Jack, you and Sam go first. Then Stan and I. Now, while we're changing into the BEs, the girls are parked in the car with Vardakis. His window will be open on the driver's side. Naturally, he, and you ladies, won't see us, since we'll be invisible. When we're ready,

I'll reach inside the car and blast the horn. One long, two shorts, and a long."

"That's when we go into action," Jen said.

"Yes, and we come in right behind you. When you go upstairs, we wait fifteen minutes, just to be sure you had the chance to eliminate the two men. Then we kill the three guards downstairs. Silently, with the knives. Then we come upstairs and do the three men in the hallway. We enter the two rooms where you ladies are with what should by then be corpses. Next we disarm the bomb, take it with us, and get the hell out of there."

"What about the desk clerk?" Sam said.

"That poses a dilemma. We don't want to hurt him, but we don't want him sounding an alarm."

"So what do we do?" Sarah said.

"Look, it'll take only three of us to kill the three guards. That'll be Stan, Jack, and me. Simultaneously, Sam, you'll gag and tie up the desk clerk and shove him into the back office."

"What about if the four local ladies of the night arrive a little early, before we get out of there, and see the corpses in the lobby?" Jen said.

"I've spoken to Stavros. There's a change in plans. He's going to send a friend of his, an off-duty policeman in uniform. He'll stroll back and forth in front of the hotel entrance. If he sees the prostitutes heading his way, he'll sort of 'arrest' them, put them in a borrowed paddy wagon, drive them across town, and then turn them loose."

"That's if all goes as planned," Stan said. "Of course, it never does with Mr. Murphy always hangin' around ready to shaft a guy."

Sam said, in a solemn tone, "Plans are a basis for change."

Stan said, "Confucius, right?"

Jack said, "Sounds more like Sun Tzu, *The Art of War*, but it isn't."

Sam opened his mouth to speak, but was cut off by Travis who said, "Gur Golani, colonel, Israel Defense Force, retired."

Sam looked surprised.

Travis said, "I've met the man." Then he checked his watch and said, "The bomb is supposed to be detonated at

2359 hours tonight. That's ten hours and twenty minutes from now. We're going to get to the Paradissos at 1730 hours, which is four and half hours from now. It could take up to half an hour to get there, but that's rush hour. We'd better be right in the neighborhood an hour earlier. The stimulants we took are still operative, so there's no use trying to get any actual shut-eye for now. Let's get room service to send some sandwiches."

Travis was about to tell Sam to ring Vardakis's cell phone when he saw that Sam had already picked up the phone and was punching in the numbers the Greek private eye had given them.

Sam waited for Vardakis to answer, then, "Stavros, Sam here. The show starts at five-thirty. We'll be hanging around the theater from around four-thirty. Right. See you there."

1510 hours
Hotel Paradissos, Athens, Greece

Edip Bir, a thin twenty-eight-year-old man with gaunt features, was smoking as he lay fully clothed on his rumpled bed. His hand trembled as he brought the smoldering joint to his lips. His open shirt revealed the black device strapped to his chest. An equally thin young man, Alper Gunel, nervously paced back and forth in the hotel room. The door opened, and Zafer Yazoglu, a short, stocky forty-year-old with crew-cut black hair, entered and sat down in an armchair. He sighed.

Alper Gunel suddenly stopped pacing. "What!" he said. "Mehmet. He's gone."

Edip Bir stared at Zafer Yazoglu and took another drag on the joint.

Gunel said, "Gone? What do you mean?"

Yazoglu stretched his legs out in front of him, leaned back in the chair, and matter-of-factly said, "The two downstairs, Erdogan and Ismail Hakki, say he went to the men's room an hour ago and never came out. Erdogan went to investigate a half hour ago. The room was empty and the window was open. I expect the cowardly piece of shit is about to board a plane to who-knows-where at this very moment."

"What now?" Gunel said.

Yazoglu sneered at the question. He folded his muscular arms in front of his chest and said, "What do you mean, 'What now?' It makes no difference. We proceed according to plan."

"Plan?" Gunel said, "The plan is fucked. There has been no nuclear explosion in Tel Aviv."

"Bah," Yazoglu said, "there has probably been a total news blackout. It is being kept a secret for the present. I am sure that the Zionist entity is mortally wounded."

"And there is no communication with Kara Kale or with Rauf Pasha from any location."

"He was to communicate with us only if our mission was to be called off. Obviously, the satanic government in Ankara has still not complied with our leader's holy demands. Therefore, the mission has not been called off."

Yazoglu studied the man on the bed. "Edip," he called to Bir, "you don't look well."

Bir, without turning his head toward Yazoglu, mumbled, "What . . . ?"

"I said, you don't look well."

"Well, then, I look like I feel."

Yazoglu stood and strode toward the bed. He spoke cheerfully. "*Haydi, Edipcik*! Come on, Edip, my boy! Buck up! Soon we will be in Paradise, out of this miserable world, waited on hand and foot by the beautiful *houris*, our every desire satisfied. And even before we get there, there will be no suffering, no lingering death, like your mother who suffered with excruciating disease for two years before succumbing. You just push the button, and the next thing you know, you are among the other blessed martyrs. God Himself will welcome you."

Bir turned his head toward Yazoglu. "Yes, Zafer. I know. I know. It's just this accursed waiting and waiting . . . I'd like to push the button right now and have done with it."

Yazoglu looked from Bir to Gunel and back to Bir. "Well, maybe it would be a good idea after all . . ."

Gunel said, "But Zafer, we need to follow Rauf Pasha's

orders. Perhaps the Turkish government will yet surrender to our demands."

"It is getting very late for that."

"But we must be disciplined. Things can change at the last minute. Besides, we need to follow our leader's commands."

"Yes, Alper, you are right, of course. But, at this point, I can't wait to destroy this hotbed of infidels, our ancient enemies. I can't wait to look down from Paradise and know that this immense stinking dung heap has disappeared from the earth."

Gunel said, "I am very nervous too, and I'm anxious to get this over with. But I can wait a few hours more. Let us at least have some fun with the infidel women who will be here shortly. Since it will be the last time with them, we can torture the filthy infidel whores slowly as well. Then, after we have our pleasure with them, we will all leave this wretched world, knowing that while we will be in eternal ecstasy, those swinish women, and the rest of Athens, this Sodom and Gomorrah, will descend straight to the everlasting fires of hell. *Evet! Hay! Hay!*"

Yazoglu turned to Bir. "Do you hear what our friend said, Edip? Can you hold out?"

Bir seemed distracted.

Yazoglu prompted him, "Edip, can you hold out?"

Bir turned to Yazoglu and stared at him, or beyond him, for several seconds before answering. Then, *"Evet.* Yes." His voice sounded distant. He turned away from Yazoglu to stare at the wall across the room, and with a trembling hand brought the marijuana cigarette to his lips. He took a deep puff, then he looked down at the button on the device under his shirt, closed his eyes, and exhaled the pungent smoke with a sigh.

Chapter 16

1723 hours
The Kali Orexia Restaurant, next door
to the Hotel Paradissos, Athens, Greece

A middle-aged man in work clothes got up from the table and made his way back to the men's room. His shoulder glanced against something solid that he didn't see. He stopped for a moment, puzzled. Then he shrugged and continued to head for the bathroom. He thought he saw the door open and then close, yet he saw no one go in or come out. He thought he saw some kind of shimmering, like heat waves, in front of the door. He stopped, removed his glasses, and rubbed his eyes. Then he took out a handkerchief and rubbed his eyeglass lenses. *I must go to the ophthalmologist more often,* he told himself, *or stop drinking so much retsina wine with my dolmadakia.*

Two men with seven-days' growth of beard lounged in arm chairs in the lobby of the Hotel Paradissos. They had arranged the chairs so that they faced the entrance. The bulges under their jackets suggested pistols in shoulder holsters. The elderly Greek desk clerk sat on a stool behind the reception desk watching an old Cary Grant/Audrey Hepburn movie on the little screen. Cary Grant spoke perfect Greek, but his voice was an octave higher than usual. The younger of the two Turks looked about twenty years old. He kept craning his neck to watch the TV screen. The other man, about thirty years old, said something to him in Turkish. The younger man then turned back to look out at the street.

Erdogan, the younger man, smiled and stood up in his enthusiasm. "Here they come!"

Ismail Hakki, the thirty-year-old, stood and said, "Well, open the door for them, kid."

The two women, followed by Stavros Vardakis, strutted into the lobby. Sarah wore an outfit that resembled the classic French maid's uniform: black dress reaching down only to midthigh, slit to a point just three inches below the hip, tiny white apron, black fishnet stockings with seams in the back, and high-heeled black pumps. Jen wore black too: black leather hip-hugging short shorts and a black leather halter that lifted, separated, and presented her ample breasts as though they were honeydew melons on a black tray. She also wore a black sea captain's visored cap and high-heeled black leather boots.

Vardakis, trying not to look like the private eye that he was, wore borrowed clothing. He sported wide black trousers, a red shirt, and a white jacket, which concealed his Colt .45 pistol.

The elderly desk clerk's mouth fell open, showing yellow teeth and blank spaces when he turned around to look at the women. Then he rubbed his eyes when he thought he saw the entrance and the walls near it seem to move. He felt as though he could see air moving. He told himself he shouldn't watch so much television. Then he looked back at the women.

Vardakis walked over to the desk and spoke to the clerk in Greek. Ismail Hakki and Erdogan stared at the women approvingly.

"Where other women?" Ismail Hakki asked in broken Greek.

"I suppose they'll be here pretty soon. We're a few minutes early. But what the hell do I know about the other ones?"

Ismail Hakki continued in broken Greek. "You," he said to Jen, "go room two-two." To Sarah he said, "You, go room two-three."

Vardakis explained that the women were foreigners, the tall blonde from Sweden, and the petite brunette from

France. Then he gave the two women their instructions in English.

The women took the staircase, with the men staring after their sculpted legs and swaying behinds. Vardakis went out into the street.

Erdogan commented to Ismail Hakki, "*Bu kadinler çok güzel!*"

Ismail Hakki said with irritation, "Yes, these women are very beautiful. Your turn will come. Now keep your eyes on the street."

Erdogan turned toward the door and window. "Ah, here come the other women, the ones from yesterday."

The two Turks watched with anticipation.

"Wait . . . What the hell is this?" Ismail Hakki said.

Erdogan answered, "The policeman is approaching them. He has stopped them. He's saying something to them. One of them just gave him the finger. He smacked her. He's taking them back down the street to a police van."

"Shit," Ismail Hakki said. "Pain-in-the-ass Greek sodomite police. What the hell do they care if some real men want to have some fun? Sons of bitches!"

"What now, Ismail Hakki?"

"We'll just have to share the two upstairs."

"Wonderful!"

"Yes, but it means waiting around. Less time with them. Too much time to kill before . . . Too much time to think."

1735 hours
Room 23, Hotel Paradissos

Sarah, in her French maid costume, knocked on the door. Zafer Yazoglu, wearing only a pair of undershorts and a shoulder holster containing a Brazilian-made Taurus 9mm pistol, peered through the peephole, then eagerly removed the chain and unlocked the door. He opened the door, stuck his head out, and looked both ways along the corridor. He saw Jen entering Edip Bir's room, and Alper Gunel leaving, to give Bir his privacy.

He grabbed Sarah by the arm, pulled her in, and shut the door, remembering to lock it and replace the chain.

Then he seized her around the waist and pressed against her. In Turkish, which he knew she didn't understand, he said, "I'm going to bang it home until you scream for mercy, you European bitch. Then the others can have you. Finally, we'll slowly torture you to death before the big blast." It gave him a charge to be able to tell her what they were going to do, even if she didn't understand.

Sarah had no idea what he was saying, but she smiled as lasciviously as she could. As his hands moved down, slid under her skirt, and caressed her behind, Sarah slipped her hand into the pocket of her white apron and extracted the small hypodermic syringe. She lightly seized his right earlobe between her teeth, a move that excited him while distracting him from noticing the slight prick of the needle on his left buttock. She swiftly replaced the syringe in her pocket.

Yazoglu leaned back and began to fumble with the buttons at the top of her dress. Suddenly, he stopped. He put his hand to his forehead and a look of puzzlement covered his face. Then his eyes rolled up into his head as he sagged to the floor. Sarah reached down and took his Taurus from the holster.

1735 hours
Room 22, Hotel Paradissos

Edip Bir opened the door for Jen. The slim young man's eyes bulged when he saw the statuesque blonde beauty in black leather. He stood transfixed for a couple of moments, staring at her. She put out her hand to caress his stubbly face, but he backed away while raising his hand as though to say "wait."

Jen noticed the odor of sweat mixed with cannabis and spotted the brown cigarettes on one of the nightstands. She waited as he took off his shirt, baring the apparatus harnessed to his chest. The size of a portable Japanese radio, it was black and ugly, and had two red buttons. Bir undid the harness and placed the bomb on the table next to the bed. He pointed to it, then wagged his finger back and forth and brokenly repeated the phrase he had memorized in Greek, English, and French that meant "Do not touch."

Then, standing by the bed, he motioned for Jen to come over to him. She took off her cap and let her blonde hair hang free. She walked over to him and lightly shoved him so that he fell backward onto the bed. Then she straddled him. Looking up at her face, her hair, her breasts, he stroked her thighs.

The young man seemed so harmless, Jen had to psych herself to kill him. This was the first time this had ever happened to her. All the other enemies she had faced were shooting at her, or attacking her in one way or another. Or at the very least looked tough. She especially hated using her sexuality for this purpose. Then she looked at the ugly black box on the table.

She lay down full on top of him and slowly began to kiss his face, his neck, his ear . . . He closed his eyes, sighed, made little whimpering sounds like a puppy begging for dinner, and put his arms around her. *At least he'll feel good before he feels nothing.* She extracted the syringe from a small pocket in the leather skirt. Then, so he wouldn't notice the needle prick, she inserted her tongue into his ear and pressed her nails in the flesh of his left shoulder as she pierced the skin of his right shoulder.

But he did notice. In a sudden burst of energy, he pushed her off him and onto the floor, reached out to the bomb, and pushed one of the red buttons. Jen reached up and grabbed his wrist before he could push the second button. He struggled for one second, then his arm went limp. His eyes rolled up, and he fell back to the bed.

My God! He's pushed the button!

She sprang to her feet, ran to the door, and opened it as she saw Sarah emerging from the room across the hall.

"Travis," she called down the staircase, "do the job now! Fast! But send Sam up here right now!"

1752 hours
The lobby of the Hotel Paradissos

Ismail Hakki and Erdogan jumped out of their seats and jerked their heads toward the loud voice of a woman speaking English at the head of the stairs. They drew their weapons. The old man at the desk called out *"Ti thelis? Ti thelis?"* asking in Greek what Jen wanted.

Stan, invisible and from behind, clapped his left arm tightly against Ismail Hakki's nose and mouth to cut off his breathing and any cry that might be heard by other possible guards, or other guests or passersby. He followed up immediately by plunging the knife downward into the area between the neck and the shoulder bones, severing the man's jugular vein and carotid artery simultaneously. Ismail Hakki's blood immediately began to drain down his windpipe and into his lungs, drowning him in his own blood. He quickly lost consciousness as his brain's oxygen supply was cut off. He went limp and sagged in Stan's arms.

Stan hated this kind of hands on, personal killing, where he was practically embracing the man he was butchering. But it was silent, if done correctly, and efficient. So it had to be done. When he first learned the technique and practiced with dummies, it seemed almost fun. But the first time he actually performed the operation on a real human being, he puked and almost gave away his position to the enemy. The second and third times were slightly better. By now, it was a job, and he was good at it. But he liked it about as much as he liked having his prostate examined.

At the same moment that Stan grabbed Ismail Hakki, Jack, standing behind Erdogan, seized the young man's hair in his left hand, and with his right hand plunged his knife into the base of his skull at the point where the spinal column begins. The man died instantaneously and collapsed to the floor.

The elderly desk clerk was horrified and overwhelmed with shock. He saw only two other men in the lobby. Suddenly, their heads snapped back. Blood gushed like a geyser from a wound opened between one man's neck and shoulders, and he floated downward to the floor. A thin line of blood appeared at the base of the other man's skull and he dropped like a bag of lead to the floor. All this as if caused by ghosts or evil spirits, and without even a single sound from the victims' mouths.

He heard the sound of feet pounding up the staircase, but saw no one on the stairs. Even while watching these uncanny phenomena, he felt something cover his mouth and shove him into the back office, and then lock the door. It was Travis, yet the clerk saw no one. He thought he must be going mad. This idea was reinforced by seeing, or thinking he saw, the walls and even the staircase move again. And then the telephone wire being ripped out of the wall. Perhaps he was seeing ghosts, actual ghosts?

The entire operation, from the time Stan hooked his arm around the guard's neck until he gently deposited him on the ground, took five seconds. The adrenalin generated by this act made his heart race, and he waited five seconds before dashing up the stairs two steps at a time right behind Jack and in front of Travis.

As soon as Sam had observed Ismail Hakki's and Erdogan's heads snap back, he raced up the stairs and was the first to join Sarah and Jen.

"I'm here, Jen," Sam said. "What is it?"

"In there," she said, pointing to the open door of room 22. "He pushed one of the two buttons."

Sam rushed into the room.

As Jack, Stan, and Travis reached the top of the stairs, they heard footsteps hurriedly clomping down from the third floor. They looked up and saw two men, guns in their hands, rushing down the stairs, yelling in Turkish. They sized up the situation. Jen, Sarah, and Sam were in room 22 with the door open. Travis had to make a split-second decision. In one second they would see the bodies of the men on the floor of the hotel lobby and would see Jen and Sarah in room 22 with the deceased martyr.

Travis whispered through the transmitter of the Battle Sensor Helmet, "Jack, I'll kill the first guy. You take the second. Knives."

The first man landed on the carpeted corridor of the second floor. Travis stepped in front of him and jammed his knife directly through the man's throat, cutting off the flow of air to the lungs and severing his vocal cords in one fell swoop. The man's eyes opened wide, and he sank to the floor.

The man two steps behind him stopped suddenly as he saw his comrade fall. He heard gurgling sounds as the man squirmed on the floor, spraying blood from his throat. He could see no one else around and started shooting wildly in a panic. Bullets whizzed by Travis, Jack, and Stan and went through walls and the floor.

Jack rushed toward him and thrust his knife into the man's chest cavity just below the sternum, blade up, the tip of the knife slanting upward to penetrate the heart. The man sank to the stairs and tumbled the last two steps to land on top of his dead partner.

Stan spoke through the microbio-chip communicator, "Shit, how many more of these suicide fuckers are there around?"

Travis said, "Don't know. But those gunshots . . . We didn't want any noise. We've got to hurry." Then he addressed Sam over the communicator. "Sam, what's up?"

"The guy managed to push one of two buttons."

Travis said, "Okay, I'm coming in. Jack, keep watch on the staircases. Stan, come with me to room 22 and keep watch on the hallway."

Travis entered room 22 and saw the black box with two red buttons. It was rising in the air, and he knew that Sam was handling it.

"Sam, what's happening?"

"This guy," Sam said, indicating the dead man, "pushed one of the two buttons. That's like cocking a gun, so to speak. All you'd need would be to have the other button pushed, and . . . I mean, someone could just lean on it accidentally. So I disabled it with the HERF gun."

"Yeah," Travis said, "but we've still got to disarm it."

"Without setting it off," Stan said.

"How about it, Sam, can you do it?"

"I think so, Boss."

"Look," Travis said, "we want to get the hell out of here as soon as possible, so we don't want to work on the damn bomb here."

Stan said, "Yeah, but how do we get it out of here without the chance of pushing the other button, and without anyone seeing it?"

"I can stick it under my camouflage suit. We still have plenty of time before our Low Observable capability is exhausted. As far as pushing the button . . ."

"Okay," Travis said. He took the device and put it under his uniform. "Jen, Sarah. Our cars are parked right down the block. Here are the keys to the blue Twingo. Your touristy sports clothes are in the trunk. Get them and go change in the ladies' room of the restaurant next door. Sam, you lock yourself in the men's room and work on that bomb. We'll see to it that no one tries to go in."

"Right, Boss."

As they left, still invisible, ordinary Middle Eastern businessmen and tourist family groups were cautiously peeping out of their doorways.

1753 hours
The men's room of the Kali Orexia Restaurant

The entire team had used the restrooms to change into civilian clothes. Except for Sam, they had ordered something to eat, in order to look natural. They could hear the sirens of police cars converging on the Hotel Paradissos next door.

Sam now occupied the men's room. He sat on the lid of the toilet seat in one of the two stalls. He had the nuclear device on his lap. His tool kit was on the top of the toilet tank. With a Phillips screwdriver he removed the lid, reached back and placed it on the tank cover. He studied the mechanism. He saw that a tiny lever had been cocked and that the second button's being pushed would release it, allowing it to make contact with the ignition.

At that point, pressure on the second button would set off the explosion. But even now, there was no guarantee that if he accidentally jarred the cocked lever, it might not connect with the ignition.

Beads of perspiration appeared on his forehead and trickled down into his eyes. His glasses tended to slide down from the bridge of his nose, and he had to constantly push them back up. His Hawaiian shirt was damp with perspiration. He was not familiar with this particular type of apparatus, but was the most qualified in the group. Two wires, one red, one green, led from the cocked lever to the primer, which would then set off the nuclear explosion. One of the wires had cocked the lever. The other one would set off the primer. But which was which? They both seemed to connect the lever to the primer and to both red buttons. Why? To throw off anyone who tried to disarm it? The hand that held the wire cutter began to tremble.

He carefully placed the device on the top of the tank, left the stall, and opened the door. He looked out and called to Stan, motioning for him to come in.

Stan got up and went to the men's room. "What?"

"Stan," Sam said, "I'm the technical man, but I've never seen this kind of setup. You're our demolitions expert. You might know more about it than I do."

"Never send a techno-weenie to do a demolition man's job. Stick that in your Sun Tzu. Okay, let's put the damn thing out here on the sink. More room for two guys to work."

Sam brought the device and the tool kit out of the stall and placed it on the sink.

"Shit!" Stan grumbled. "Who the hell built this fucking thing?"

"Complicated?"

"No, too simple. Those crazy bastards made it so simple, you could set the damn thing off by farting too close to it." He took the smallest screwdriver and said, "Sam, hold the lever with your finger. Don't let it release."

Stan inserted the screwdriver into the Phillips head screw that held the lever to its metal platform and unscrewed it. "Okay, Sammy, lift the lever up and away."

"What should I do with it?"

"Just stick it in your pocket. Now, by the way, we do not want to put any pressure on these wires, but we do want to sever them. One at a time. The correct one first. The problem is, if I sever the wrong one first . . . Well, it's *luti, luti, luti/dobre, dobre buti,* as they say in Polish."

"Meaning?"

"If it's raining, you ought to wear your boots. Shit, it rhymes in Polish."

Sam stared at Stan uncomprehendingly.

"Never mind. You know what I mean." He took a deep breath. "Okay, hand me the wire cutter."

Sam handed it to him. Stan grasped it and stared at the wires for a full five seconds. Then he placed it on the green wire, sighed, and cut. He sighed again.

Sam said, "Great!"

They heard a humming sound emanate from the device, and looked at each other.

Sam said, "It's activated again."

"Really?" Stan's tone was ironic. "This goddamn apparatus is so simple that there are fewer parts to interact with each other, and mutually fuck each other up. Maybe the blast from the HERF gun didn't actually short it out."

"So now we cut the red wire."

"Yeah, except . . ."

"What?"

"Look. Since we thought the device was deactivated when I cut the green wire, I don't know if it was the one that cocks the lever, or the one that ignites the primer. So the red one could have been either one too."

"So, now that it's activated, cutting the red one should sever the connection if it's the one that sparks the primer, right? And if it's the one that cocked the lever, it doesn't really matter. Right?"

"Theoretically. But this device is so crappily made, there's a possibility that cutting the wire might set off the primer."

"Then what . . . ?"

"We don't have any choice. If we don't cut it, and we transport it in that condition, any little thing might set it off."

"Then . . ."

"Then pray, 'cause I'm cutting." He placed the wire cutter on the red wire, looked at Sam for a second, turned back to the wire, held his breath, and cut. The hum ceased. Then he closed his eyes and exhaled. After a moment, he looked at Sam and said, "Okay, shove the whole thing in your gym bag so we can take it back home."

Epilogue

They could hear the rhythmic crash and shushing of the surf and felt exhilarated by the smell of the salt air and the scent of tropical flowers wafting through the open windows.

They had been unwinding for several days on a secluded Government-owned compound on Virgin Gorda Island in the U.S. Virgin Islands. Their accommodations on the beach consisted of small, pastel-colored stucco lodgings, but these little bungalows contained the most modern comforts and facilities.

There was a main building for group activities, which contained a bar, pool tables, Ping-Pong tables, a library, comfortable furniture, and a wide-screen television set. On the premises were a golf course, a swimming pool, tennis courts, and a sauna. A yacht suitable for deep-sea fishing was docked at the wharf.

One evening, after a day of fishing, swimming, and tennis, Jennifer Olsen, Jacques DuBois, Hunter Blake, and Stan Powczuk were sitting around a pine table in the main building, playing poker.

Across the room, Sam Wong was about to checkmate Sarah Greene's king, when Travis Barrett, sprawled out on a leather-upholstered couch before the TV, said, "Hey, y'all, listen up!"

Jack, his hands cupped around a pile of chips he was about to pull in, looked toward the screen, as did Sam, his right hand holding his queen in midair, his left hand in a death grip on a can of Mountain Dew. Everyone gave their attention to the tube.

On the screen, wearing his signature bad hairdo, as well as his habitual look of sincerity and concern, was Ted Koppel. They heard Ted say, ". . . to elaborate on this affair, we have with us tonight the Turkish Ambassador, His Excellency, Mr. Turhan Ecevit."

Ted turned to the ambassador and said, "Mr. Ecevit . . . Am I pronouncing that correctly, sir?"

"Yes, Mr. Koppel, perfectly."

"Mr. Ecevit, by now, just about every American knows about the destruction of the bridges across the Strait of Bosphorus during the crossing of Turkish troops and armor on April 2 and the events following it."

"You know, Ted, this kind of behavior simply cannot be tolerated in a civilized society. We do *not* tolerate it."

"Of course. Now, Mr. Ambassador, there have been some alarming rumors, or unofficial reports, that nuclear warfare was somehow in the offing."

Ambassador Ecevit took off his steel-rimmed glasses to wipe them with a handkerchief. He sighed and said, "Ted, it is truly incredible, and yet, absolutely true."

"Could you explain, Mr. Ambassador?"

Ecevit sighed once more and said, "The as-Saif al-Islam demanded that our democratically elected government stand down in favor of their own rule. Otherwise, they said they would attack Athens and Tel Aviv with nuclear missiles."

Ted Koppel stared in silence at the Turkish ambassador for five full seconds. When he was again able to speak, he said, "Did I hear you correctly, Mr. Ambassador? They threatened to nuke Athens and Tel Aviv if you did not turn the Turkish government over to them?"

"Yes, that is exactly correct."

Koppel nodded his head in disbelief. "That's . . . That's . . ."

"Yes, Ted. It is too horrible to contemplate."

"Well, Mr. Ambassador, in view of the specter of nuclear catastrophe, would it have been better, perhaps, to have surrendered to their demands?"

For several moments Ecevit looked at Koppel the way a kindly teacher looks at a student who sincerely tries to learn, but seems incapable of understanding. Finally, he said, "No, Ted. In the first place, we Turks have no wish to go backward into misery. We are Muslims, and are proud to be Muslims, but we are Muslims of the twenty-first century, not the seventh century. Our desire is to advance, to join the Western World in paving a bright new future for our people. The as-Saif al-Islam organization would pull us down into the quicksand of the past, stifling our aspirations, our personal freedoms, our human rights, our initiative for moving forward. It would negate all that has been accomplished by our beloved Atatürk, Mustafa Kemal Pasha, at the end of World War I, and by subsequent governments following in his footsteps up to the present time. Turkey would have become an extension of Iran. And, don't forget, Ted, the United States is considered the Great Satan by those people."

"But, Mr. Ambassador, in view of the horrific alternatives . . ." Koppel sounded appalled by the prospect.

"Yes, Ted, I understand from what direction you are arriving but you must understand . . . The Greeks, the Israelis, the American people must understand . . . Our submission to the demands of these terrorists would not have led to peace. In fact, it would have ultimately led to nuclear holocaust."

"How is that, Mr. Ambassador?"

"If they controlled Turkey, they would have used the military and economic power of a sovereign nation to blackmail the West, the world, into submitting to their every demand. There can be no compromise with such people."

Koppel looked thoughtful for a moment. Then, "Well, Mr. Ambassador, what has prevented these people from carrying out their threats?"

The Ambassador smiled. "After concentrated investigation by Turkish intelligence services, working night and day, we came upon their main base of operations . . ."

"Where was that?"

"I have not been made privy to that information. It is top secret. Anyway, Turkish commandos, acting on classified information, stormed their fortress, disarmed the nuclear devices, and destroyed them. Since the members of this group put up a strong resistance, and were about to launch the missiles once they knew they were under attack, all the members present at this site were neutralized."

"Killed?"

The ambassador raised an eyebrow. "Yes. About two hundred men."

"Does that end the threat"

The ambassador sighed. "For the present, yes. However, our intelligence services believe there are many sympathizers in my country with the ideals of this group. This represents a tiny minority among the Turkish population. Still, it is a lot of people from which to draw fighters. And there is an international Islamic organization based in London at present called Al-Muhajiroun that actively recruits sympathizers worldwide to join the *jihad*, with the ultimate goal of establishing the *khilafa*, the strictly Islamic state, and conquering the entire world. This is what the organization's founder and leader, Sheikh Omar Bakri Mohammed, has openly said."

Ted Koppel said, "Mr. Ambassador, some kind of explosion has been reported in Iran, very close to the Turkish border. Do you know anything about that?"

"No, Ted. I understand that the Iranian government has reported some kind of earthquake in the region. It must have been that."

The camera shifted to a close-up of Ted Koppel, who turned from the ambassador to look directly into the camera. He said, "Thank you very much, Mr. Ambassador. In the next half hour . . ."

Travis pointed the remote at the television set and the screen went black.

Jack shook his head and said, "So now we're Turkish fucking commandos . . . ?"

Hunter said, "Someone has to get the credit, Jack. It sure as hell can't be us."

Sam solemnly intoned, "A job well done provides its own exquisite gratification."

"An inspirational quote." Jen sounded ironic.

"Confucius?" Jack asked.

"No. Jane Tolliver."

"Who the hell is Jane Tolliver?" Jennifer said.

Hunter said, "Don't you people read the paper or listen to the news? Jane Tolliver is the three-thousand-dollar-a-night call girl who was shot in San Francisco about a month ago. Apparently, she decided to take a twenty-five percent tip, without her john's permission. And this guy was some Texas oilman who never went anywhere without his silver-plated, ivory-handled .38 revolver. It seems he took offense."

"Yeah, what was his name?" Sam asked.

"Billy Bob Hutchings."

"Billy Bob Hutchings?!" Travis said as he sat up, turning to face the rest of Eagle Team. "I went to high school with him! Damn, that Billy Bob always was one cheap son of a bitch."